The Land of the Lost

By

William Satchell

ISBN 978-0-473-55244-2

Cover photo: Gum Digging. Courtesy Alexander Turnbull Library.

The Land of the Lost
Author - William Satchell
Published by AG Books
Whanganui 4501
New Zealand

Foreword

William Satchell is known as a major New Zealand pre-World War I poet and novelist. Most of his novels describe the stunning New Zealand landscape and the struggles that both colonizers and Maori faced. Some would consider him a romance novelist as relationships play an important role in his plots.

Satchell was born in London, England on 1 February 1860 to Thomas and Hannah Satchell. Thomas Satchell influenced his son with his love of books, editing and publishing. Thomas Satchell occasionally contributed to what is now known as the Oxford English Dictionary and became Surveyor-General before his death in 1887.

William Satchell went to St. John's College, Hurstpierpoint in Brighton and in 1877, he attended Heidelberg University in Germany. By 1879 however, he was back in England working with his father at his publishing company "W. Satchell and Co.", which published various art books and two periodicals. Satchell also tried his hand at writing.

There were no profits in the publishing company and disappointed with his writing, having no occupation and being in poor health, Satchell decided to emigrate to New Zealand. He advertised for a hired man and on 21 May 1886 Satchell sailed with Elmer J. Brown on the *Arawa*. His brother and cousin followed a year later and were financially supported by Satchell.

He spent time looking for land in the Waikato and Whangarei districts, but influenced by John Lundon of Rawene, Satchell settled in Waima in the Hokianga region in November 1887. He purchased 300-400 acres of land and actively turned it into fields of orchards and built a double storey house and outbuildings. He was well-known in Waima as Satchell founded a cricket club and helped build a hall there. He was still every bit an English patriot at this time. This allegiance to England along with his bearing, shyness, and mannerisms earned him the nickname "The Little Duke".

On 15 November in 1889, Satchell married Susan Bryers, the grand-daughter of Joseph Bryers and Kohu Whareumu. His marriage would quietly influence Satchell's writing as it gave him further insight into Maori culture and community. This only begins to appear in his novels *The Toll of the Bush* and finally in *The Greenstone Door* more than twenty years later. His daughter Edith was born in 1890. Three more daughters and five sons would follow.

In 1891, Satchell discovered that he did not own his land as the person who sold it to him was not the sole owner. He was refused a refund and after receiving legal advice, Satchell was forced to give up the land and work as a local storekeeper. The store closed and in 1893, Satchell left to find work in Auckland, leaving his family behind in the care of his wife's aunt.

Satchell began to write again. He earned money through clerical work and journalism. In the years that followed, he was published in the *New Zealand Graphic, Auckland Star, New Zealand Herald* and Sydney *Bulletin*. He wrote under various pen names such as Samuel Cliall White, Warwick Simpson, William J. Stewart, William Sage and William Scott. Satchell became known as a minor colonial poet.

He was reunited with his family and because of his investments in the *Auckland Free Stock and Mining Exchange* as well as his work, he could afford to buy a home on Grange Street in Mount Roskill. His first published book *Patriotic and other poems* was released in 1900 and was well received.

In 1901 Satchell started the weekly magazine *The Maorilander* which he wrote, edited, collected advertisements for and supervised its circulation. It was short-lived and survived for only two months. The magazine showed Satchell's interest in literature for New Zealanders written by New Zealanders. Though it was only briefly published, it is often cited as one of Satchell's major accomplishments.

Satchell began to write novels and in 1902 *The Land of the Lost* was published, followed by *The Toll of the Bush* in 1905 and *The Elixir of Life* in 1907. Bad investments caused Satchell to sell his Grange Street home and move to Birkenhead. He settled in Northcote on 5 acres of orchard.

Satchell worked in horticulture and poultry farming and became the part-time secretary to the Auckland Horticultural Society in 1909. He continued to write and published *The Greenstone Door* 1914. It was not well received due to the public's preoccupation with the impending war as well as the questioning of British patriotism in the novel. This disappointed Satchell so much that he never wrote another novel.

Instead he found work as an accountant for the Robert P. Gibbons Timber Company first in Kopu, Thames and then in Auckland until 1936. His novel *The Greenstone Door* became popular and it was reprinted in 1935. *The Land of the Lost* was reprinted in 1938 a year after Satchell's wife died.

Satchell lived in semi-retirement in Mount Roskill until he was awarded a Civil List pension for his contribution to New Zealand literature. He accepted it due to his poor royalties. He cared a great deal about his family and "never took up his pen to write without a feeling of guilt." He died on 21 October 1942. As part of his obituary the Sydney *Bulletin* wrote "he was one of his adopted country's best novelists, if not with his *The Greenstone Door* the very best."

Satchell's first novel *The Land of the Lost* is set in the Kauri gum fields in the Hokianga region where Satchell himself had experienced the difficulties of farming. The region and lifestyle could be compared to the harsh life of the cowboys in the American "wild west" where many are hiding a troubled past and one can never be sure who are friends or foes. The novel however, is distinctly New Zealand as Satchell conveys the life and land of gum diggers with poignant accuracy:

"To the right he [Clifford] could perceive the track of the creek, indicated by an occasional cabbage tree or flax bush, gradually making in towards the road, and about a mile from the inn he struck across the rough, grey gumland to its banks."

Although Satchell's plot is quite Victorian, it interweaves well with descriptions of the desolate day-to-day living in this region. Satchell's description of the gum fields are probably one of the best of this time and place in New Zealand.

Maori are portrayed as an integral part of the economy and lives of these early settlers as you see in the horse races, and the maid Maria who serves her own opinion with relish as well as the meal. The dispute between the local Maori and Roller over a lumber contract show the beginnings of financial integration between the two communities.

This world is dominantly male, ruled by male relationships and a vigilante code of conduct. This is shown from the very start of the novel as the first setting is indeed the local pub and inn called "The Scarlet Man". The scenes from "The Scarlet Man" where we first meet, Cuthbert Upmore, Hugh Clifford and "Bart" also known as Sir Charles Medway show the bleakness of life which very few can escape. This male dominance and power is also shown near the end of the novel during the search for Bart. However, unlike the "wild west", inspectors from Auckland are called upon to restore order and balance.

Clifford, the protagonist, is a young twenty-three year old trying his hand at gum digging. In the small town whilst shopping for supplies, Clifford meets Albert Roller and Robert Brice a shop keeper and supplier. Clifford brings a youthful breath of fresh air to the village, which is not necessarily welcomed by its inhabitants. On his first visit to his plot of land Clifford is befriended by Jessame Olive, "King of the diggers" and becomes quite proficient at digging under Olive's tutelage. Olive is later subjected to degradation and torture by Brice and Roller.

Although, we do not know where Clifford has come from, we are aware that he is a "gentleman" as he comes to the aid of an injured person whose horse had been spooked. This person is revealed to be a young woman named Esther Hamilton who had a badly sprained ankle from the incident. Clifford tends to her with sensitivity and honour, and a mutual attraction is formed from that encounter. Esther's father does not treat Clifford kindly as he feels that Clifford is beneath his station. His daughter is also already engaged to Roller, a man, Dr. Hamilton feels, is a more suitable match. Esther feels differently and supported by her cousin Wilfrid, has Clifford come to visit at her father's house. Love blossoms and both Clifford and Wilfrid tries to get Esther and Dr. Hamilton to see reason. The facts remain though, that Esther is a doctor's daughter and engaged to Albert Roller and Hugh Clifford is just a gum digger, or is he?

An interesting plot and intriguing read, Satchell uses mystery, subterfuge and romance to create a compelling page turner of a story.

CHAPTER I

BETWEEN two and three hundred miles to the north of the city of Auckland stands a lonely inn. No other house is in sight, and the nearest building worthy of the name is removed from it a distance of seven miles.

This inn, which, with that disregard of probabilities for which houses of entertainment are famous all the world over, is called the "Scarlet Man," stands in a hollow by the roadside among the undulations of an extensive gumfield. In every direction the field stretches itself out to the horizon, and in the whole vast circle it meets the skyline saving at two points. The first of these lies immediately in front of the door of the inn, at a distance of five or six miles, where is to be discerned the dark roof of the forest, the trunks of the trees being concealed by a low, level ridge considerably more in the foreground and running like a rampart from the extreme right to the extreme left. The trees, chiefly kahikateas, stand motionless and sharply defined against the clear sky, forming pyramids of black foliage suggestive of the wooden toy trees of childhood. The only other point where, as viewed from the neighbourhood of the inn, the gumfield fails in its clear line on the skirts of the sky is to the left of the building, where the mountain ranges of Waima and Waimamaku are visible like a blue and unchanging cloud, their peaks delicately plumed with foliage of the same unsubstantial appearance. Through the low brushwood, with its undergrowth of coarse, stunted fern and patches of green and orange-coloured moss, runs the Great North Road. Here, where it crosses the gumfield, it presents from the inn door the appearance of a chalk line drawn unsteadily but in one direction from the extreme right of the rampart before the forest to the summit of a low tableland on the skyline to the left, where its sharply defined edge, under the motion of the atmosphere, glitters and sends forth spokes of light continually fading and springing into existence. For it will be found on lifting some of the chalk-like soil of which the gumfield is composed that the whole basis

9

of the vegetation is a white and infinitely fine sand like the dust of porcelain. At this period of the year—the beginning of summer—the road is rough and hard as iron. The traffic of winter-time, when horses and bullock drays moved along a track apparently metalled with cream cheeses, has left ruts and holes, subsequently baked and solidified by the sun. Later on in the season, before the advent of the winter rains, the track will be pounded smooth by the scurrying feet of native riders, who have passed all the summer and autumn through to and from the gum store on the edge of the rich vale of Parawai; but during the month of December it has more the appearance of a ploughed field than the main road which it purports to be.

The gumfield might also be described as an immense fallow suffered to become clothed with a weedy vegetation. Throughout the vast circle hardly a spot can be found which shows no trace of the digger's spade. Yet so invincible is the manuka—or tea tree of the settlers —that despite the constant interference to which it is subjected, it covers the field from horizon to horizon. All the year round the manuka may be seen putting forth its pretty white flowers and ripening its purple pods of seed. Seen from a distance and in masses, the white flowers give to the vegetation a grey look, the effect of which is enhanced by the dust which accumulates on the leaves in dry weather. The brilliant sunlight is powerless to redeem the colourlessness so created, and the effect is that of a wide sea of vegetation withered by the fierce beams of the sun.

Beneath this dreary-looking carpet is concealed the precious gum.

One or two thousand years ago this sun-bathed plain was shadowed by a forest of gigantic trees, as certain other parts of the province of Auckland are to this day. These trees reached an elevation of two or three hundred feet. Many of them were sixty feet in girth and built up in tremendous columns for eighty feet without a branch. Their trunks were tan-coloured and curiously dimpled, as the bark continually peeled and fell to the ground in small hard flakes. Here and there on these huge pillars the gum exuded, pearly and plastic, and crept slowly earthwards. There was no undergrowth of any size, but the handsome umbrella fern spread its tender carpet along the aisles, rejoicing in the shadow which preserved a continuous moisture at its roots. Such was the kauri forest. As centuries went by many unrecorded disasters befell it. Strong gales blew from the east and the west, and the aged giants on the highlands fell into the hollows, crushing the young trees in their fall. The earth, exhausted by the demands of its children, grew less and less able to support them; the young trees starved and died, the older became more economic of leaf and branch. Occasionally at rare intervals the god of fire drew his toll from the forest, devouring some, wrecking many. Still more centuries went by. Slowly the forest withdrew like the shadow of a cloud. Splitting itself into two battalions, it travelled westward and southward, and the manuka crept down from the highlands to the north and burst into impudent flower at its very gates. The inexorable march of the centuries continued, the dogged withdrawal of the forest went on. At length there came a day when the last dolorous giant disappeared over the hill and the tiny manuka held the land from sky to sky. Still the centuries continued their march, countless generations of manuka sprang and bloomed and died, and nothing further appeared from over the hills. The forest had been long gone and forgotten; no imagination could, unassisted, have conjured from the barren wilderness a dream so majestic, yet the proofs of its previous existence lay all the while indelibly written in the earth. Beneath the white and exhausted soil, carefully piled in heaps, lay the nuggets of amber-coloured gum, petrifying and perfecting itself against the day when it should again come to light.

The "Scarlet Man" stood alone in the solitude, a two-storeyed, weatherboard building, somewhat disreputable in appearance. Three windows faced the road on the upper floor. Beneath the central window, the swing-doors of the bar, held back by a couple of rust-eaten iron weights, opened on to a crazy verandah, whence a single block of hewn wood formed a step to the road. On either side of the door was a window, that to the left looking out from the bar and that to the right admitting the sunbeams to a small, darkly furnished chamber, used as a dining and sitting-room. Facing the swing-doors at the other side of the bar was a narrow passage leading into the back part of the house, with a steep flight of narrow, uncarpeted stairs breaking upwards immediately within the entrance. The inn was crowned with a steep roof of moss-grown shingles, black with age, and forming but a poor re-commendation to the weatherproofness of the upper storey. The weatherboard walls, originally painted white, were now of a piebald appearance, the prevailing hues being black, grey, and green where patches of moss had managed to thrust their delicate rootlets into the decaying wood. On the left side of the building, being that from which the inn was more usually approached from the road, was a framed canvas picture of the "Scarlet Man," representing a native heavily tattoed but otherwise as turned out from the hand of nature. He was a good deal the worse for his long vigil, having yielded to the elements the greater part of his chest and stomach, as well as the whole of the top of his head. His pristine hues, also, which originally justified the name he still bore, had faded to a dull orange and in places showed signs of vanishing altogether.

Behind, and to the sides of the building, a piece of land, about an acre and a half in extent, was inclosed in a rough puriri fence, and within this again a small portion had been paled off to the rear of the house, where an abortive attempt had been made to form a garden. Outside the pale the fenced land was evidently designed to answer the purposes of a grass paddock, though what grass there was was everywhere nibbled to the roots, and large patches of the soil had been bleached absolutely bare by the sunbeams. The earth thus revealed was of a bright red colour, approaching vermilion, and a person sufficiently curious to reflect on this fact might have discovered with a little search that the land on which the inn stood, and for a few chains around, was everywhere of this same vivid hue. Following up his discovery, he would have found further that this same soil continued in a winding line along the deepest hollows of the gumfield, and that it led him ultimately to the rich red soils of Parawai. From these discoveries he might have formed the theory that here, in the days of the kauri forest, had been a blind creek or swamp, periodically charged with the flood-borne mud of the rich district beyond the horizon.

It was a day in the middle of December. The altitude of the sun showed the hour to be close on noon. The atmosphere was perfectly clear, cloudless, and without wind. Not a sound was to be heard.

CHAPTER II

ABOVE the swing-doors of the inn was nailed a narrow strip of blackened tin, on which was painted in white letters the legend: "Cuthbert Upmore. Licensed to sell Wine, Beer, and Spirits."

Cuthbert Upmore himself leaned negligently against a post of the verandah and looked along the road. He was a tall spare man of dark complexion, with a long thin nose. He wore a heavy black moustache, but no side whiskers or beard, the stubble on his face and chin merely denoting that it was approaching the end of the week and drawing nigh to Sunday, the weekly shaving day. There was no particular reason why Cuthbert Upmore, who had little to do at any time, should not shave on any or every day of the seven, but he had fallen into the common habit of the people around, and clung there steadfastly. Indeed, the weekly shave assumed in these parts something of the nature of a religious observance.

Presently the man yawned, and relinquishing the support of the post, strolled round to the back of the inn. The ground here sloped gradually upwards for a quarter of a mile, where was reached the highest point in the near neighbourhood of the hostelry. Upmore, after moving irresolutely for some time, made his way to the summit of the elevation. From this point a considerably wider extent of country was visible, and several new features were added to the scene. The additional height had the effect of levelling the billowy undulations of the gumfield. The kahikatcas, whose summits only were visible from the verandah of the inn, were now revealed in their entirety, clouding the skyline in that direction with their sombre foliage. The curve of the top of the forest showed the formation of the country on which they existed, which was that of a cleft between two hills, the trees having possession of the cleft and part of the hill-slopes on either side. They were advancing on the gumfield in the form of a wedge, the point lying immediately in front of the dip, and the base spread across from hill to hill. At several other points round the horizon the forest could be seen breaking through the crevices of the hills, as though with the intention of resuming its ancient abode.

In the opposite direction, that, namely, which lay to the rear of the "Scarlet Man," the gumfields stretched out as far as the eye could see; but about a mile from the elevation on which Upmore stood could be descried a sudden dip, forming a narrow crevice, traceable for a considerable distance through the manuka: this was the bed of a creek. At one point a slump of cabbage trees brandished their sword-like leaves above the hollow. Further along was a square vivid green patch, glancing brightly in the sunlight with pale curls of blue smoke rising from the earth close beside it. This Upmore decided to be a hut of native construction, the freshness of the palm thatch betraying it to be of recent origin.

The watcher seated himself and continued his observations. This great, dreary circle, which at first appeared absolutely tenantless, seemed, on long scrutiny, well-nigh as populous us a rabbit burrow. From the one extreme of emptiness the mind drifts into an equally erroneous opinion at the opposite extreme. Every thick tuft of manuka is conceived to be the lurking-place of a digger, every slight rustle and stir of the brushwood an indication of his presence. At times the quick eye of the innkeeper discerned a head bob up from the thick growth, or the complete body of a man pass slowly from one clump to another. Once or twice a figure bearing an empty, or partially empty sack on its back, a spade across its shoulder, and a thin spear, shining like a splinter of glass in its hand, came into an open space and prodded the ground here and there. This was a digger spearing for gum. At other times a man might be observed throwing out the soil with his spade; but no single figure remained in view for longer than a few minutes at a time.

Apparently surfeited with the view in this direction, Upmore now turned his face towards the inn and scanned the long white line of the road. Away on the summit of the low tableland the glittering, as of a glass wheel with rimless spokes, still went on, but a small black speck was now discernible in the heart of it. This speck moved steadily downwards for about ten minutes, and then suddenly disappeared. Upmore took out his watch and made a note of the time. There was generally a good deal of this commodity on his hands and a very limited number of ways of employing it. Ten years or so ago he had discovered the particular method which he now put in practice at the moment he pulled out his watch. From the spot where the speck had disappeared to the point where—from the winding of the road—it would again come into view was a distance of two miles. According to the time takenby the traveller in covering this distance was the good or ill fortune in store for the watcher from that period to the next occasion chance suffered him to behold a similar event. There were several other more or less absorbing speculations to be got out of the business, but the main and most exciting point was the dependence of his own destiny on the speed or otherwise of the unknown.

Lonely men light on strange ideas; the pressure of solitude drives them home; time rivets them fast: they become credible facts, as things seen and heard are credible facts—the one being, not impossibly, on as sound a basis as the other. Upmore had formulated his creed as the result of experience; it had been of a tentative nature once, owing to the complexity of the experience, but it had long since settled into dogma and become as a consequence indisputable. On one occasion a man had spent an hour and a half between the two points and brought him ill-luck. He had remained at the inn for two months, stupidly drunk the whole time, and had ended by dying suddenly in the dead-house, putting Upmore to the trouble of burying him outside in the paddock, for the whole of which—board, drink, funeral expenses, and anxiety of mind— he had never received a penny to this day. Upmore thought of this now as he sat on the hill with his watch in his hand waiting for the reappearance of the speck. But there had been a worse occasion than this—that of a man who had done the distance in thirty-six minutes. Never was there such a devil of a business as followed the advent of the man who did the distance in thirty-six minutes! He brought worry and disaster with him, compared with which the board and burial of a dozen hour-and-a-half men were things to be prayed for and rejoiced in. This man also had turned aside through the doorway of the "Scarlet Man." He had slept there one night, and risen the following morning swearing that he was robbed—robbed of a hundred single pound notes. Here was an aspersion to cast on the good name of a defenceless "Scarlet Man," licensed to sell wine, beer, and spirits! And the tremendous to-do that followed! The dreadful excitable nature of the robbed man; the wild and humiliating theories put forth by him to account for the fact of the robbery; the extraordinary interrogativeness of the police, who haunted the landlord's dreams for months afterwards in the shape of query marks in official uniform. Never was a man so cornered and bullied with embarrassing questions. He was considerably out of pocket, and had lost a great deal in weight before he saw the last of the man who did the distance in thirty-six minutes, and even now as he thought of him he shuddered. Disasters of a milder type had befallen him on other occasions, but they were always associated with a traveller unduly slow or swift in his movements.

Upmore glanced at his watch; thirty-two minutes had elapsed. The possibility of his having to wait another twenty minutes before the reappearance of the figure made no call on his patience. In a solitude such as this, with a daily average of two or three travellers, and perhaps as many visits from those digging in the locality, any employment which was not actually loafing assumed a dignity comically out of proportion to its true value, and had thus the advantage of diffusing that glow of self-satisfaction which follows on exertion at the smallest imaginable cost to the labourer.

Another minute passed, and another. Suddenly the curved white edge of the road, sharply outlined against the darker background of brushwood, became at one point slightly blurred and uncertain. He rubbed his eyes and looked again. The uncertain had now become the certain, the body of a man was rapidly rising into view, surrounded by a halo of scintillating

17

dust: in a moment he reached the brow of the elevation and began his descent towards the inn. Upmore looked at his watch—barely thirty-five minutes had elapsed since he lost sight of the speck two miles away. He rose and stood as one thunderstruck, helplessly gazing at the approaching figure. What disaster was this that advanced on him with a speed hitherto unprecedented in his experience? And here a circumstance occurred which to the superstitious mind of the innkeeper suggested all the irony of a malignant fate. The man, having completed the work of prophecy, deliberately sat down by the roadside and lit his pipe.

To Upmore's mind this was adding insult to injury —an overwhelming confirmation of the exactness of his theory of devil-worship, which in his present state of gloomy anticipation he could readily have done without. Upmore gazed on the unconscious smoker as he sat blowing the blue tobacco-cloud from his lips with less of hatred than curiosity. The creature before him was to his mind but the irresponsible instrument of something hateful behind. A less superstitious man might have taken steps to avoid an encounter with the traveller; to Upmore's mind this would have been merely working on the side of destiny. The correct attitude was that of an automaton, to be set going, shifted about, and stopped at the pleasure of its maker, if not with indifference, at least with avoidance of those struggles which have to be carried on entirely at the creature's own expense.

With a philosophy worthy of a better cause, Upmore made his way back to the inn, creeping under the puriri fence and entering the house from the rear. The kitchen of the establishment lay to the right of the passage, and here the innkeeper, after glancing rapidly round and listening attentively for a few moments, commenced knocking the ceiling violently with a piece of wood. The sound of a step moving from place to place with that apparent aimlessness which conveys to the initiated the process of making a bed, suddenly ceased; and a moment afterwards the person above commenced the descent of the stairs. Upmore laid the wood on the fire, and blew it into a blaze.

As he completed his task a woman of between thirty and forty entered the room and stood without speaking, looking inquiringly into his face from a pair of exceedingly bright and watchful eyes. Upmore, standing with his back to the fire, gazed fixedly at, or rather beyond, her with the air of one engaged in abstruse speculation. The heavy, drooping, black moustache gave a drawn and anxious expression to his countenance.

"Did you knock?" asked the woman at length in the low monotone occasionally observable in very deaf people.

Upmore, becoming conscious of her presence, pointed his finger in the direction of the road and shouted, "Someone coming!"

The woman nodded her head, and her lips parted in a slight smile.

"Have you any meat?" asked Upmore.

The woman gave a sign in the affirmative. "Peter brought some beef this morning, but very tough and no fat. There never is any fat on the Maori cattle." Upmore nodded, and pointed to the fire.

Thus directed, the woman ceased in her watchful gaze on his face, and going to the fireplace, swung the huge kettle on a hook up the chimney. She then placed a large frying-pan on the bars.

Upmore now left the kitchen and took up his position in the doorway of the inn. The only moving object in the landscape was the figure of the stranger advancing rapidly along the white road. He was apparently heavily laden, and bore a spade and spear across his shoulder. His stalwart limbs were encased in a pair of snowy drill trousers, turned into a pair of yellow cotton socks. He wore a blue Crimea shirt open at the throat, but no coat or waistcoat. A broad-brimmed hat, woven from the kiekie of the forest, completed his attire. As he drew nearer Upmore could see that his face—that of a young man of two or three-and-twenty—was tanned scarlet by the sun; and a few moments later he was aware of a pair of frank blue eyes

19

looking into his own and a pleasant voice giving him a good-natured greeting.

Could this handsome, innocent-looking creature be the messenger of the Implacable Fates?

CHAPTER III

THE new-comer loosened the straps at his shoulders and allowed his baggage to fall upon the verandah. "I have to go back to Parawai for my tent," he explained; "but I should like something to eat and drink first, if it is to be had."

"There may be something," said Upmore, without stirring.

"Anything to stay the pangs," said the young man cheerfully. "shall leave these things here," he added, "and be back in the morning,"

Upmore turned on his heel and led the way into the dining-room, where the table was already spread with a not overclean cloth, a battered castor, and some knives and forks. The visitor threw himself on the worn horsehair sofa, and looked on while the woman completed her preparations for dinner. Upmore meanwhile, with a cat-like tread peculiar to him, wandered restlessly in and out, as though he were looking for someone. "Where is that boarder?" he asked of the woman at length.

"In the dead-house," she replied.

The innkeeper looked relieved, and taking his seat at the table, began to cut up the steak.

"Someone dead?" asked the young man sympathetically.

Upmore turned the steak over as though in search of a more vulnerable point than that he had at first attacked. "No," he said thoughtfully, "we have to put him in there at times; he won't keep out of the bar!"

"I see," said the young man. "What is he?"

"Well, when he's drunk he says he's Sir Charles Medway, but when he's sober he doesn't let on who he is."

"And how does he live?"

"Like everyone else about here," replied Upmore, "digging gum."

"I suppose a man can get a living at it all right?" the young man inquired a little anxiously.

Upmore looked at him reflectively and nodded.

At this moment sounds as of someone violently kicking at a closed door became audible from the rear of the house, and a minute or so later a man appeared in the doorway of the dining-room. He was a dishevelled-looking creature of about thirty-five, dressed in the ordinary rough clothing of the digger. His hair was long and unkempt, and there was a week's growth of stubble on his chin. His features were clear cut and aquiline, and might originally have been termed refined, but there was a bloated look about the cheeks and around the bloodshot eyes.

"Why do you keep shoving me in that beastly hole?" he asked sulkily, as he took his seat at the table.

"Just so no one shall interfere with you," said the innkeeper in a conciliatory tone. "It's handier than taking you up to bed, Bart."

Bart looked furtively at the other guest, who was regarding him with frank curiosity. "Drop your Barts," he said. "You know what my name is well enough. Who's your friend?"

"My name is Clifford," said the young man, smiling.

"And mine is Higgins," said the other. "Some of them call me Sir Charles, or Bart, but that's merely the local substitute for a joke. What are you doing here?"

"I am going to start gum-digging," said Clifford apologetically.

Bart sniffed and pushed away his plate with an air of disgust. "Where do you get your beef, Upmore?" he asked savagely. "I believe this is the same blooming bull you served up yesterday. Call this a hotel? For God's sake let us have some beer—none of your cask stuff. Bring a couple of bottles and let me see the corks before you open them."

Upmore rose obediently, and presently returned with bottles and glasses. Bart satisfied himself that the flasks had not been tampered with, and permitted them to be opened.

"Will you join me, Mr. —, I forget what you said your name was."

"Clifford," said the innkeeper, looking sideways at the man whose name he mentioned.

"Allow the gentleman to speak for himself," said Bart; "he may have changed his mind."

"Not I," said Clifford, laughing and accepting the proffered hospitality. "Is that also the local substitute for a joke?"

"There's no joke about that," said Bart, "it's a necessity. When you have knocked about here for a bit you will probably find that your real name is worse than no good to you. There are a few, I can tell you, who have had so many aliases that they have forgotten their correct patronymic, and wouldn't remember it if they heard it; and there are others," he added gloomily, setting down his empty glass, "who would only be too glad to forget, but can't. Your name may be Clifford, but you don't suppose that chap's name is Upmore, do you?" he concluded, with a vindictive glance at the innkeeper.

Clifford, detecting signs of annoyance on the face of the person alluded to, hastened to change the subject. "You have had a good deal of experience at gum-digging, I suppose," he said.

"I suppose I have," was the curt reply; "and I would pay you a good round sum to take it off me."

"I can't see why gum-digging shouldn't be as respectable as anything else," argued Clifford,

"You can't," said Bart, "but you will. Respectable! Good Lord! Listen to him!" he went on bitterly. "Why, this is the stranding-ground of the dead-beats of the World; this is where all the wrecks of the earth are thrown up to rot—and you talk about respectability! Every inch of this north country is poisoned with dead hopes, and it will never be any good till the gum is gone out of it. Do you mean to tell me that you come here voluntarily and of your own free will? Rubbish! This country is peopled under the lash." He rose as he spoke and made his way in the direction of the bar.

"Bart's a curious chap," said the innkeeper. "He can only be agreeable when he's drunk; he's not the same man then. What part of the country do you come from?"

The question was put abruptly, and the young man seemed slightly staggered under it. "Down south," he replied vaguely.

"Taranaki or Hawke's Bay way?" asked the innkeeper insinuatingly. "I used to know a Clifford in Hawke's Bay—I knew of him, rather—a station holder in a big way."

"The name is not a rare one," said the young man, pushing back his chair.

Upmore was about to make some further remark when a sound of glass jingling in the bar interrupted him, and he rose. "I believe he's found the bottle," he said *sotto voce.*

"Do your customers help themselves?" Clifford asked.

"Only when there's no one about to attend to them, you know," the innkeeper replied cautiously. "Bart's like one of the family," he added; "he's a contract boarder."

"Does he live here altogether?" the young man inquired.

The innkeeper peered across into the bar and partially closed the door, "It's a good system," he said a little eagerly. "You just pay your cheque down, you know, and you get *carte blanche.* It might be an advantage to you if you are going gum-digging. What? Just a trifle on account."

He approached quite close to Clifford as he spoke, and the young man noticed that his long, lean hands were closing and expanding in a manner that promised a warm reception to the "trifle on account."

"I think I'll try the open air," he said; "thanks all the same. But I'll remember your system in case I should require to take advantage of it."

"Quite so," said Upmore, drawing back and slowly resuming his ordinary demeanour. "We'll make you welcome. What might your age be now?"

Again the personal question came so abruptly that the young man hesitated before he answered. "I have just turned twenty-three," he replied at length.

The innkeeper reflected an instant and then nodded. "Well," he said, "think it over when you come back. I'll go and look after Bart. I believe he's found the bottle."

As Clifford had noticed quite a number of bottles on the shelf over the counter, he was curious to know what was intended by the use of the definite adjective in conjunction with the word bottle, and he followed Upmore into the bar.

Bart was sitting on a stool behind the counter with a bottle clutched between his knees and a long glass beside him.

"Come on, Clifford," he called in high glee. "I've got the beggar now. Get a glass and join in. This is the mother-tincture, my boy—the true *aqua vita*—the parent spirit. All the rest, except the bottled beer, is water and fusil oil and logwood and the very devil. Would you!"—he broke off as the innkeeper anxiously endeavoured to secure possession of his property—"Hands off, or I'll waste it over your skull. Look at the beggar frothing at the mouth! Now I'll just let you into the secrets of the trade, Clifford, my boy. That bottle over his head is Rum Number One; it's given to white men, and it's non-poisonous. The next—Number Two—is reserved for low whites and diggers; it'll drive you mad, but it won't kill you. Number three is logwood, fusil oil, painkiller, and treacle, and he gives it to the natives, and they die suddenly or kill one another. Then he and the old woman hank them into the dead-house, and sometimes there is an inquest and sometimes there isn't. And when there is, the jury bring in a verdict of consumption complicated with influenza, and add a rider deploring the foolish conduct of the Maoris in getting their clothes wet and sleeping in them. Those bottles up there are schnapps—you notice that they have both got their corks drawn, and when you see a bottle with the cork drawn in this establishment stand off. Just up here is the whisky department. Looks well, doesn't it? Well, stand off that too. Some day, when I can get hold of the key, I'll show you the laboratory where these things are made—it'll interest you. Now where's your glass?"

"Don't be a fool, Bart," said the innkeeper, looking slightly white about the gills. "People who don't know you might think you are speaking the truth."

"Hark at the cunning wretch!" exclaimed Bart, after emptying half a tumblerful of the raw liquid down his throat. " Every word of it is gospel, and he knows it. He's going to get a cemetery of his own some day and collect his dead.

 " 'He's getting his dead from their lonely graves
  And lumping them all together;

There's some of them fools, but more of them knaves,
     And he's yarding them all together.
He's yarding them all together, they say,
     Whisky and gin and rum,
And there they'll stay, the green and the grey,
     Waiting for Kingdom Come.

" 'Waiting for Kingdom Come,
     Rotten with whisky and rum,
There they'll lie while the world goes by,
     Waiting for Kingdom Come.'

"What do you think of me, you, Clifford? Did you ever hear Upmore's hymn to the mother-tincturethe basic salts of the bush pub?—

" 'O Mother of all the Spirits, one in a million miles.'

Fine thing that! And then the dashing chorus—

" 'Only a drop to the gallon,
     Only a dram to the tun,' etc.

Come on, Clifford, and be sociable. We shall be a damned long time dead."

Clifford shook a smiling negative, "I've a long tramp before me," he replied, "but I shall be back again to-morrow."

Upmore, after a last reluctant look at the bottle, accompanied Clifford to the verandah. "Bart gets very pleasant when he's drunk," he remarked, rubbing his hands and looking furtively at his companion. "Did you notice it?"

"He seems to be in high spirits," said the young man drily.

"Of course, it's only his nonsense about the bottles, just his pleasantry. Did you come straight here from Hawke's Bay?"

Clifford looked intently at the speaker. "Aren't you jumping to conclusions rather?" he asked. "I don't remember saying that I had ever been in Hawke's Bay, and anyway, from the description of the gumfield I have just heard, I should imagine that it is a place where it is best to ask no questions."

"No harm meant," said the innkeeper. "I understood you to say that was where you came from."

"It's all right," said Clifford as he turned away.

The innkeeper stood watching the departing figure of his guest until it became concealed by the winding road. "I wonder—" he mused half aloud. "It would be an extraordinary piece of good luck if—" He broke off and re-entered the house, pulling thoughtfully at his long moustache.

CHAPTER IV

DURING the innkeeper's absence Bart had seized the opportunity to decamp with the mother-tincture and not a trace of him was to he found. Upmore wandered about for a while in fruitless search, then made his way into the dining-room. In a corner lay his late visitor's luggage, consisting of a flour-bag and a haversack, as the young man had thrown them down when he came in. The innkeeper's attention was arrested by the sight of these objects, and closing the door, he commenced a hasty examination. The flour-bag, he soon determined, contained nothing but clothes, and this he tied up again after thrusting his hand to the bottom. The contents of the haversack were of a more miscellaneous description, but still consisted mainly of wearing apparel. A couple of volumes of the "Canterbury Poets" furnished him with the information he sought, having inscribed on the flyleaf the name "Hugh Hilton Clifford" in a round, boyish hand. Upmore sucked in his breath and whistled softly as he read the name.

At this juncture he was disturbed by the sound of a horse cantering up to the door of the hostelry, which was immediately followed by the loud tapping of a whip on one of the verandah posts. Hastily restoring the contents of the haversack to their places, Upmore made his way to the verandah.

Drawn up close to the house was a man of between thirty and forty on a flea-bitten grey. He was well clad, and had the appearance of a person well to do. In figure he was slightly below middle height, broad-shouldered, and well-proportioned. His face was ornamented with a moustache and short, curling, brown beard. His eyes were handsome and well opened—they were, if anything, too well opened, and lent to his physiognomy a somewhat insolent and overbearing expression. He spoke in a strong, swift, slightly authoritative voice.

The innkeeper greeted him by the name of Roller.

"I am going on," said the new-comer, "as far as the Maori settlement. The beggars are not keeping to the terms of their contract; there have not been half a dozen logs drawn this last fortnight."

"There's been a death there, Mr. Roller," said the innkeeper apologetically.

"That's neither here nor there," returned Roller. "If a friend of mine were to die they would not consider it a sufficient excuse for my withholding payment. A contract's a contract."

"Well," said the innkeeper, "no doubt they'll put things straight when the *tangi* is over."

"They're twenty logs behind," said Roller.

Upmore was silent.

"Well," said the other, wheeling his horse, "I thought I'd let you know as you are interested in the business. I am really doing your work in rowing them up."

"I don't see that," said Upmore quickly.

Roller looked slightly aggressive. "Not after guaranteeing completion?" he asked.

"That's a mere matter of form," said Upmore uneasily.

"Form be hanged!" said Roller; "you know better than that. But we'll talk it over when I return."

"Very good, Mr. Roller," said Upmore mildly.

"I'll sleep here as usual," said Roller, moving off. "I have to catch the Auckland boat in the morning." He touched the horse with a long, bright spur and cantered swiftly along the road, his form being shortly concealed by the cloud of dust that rose in his tracks.

Again Upmore entered the dining-room, and again he was disturbed in his employment—this time by the sound of a heavy step entering the bar.

His second visitor was a man over six feet in height, massively framed, with long, sinewy arms, and large, hairy hands. His head was singularly out of proportion with his body, being remarkably long and narrow, and the incongruous effect thus created was enhanced by the manner in which his hair was cropped close to his skull. His eyes were small and light in colour.

" 'D evenin', boss," he said, looking keenly at the innkeeper.

Upmore nodded reflectively.

"I'll take a nobbler of rum," said the man.

The innkeeper supplied him, and while he drank it looked curiously at him as though endeavouring to arouse some sleeping memory.

"Seem to recollect me, boss?" asked the fellow, setting down his glass and wiping his lips.

"I seem to have met you before," said Upmore slowly.

The man nodded, winked one eye, and set his elbows on the counter. "How about the price of gum those times?" he said.

The innkeeper looked puzzled. "The price of gum?" he repeated.

"You never heard of New Caledonia," said the other, "not you."

Upmore started and looked more closely at his companion. "It's Robert Brice," he said under his breath.

Brice laughed. "There used to be a bit of a fringe round it them times," he said, stroking his face and chin. "But I knew you wasn't the sort to cut an old pal."

"I thought you got five years for some affair or other," said Upmore.

"Five and fifteen months' conduct makes three nine, and I'm through with it."

"Fifteen months," said Upmore, in a voice which despite himself had an aggrieved ring; "that is a big allowance to make."

"Not so big, after all, guv'nor," said Brice, "when it's yourself as is gettin' it. You've got to 'sperience these things to get the hang of them."

"And what are you doing out here?" Upmore asked, after a pause.

"Gum-digging," replied Brice. "That and lookin' round for a soft thing."

"You've come to a poor place," said Upmore. "Why didn't you stay in town?"

"Overdone," said Brice, with a nod. "Four years ago," he went on reflectively, "I was in a fair way to a pile. If it hadn't been for that blamed cheque cropping up six months after I had forgotten it, I'd have a full pocket now. There was whips of money in it. It couldn't last, you know, but while it held out it would be a fair pour."

"You are talking of the Caledonian," said Upmore.

The Caledonian— Give us another nobbler. Now see 'ere. I'd got the thing on the move, you understand. There was a schooner in it. We could land the stuff comfortable at ten pound a ton. What was the price of kauri? Don't you make no mistake, there was twenty pound profit on every ton we shipped, and no risk."

"It couldn't last," said Upmore; "it would have blasted the kauri trade in less than a year."

"Let it last six months," said the other; "it's enough."

"Ah, well, it's no good talking of it now; the thing has been blown on. I don't see what you can do with gum, anyhow, these times. You've come to the wrong place."

"Ain't there a lay of any kind?" asked Brice. "If so, I'm on it."

Upmore shook his head. "Where are you camping?" he asked.

"'Bout a mile down the creek. Got a doss with a man they call Sandy George."

"Well," said Upmore after a pause, "come up again some other day. I'm busy now. Besides, I am expecting Roller every minute."

"What of that?" exclaimed Brice. "I am not afraid to face him."

"Perhaps not, but there might be some unpleasantness in meeting a man whose cheque you had altered and who got you gaoled for it."

"There might so," said Brice significantly.

"But I'll have none of that here."

Brice reflected and changed his tone. "Revenge is a poor lay," he said; "it never filled a man's stomach, There's ways of gettin' even in business, and they do a man more credit. Mind you, I don't say Roller and me 'as played our game through;

31

there's cards yet on my side, anyway."

"I know nothing about that," said Upmore, "and don't want to. All I've got to look after is the respectability of my house."

"Just so, boss," said the man cheerfully. "Respectability's a good draw. Well, 'ere's to you." He drained his glass, put down the money, and moved to the door.

Upmore, mollified by the obsequience of the other, followed him. "Come back some other day," he said; "any time when you have nothing better to do."

"Right yer are, boss," said Brice. He swung away as he spoke with a strong, ungainly stride, his small head swaying on his long, willowy neck.

Something in the henlike motion of this part of Brice's anatomy stirred the sombre imagination of the innkeeper till, clutching his own throat, he turned back into the house.

CHAPTER V

THE young man who had formed an object of such pronounced interest to the innkeeper reached his destination at sunset.

The village consisted of two stores, a church, a school, and about a dozen weatherboard cottages set on either side of a piece of metalled road a quarter of a mile in length.

The two stores stood at opposite ends of the township, one being kept by a person of the name of Armitage, who was a comparatively new corner, while the other and larger was the property of Albert Roller.

Roller's store was a collection of low, wooden buildings, connected by covered passages and comprising, in addition to the main store, a dwelling-house, houses for sorting and storing gum, a butcher's shop, and, removed some little distance away, a group of stables. It was, in fact, a typical up-country store, where the settler might supply his every need from a needle to the proverbial anchor.

Roller's storekeeper, Wilson, attended to Clifford's wants, and liking the appearance of the young fellow, took him into the house instead of consigning him to the shed reserved for sundowners.

"I suppose this is all pure enjoyment to you?" he said in allusion to the purchases the young man was making.

"Why should you think so?" asked Clifford.

"Oh, it's easy to see yours is not a case of necessity. As a general thing, the digger only wants a spade, a spear, and a small stock of provisions; and he wants them on tick."

By daylight Clifford was afoot, making his way back to the inn. On arrival he found Upmore at his accustomed post on the verandah, standing in his accustomed attitude, with his hands in his pockets and one leg crossed over the other. The innkeeper regarded him critically, as though his visitor had awakened in him a fresh interest since their last meeting. However, he merely nodded in response to the young man's greeting, and made no motion to accompany him into the house. While securing his baggage Clifford looked about for the contract boarder, but he was nowhere to be seen.

"Is he in there again?" he asked as he came out.

"Bart? I expect so," Upmore replied indifferently.

"It's a wonder he survives it," commented Clifford. "How long has he been going on like this?"

"His time is nearly up," said the innkeeper. "Most men would have turned him out before this, but I like to give full value."

Clifford could not avoid reflecting on the sort of value Bart was receiving, even with occasional access to the mother-tincture; and there was a good deal of contempt in his face as he turned away and began to load himself with his various possessions. This was a task of some difficulty, and finally the innkeeper took his hands out of his pockets and assisted him.

"Why, you're as strong as a bullock!" he remarked when the job was completed. "How far are you going?"

"Not very far, I expect," said Clifford, laughing and turning away; "the first suitable camping-ground will be far enough."

Upmore stood watching him till he was aware of someone stepping on to the verandah behind him, when he turned to find Brice, his visitor of the previous day.

"Who's the bloke?" asked Brice, looking over the innkeeper's shoulder.

"A new chum," said Upmore, "starting digging."

"Gum-digging, eh?" said Brice, scratching his nose.

The innkeeper's gaze followed the retreating figure. "White drill trousers," he remarked musingly, "yellow cotton socks, a blue Crimea shirt—rather a curious pattern on that shirt."

"Sort of circles like," said Brice.

The two men looked at one another, Brice being the first to shift his glance.

"Come inside," said Upmore after a pause, leading the way into the bar. The innkeeper poured out a liberal dose of rum for his visitor and helped himself to an inch of cold tea. "How are you getting on?" he asked, sipping his beverage.

"Getting on!" exclaimed Brice. "How is a man to get on in a

hole like this? It looks as though it would end up in my having to work. Here's to you." And he tossed the fiery liquid down his throat.

Upmore repeated the dose, and put the bottle back on the shelf. "Come into the parlour," he said.

Brice took a sip at the fresh allowance, winked solemnly behind the innkeeper's back, and followed him.

On the table lay a pack of soiled cards, and drawing up his chair, Upmore began at first to finger them idly; then suddenly he drew them out like a concertina, and ran them together again.

His visitor's jaw dropped, and he sat regarding the performance with open mouth. "Well, that's the most miraculous thing ever I seen!" he said at length.

Upmore started as though he had been unconscious of what he was doing. Then, observing his visitor's interest, he took the pack in his left hand, drew a swift circle in the air with the cards, and allowed them to fall into his right.

Brice drew back as from something uncanny, and the innkeeper, smiling enigmatically, began to drum the pack lightly on the table,

"I suppose you have a fair memory, Brice?" he said at length.

"Fair to medium," replied Brice, watching the innkeeper's long hands with a sort of fascination.

"Do you remember a man called Drayton whom the lawyers were anxious to find about seven years ago?"

Brice seemed to shrink suddenly together, and his gaze rose from the lean hands and became riveted on the lean face. "Can't say I do," he replied after a pause.

"Try again," said the innkeeper slowly.

Brice moistened his lips, "What devil's game are you up to?" he asked in a fierce whisper.

Upmore spread out the cards face downwards, and picked one out at random. "I thought you would remember," he said, looking at the card he had drawn. "There are only two men living who know what became of Drayton—I am the other one!"

Brice half rose from his seat, and his face looked ugly and white.

Upmore fixed him with his eye. "It's no good, Brice," he said, shaking his head; "I have shared this secret with you for seven years, though you were unconscious of it. If it could keep seven it can keep longer, only now we've got to put it on a different footing. There was no reason why I should keep your secret; but now, if you are wise, there is going to be."

Brice took a pull at his glass, and it seemed to do him good. "Get it out quick," he said hoarsely.

But the innkeeper seemed in no hurry. There was, indeed, something inhuman in his slow, methodical handling of the cards as he set them up in little heaps, and drew one here and there, as though indifferent to the evident agony of his companion. At length, however, he selected some cards from the pack, and leaning over, placed them on the table one by one in front of Brice.

"What's this?" asked Brice.

"There is something very wonderful, very mysterious about cards," said Upmore. "They might almost have been designed by a superior intelligence. Why should there be four suits and four seasons; fifty-two cards and fifty-two weeks in the year? Then, counting the knaves, queens, and kings at eleven, twelve, and thirteen, there are altogether three hundred and sixty-four points, which is as near as could be got to the days of the year. Again, look at the four suits—hearts, diamonds, clubs, and spades—and you get a very good image of life." He continued to look intently at Brice as he spoke.

"Blest if I know what you are driving at," said the latter.

"There is a language in cards," continued Upmore. "Look at those in front of you and tell me what they are."

"Jack o' diamonds," said Brice slowly.

"Yes."

"Ace of clubs."

"Yes."

"King o' spades."

"Well?"

Brice bit his forefinger. "You're as deep as a well," he said, "and as dark, but I'm gettin' there. Gi' me time."

"What better image of life could you have?" asked the innkeeper. "Hearts for the affections, clubs for the passions, diamonds for wealth and all the joys of life, spades for disease and death."

"Gi' me time," repeated Brice. "F'rinstance, this 'ere jack o' diamonds, he might be a young 'un, and there might be money hangin' to 'im—I'm only sayin', mind you, but we'll turn 'im over," and he suited the action to the word. "The club's as may be and accordin' to what's most convenient—we'll turn 'im over too. As for the spade, no sense in turning' im over, for them sort never tell no tales."

He looked cunningly up into the inscrutable face of the innkeeper. "What do I get out of it?" he asked.

Upmore selected a five of diamonds. "Count that in hundreds," he said.

"Done with you!" said the other, thumping his fist on the cards and rising to his feet.

Upmore continued to watch him, breathing a little quickly. "You are sure you understand?" he asked.

"White drill trousers," said Brice, checking off the item on a dirty thumb, "yellow cotton socks, blue Crimea shirt with little circles in it."

Upmore began to collect the cards and put them away. "Have another taste before you go?" he suggested.

"That's me;" said Brice.

They went out into the bar and stood in silence while the drink was being consumed; then Brice turned to go. Half-way to the door he swung round and looked at the innkeeper. "That's a bargain about the other business," he said.

The innkeeper looked puzzled. "What business?" he asked.

Brice slowly winked his eye, then, with a horrible relieved laugh, out he went.

CHAPTER VI

MEANWHILE Clifford plodded along the dusty road, looking to right and left in search of a camping-ground. To the right he could perceive the track of the creek, indicated by an occasional cabbage tree or flax bush, gradually making in towards the road, and about a mile from the inn he struck across the rough, grey gumland to its banks. A small mound, clear of scrub, determined him to go no farther, and here he proceeded to erect his tent and establish himself and his belongings. The tent, with its fly to protect the roof from the direct beams of the sun, was soon in evidence, presenting in its vivid whiteness a sharp contrast to the monotonous hues of the gumfield. A mass of dry fern fronds for a bed completed the internal fittings.

The fireplace, erected in front of the tent, consisted wholly of a forked stick thrust at an angle into the ground for the purpose of suspending pots and billies over the flames. Having nibbled some cabin-bread and made himself a pannikin of tea by the summary process of throwing some tea-leaves into the boiling billy, the young man picked up his spade, spear, and sack and went doubtfully out into the broiling sunlight.

He had received a good deal of advice from different people, but, as is usual with advice, the difficulty was to apply it. He had been told that the presence of gum was indicated by mounds, which represented the spots where the huge trees once stood; but he found the field thrown into such confusion by the spades of innumerable diggers past and present that all trace of these mounds had, to his untrained eye, long since become extinguished.

He abandoned the search for mounds, and wandered about thrusting his spear into the ground at random. This also led to nothing. Once or twice it did seem that the spear met with opposition from a gritty body, but on these occasions the spade only turned out small pieces of charcoal. After an hour or two the job began to wear a hopeless aspect. It is true there were places which had apparently never been disturbed, but this would probably be because the experienced digger knew by external indications that no gum existed there. On the other hand, the places which had received the digger's attention were presumably quite denuded of what treasure they once contained. But if this were so, then manifestly there was no gum anywhere.

Clifford thrust his spear into the ground, and taking his spade began methodically to turn the soil over to the depth of a foot. A couple of hours of this convinced him that the gum-digger's lot was not entirely a happy one; but still be persevered, accumulating energy as he went on, determined to succeed, even if success necessitated digging backwards to the horizon.

A person who had come up unperceived stood watching the young man with a dry smile, behind which there lurked something of admiration for the tenacity displayed. He was a man of about forty, turning grey, with a pair of twinkling blue eyes. He was in his shirt-sleeves, and stood with his legs wide apart and his hands sunk deep in his pockets.

"You ought to get a good crop, young un," he remarked at length.

Clifford, interrupted in the task of breaking a clod to pieces, looked sheepishly at the new-comer, who met his gaze with a good-humoured nod. "It's not potatoes I'm going to plant," the young man explained, catching some of the other's amusement. "I am looking for gum."

"You are the right sort to find it," said the other, "and I am going to show you how to find it right away."

He picked up the young man's spade and led the way among the hillocks of the gumfield, pushing aside the scrub and running his eye from point to point as he moved.

"You see," he said as they went forward, "you've not got to look at the standing bush, but the fallen, and you need to ask yourself whether a tree could have stood at a particular point or not. No tree could have stood where you were digging, and that's why no digger has ever tried it." He was silent awhile, looking keenly at the ground, and moving backwards and forwards a short distance through the thick growth. At last he stood still and thrust the spade into the ground.

"Now," he said, "look about you and tell me what you see."

"There seems to be a little hollow in front of us," said Clifford, "and the ground rises a bit just beyond it?"

"Anything else?"

Clifford looked and shook his head.

"Carry your eye in a straight line beyond the mound. Do you notice a sort of ridge running along for thirty or forty feet?"

"There does seem to be a line of tea tree higher than the rest," Clifford conceded.

"It's higher because the ground is higher," said his companion. "And the reason for that is as plain as a pikestaff. Where this hole is once stood a kauri; the gale caught him and tore his roots out of the ground, together with a great mass of soil. The mound is all that is left of the roots, and the long ridge represents the barrel."

"I see," said Clifford expectantly; then his face fell. "But it has all been dug over," he added.

"That remains to be seen," said his companion. "You must not forget that besides the barrel there are the branches, and it is never safe to conclude because a place has been dug over that all the gum has been taken out of it. Now here," he continued, pausing at a spot some twenty yards from the mound, "is a place worth trying; it's the sort of spot I should tackle myself; and if you don't find gum somewhere close handy, I'm not the King of the Diggers."

Clifford seized the spade and began eagerly turning over the soil, while the person who had staked his royalty on the issue seated himself to watch operations.

"It's a wonderful place this," he said musingly, a far-away look in his forget-me-not eyes. "Huge trees all around us, and in amongst them the saplings springing up straight and clean, bound on a life of a thousand years' duration. Listen! You can hear the wind coming up from the sea and dying away among the leaves like a spent wave."

Clifford lifted his eyes and looked across the dusty, scrubby

40

landscape and back to the speaker. There was something at once exalted and pleading in the blue eyes looking into his own that set the young man wondering.

A few more turns of the spade, and the gum began to appear in small rusty nuggets until about a dozen pieces, ranging in size from a walnut to a turkey's egg, lay on the ground beside the hole. "1 told you!" said the man triumphantly.

"Yes," said Clifford, "of course this gum is yours."

"Keep it," said the other, "for I have plenty. All the gum on all the gumfields is mine, for I alone know where it is. That is why they call Jessamine Olive the King of the Diggers."

"Is that your name? " asked Clifford.

"Yes, but you may call me Jess—all the boys call me Jess. Why should I take your gum, who have all the storehouse of the forest to draw upon? See here." He rose, and taking the spade from Clifford, moved off through the scrub.

Ten yards further on, in a piece of marshy ground, he came to a halt and began looking critically about him. Presently he laughed merrily.

"Yes," he said, "they have found the barrel all right and most of the branches, and they have taken the gum away; but there is one thing they missed. Can you guess what?"

Clifford shook his head.

"They have missed the branch that was torn off by the tree just behind you there."

Clifford smiled expostulation.

The other seemed not to notice, but thrust his spade into the ground, and in a few minutes was throwing out the gum with every lift of the white soil. All the while he kept up a running fire of comments.

"The trees are thick here. The one behind you is dying of old age and tumbling to pieces from the top downwards; the wind will never blow him over, only scatter him about in dust and rotten flakes. Do you see the shape of the branch? It is as big as an ordinary tree. It seems to have been split up and splintered, and that is why the gum is all along instead of being in pockets. There's a piece for you, now." He lifted out a nugget about ten inches long and half as much in diameter.

Clifford looked on in astonishment. "Is it possible," he asked, "that you can gather all this information from the external appearance of the soil? Why, to me it is the most colourless and monotonous place I ever saw."

Olive ceased digging. "Put it all in your bag," he said. "It is getting late, and the bush is not a place to be in after dark." He gave a little shiver and then laughed.

"I am strangely nervous of dark places," he explained half apologetically; "it's a funny thing in a man, perhaps, but so it is."

"Not at all," said Clifford gently, a light of understanding growing up in his mind. "But surely you don't intend me to keep all this gum?—that's absurd."

"Why not?" asked Olive. "All the gum of the forest is mine for the taking; I can give and I can leave it, and it costs me nothing at all. Let us get outside," he broke off, looking about him with a vague anxiety.

The sun had set, and the brief twilight of northern New Zealand was darkening rapidly into night.

"Where are you camping?" asked Clifford, as they forced a passage through the scrub.

"On the hillside," said Olive. "I saw your tent from my cabin, and knew you would want me."

"Then you came especially on my account? That was kind of you."

"I like to help beginners," said Jess simply; "the world is not an easy place to live in if we do not help one another."

"It is not," Clifford assented.

"I do not like to be taken advantage of. Sometimes men follow me about with the idea of making capital out of my knowledge, but in the end they have to give it up. I help those I like."

"Shall I come over with you?" Clifford asked when they had reached his tent.

"No," replied Jess; "it is not so dark out here, Strange weakness, isn't it, for a grown man to be afraid of the dark?

You can go back to that place again to-morrow; there is more gum there. And keep to the swamps and damp places, you will find it easier. I shall come round to see how you are getting on. Don't forget the King of the Diggers."

Clifford gave him good-night, and watched him as he went up along the creek in the last gleams of daylight, the stars breaking out above him as he moved. It was not an altogether unaccountable freak of the imagination that he seemed to see in the long, night shadows about the retreating figure the tremendous columns of the vanished forest towering upwards into the dim sky.

In a few minutes the fire for the evening meal was crackling and blazing in the cool night air, and Clifford's first day on the gumfield had ended more successfully than he could have anticipated.

CHAPTER VI

FOR two or three days afterwards Clifford continued to visit the spot to which Olive had introduced him and daily added a few pounds of gum to his store. In the evenings he sat for an hour or two, in the light of a candle in a cleft stick, scraping his day's takings and preparing them for the storekeeper.

Now and then he was visited by stray diggers, who dropped in for what they described as a "pitch" Some of these men were fairly educated, but they had all picked up the manners of the society in which they moved, one feature of which was that every other word they used was an oath, and had it been possible to convey an intelligible meaning in such fashion, there can be no doubt that the words in between would have been in exactly the same predicament.

The subject of most engrossing interest with these men at this time was the Christmas holidays, now close at hand. Clifford did not propose to make any alteration in his way of life on that account, but he found himself listening with half-sympathetic amusement to the wild proposals of his visitors. Most of them had apparently accumulated cheques for a considerable amount, but none contemplated that these sums would last them longer than a week or ten days at the outside. They counted with perfect indifference on the confidence man, the spieler, the *fille de joie*, the predatory cabman, all of whom would swoop down on them, like so many hawks, the moment they entered the city. Nothing could have been more remote from their thoughts than to consider the conduct of these people, or indeed themselves, from an ethical standpoint. They looked forward to being fleeced and possibly maltreated with the same cheerfulness with which they regarded the memory of such adventures in the past, and the humour of these engagements was apparently the only feature which had made an indelible impression on their minds.

The mass of mankind is constructed on this plan, but we are learning how to cover up the deeps with education and various other top-dressings. Pretty and elegant flowers spring up and clothe us about, giving a smiling and respectable appearance, but the imprisoned lava below sometimes burns them off at the roots.

Out on the field Clifford came across men of this type daily. Some were from the universities of England; some were ignorant but with their wits sharpened to an extraordinary degree by experience. They were from all countries—from Austria in great numbers—and of all trades and professions. The type of the settler who had a wife and family somewhere beyond the confines of the field was also well represented. He was of a tamer species, but also of a stronger and sterner. He worked methodically, with his eye steadfastly riveted on the future; and that future would probably behold him grey-headed but active and rosy, the owner of lands and houses, of cattle and horses, and of a handsome family, living in an earthly paradise, the work of their own hands. There was also another class, less desirable in character and not so easy to define in words. These men moved rapidly from field to field, living on the gullibility of the storekeepers or loafing on the good nature of the diggers. Some of them were fugitives from justice. There was also a sprinkling of mechanics and clerks out of employment; old men for whom the world had no further use, and who preferred independence to the strict, prison-like rule of a poor man's refuge; and last, but not least, a sprinkling of natives of both sexes.

To this last class belonged Clifford's nearest neighbours on the field. A couple of families, comprising old and young men, women, and children, had built themselves a shelter of palm leaves two or three hundred yards down the creek, and thence in the still evenings he heard the sound of their voices above the liquid rustle of the stream. They were frequent visitors to the tent, especially two of the women, who on one occasion, finding him in the throes of breadmaking, took that task upon themselves, no little to the improvement of his larder. From these people he gleaned a good deal of information which was of service to him in his search for gum.

Jess Olive came also to be a frequent visitor at the tent, and the reason he gave for his coming was a peculiar one.

"What made you select this spot, young un?" he asked once.

It was a Sunday afternoon, warm, drowsy, and still, and having tried the banks of the creek, they had retired into the tent out of the strong sunlight.

"I don't know," said Clifford. "It may have been the cabbage tree or it may have been because it was the first suitable spot I came to. Why?"

"This," replied Jess, "is the grandest spot in the whole bush, and often and often have I come here to look at the noble trees. Here stands the King of the Bush, the like of whom is not to be found anywhere else in New Zealand."

"Tell me what he is like," said Clifford.

"When he was young," said Jess slowly, "he entered into partnership with the sun, and from that hour the earth and the sky were his to draw upon. God gave him an eternity of time, and slowly, hour by hour, century by century, he rose up out of the ground and stretched himself among the clouds."

"Can you see him from where you sit?" Clifford asked curiously.

Jess turned his eyes to the opening, and at the same moment it was darkened by the shadow of a man coming in under the fly.

"So this is where you are, Clifford?" said a weary voice, which Clifford recognised as the property of Bart. "And the King of the Diggers here too—save your majesty." The tone was not all a mockery.

"Sit down," said Clifford. "What news from the 'Scarlet Man'?"

"I have chucked him," said Bart, "or he has chucked me, which is the same thing. Damn the 'Scarlet Man'!"

"Don't swear," said Jess, "What good does it do?"

Bart looked at him a moment, and the harsh lines about his face relaxed. "Well," he said, "I won't, but them's my sentiments. For instance, is there a greater brute living than Upmore?"

"Why do you go near him?" Jess asked.

"God knows!" said Bart, yawning. "Ask me an easier one. Well"—brusquely to Clifford—"have you realised your ideal? What about the respectable occupation?"

"I am still of the same mind," replied Clifford.

Bart looked at him with a speculative interest. "Wait till the novelty has worn off," he said; "wait till the past begins to stretch its arms out for you and to cry 'Come back'; wait till the life hunger begins to gnaw at your heart-strings, and you know that you have placed yourself irrevocably beyond the power to satisfy it!"

"Is that the case of some?" asked Clifford.

"Of hundreds—eh, Jess?—hundreds and hundreds. When the university men and the scholars who have drifted off the track of the trade winds, and the merchant princes who have gone bung, and the geniuses who have gone bunger have trodden the cities for a year in their uppers, and the rack of necessity has broken the bones of their pride, then they come here, and the place is accursed on account of them."

Jess watched the speaker with awed fascination, a vague unhappiness in his blue eyes.

"It is not all like that," he said hesitatingly. "Most of the men who come here go away after awhile somewhere else. Some stay, and like it. I like it. There are lots of little things that keep me happy all day long."

"That's it," said Bart. "The little things make us happy because we expect nothing from them, but the big things continually disappoint us. Life is a delusion and a fraud."

"It's getting late," said Jess, rising and looking anxiously out into the glaring sunlight. "I think I will be getting home before it grows any darker."

"Good-bye, O King," said Bart. "Happy lunatic!" he added, when Jess had departed out of hearing.

"What is his story?" asked Clifford.

"Another tragedy. Wife and child killed before his eyes by a falling tree in the Wairaki bush many years ago. Mad as a March hare ever since."

"I should not call him mad," objected Clifford.

47

"Well, then, something jarred and out of tune. I grant you the ruin is picturesque. Fancy, roaming about this gaudy, howling waste, and seeing around you the original forest as he does! What a magnificent madness, after all!"

"I wonder how he would take the real bush!" speculated Clifford.

"It's been tried, but the darkness kills him. At the back of his brain there is an impenetrable blackness of horror; he resides in a sunlit chamber in front. Well, what are you making? Tucker?"

"Just about."

"Glorious existence!" said Bart, rising with a weary yawn. "Some day you may even make pocket-money." With which consolatory reflection he took himself off.

A fortnight's sojourn on the field had to some extent trained Clifford's eye to the perception of detail. He no longer conceived the place as an indistinguishable whole, but as an assemblage of places of extreme diversity, and he had discovered that, from a gum-digger's point of view, certain of these places were more desirable than others. About this time it was that he made his first good find, He had been digging from seven o'clock in the morning till four in the afternoon with but poor success, a few pieces of very jagged and almost worthless gum representing the complete result of his toil. Tired and disheartened, he threw himself down in a thick clump of tea tree, and was soon absorbed in watching a battle between two full-grown "animated straws" who, each mounted on his own twig, endeavoured to kick or haul his adversary from his position. Now one, extending a long front leg, would salute his opponent with a terrific cuff on the side of the head. This would be followed by furious blows from both sides, delivered with a blind passion that ensured their futility. Ultimately one insect decided that he had had enough, and let himself drop lower down the bush, while the conqueror, inflated with his victory, staggered off like a gouty general from a corporation dinner. The conceit of the creature was so comical that Clifford could not refrain from patting him on the back with a blade of grass.

In an instant his long antennm became glued together and rigidly extended, his narrow, straw-like body swung gently from side to side. He had become a green twig swaying in the breeze, indistinguishable, save on close inspection, from the tea tree on which he rested.

Absorbed in this miniature drama, Clifford had taken no heed of some sharp, hard substance which was making its presence obtrusively felt beneath his chest. He now turned his attention to this object, and, to his surprise and delight, found he had been lying on the edge of a piece of gum of unknown dimensions which here protruded itself through the soil. Were the whole of it visible, it would still be the largest piece he had yet discovered; but after trying it gently with the corner of his spade, he felt sure that not only was there a part concealed, but also that that part was considerably larger than the portion exposed. Digging carefully round so as to avoid breakages, he in a few minutes rolled out a fine nugget of gum weighing over fifteen pounds, but this was not all. Beneath the nugget lay several smaller pieces scattered through the soil to a depth of two feet, and when the trove was finally exhausted he found himself in possession of nearly forty pounds of first-class gum, a find with which any digger would have reason to be contented.

When finally he came to the conclusion that no more was to be found at this particular spot, he stepped out of the hole and commenced to fill his *pikau*. As he was engaged in this employment, stooping forward to lift the pieces from the ground, he was suddenly aware of a shadow flying between his feet and speeding instantaneously out of sight. He turned swiftly to find a man just behind him, holding a spade by both hands above his head. He was a powerful-looking man, with a remarkably small head, and Clifford noticed that his teeth, revealed by a sudden drooping twitch of the lips, were ragged and discoloured.

The fellow lowered his spade to his shoulder and scratched the side of his nose. Clifford stood watching him in silence, his lips closed, his eyes phenomenally dark and steady in their gaze.

"Seem to 'ave struck it this time, matey," said the man, with a desperate attempt to appear at his ease.

"Yes, you were not here soon enough," retorted Clifford swiftly, without moving. "You are no mate of mine."

"We are all mates here," said the man doubtfully.

"By God, no!" returned Clifford in the same tone. "There had need to be few mates for such as you!"

"Why, what the cuss—" commenced the other.

Clifford suddenly took a step towards him. "For two pins," he said in a deep voice, "I'd wring your ugly head off. I feel like doing it."

"Don't balk your fancy, mate," said the man, with another glimpse of his ragged teeth.

But he was mistaken in the man with whom he had to do. Clifford instantly knocked him into the hole from which he had taken the gum.

The man sat for a moment dazed by the suddenness of the attack, then, with a fierce oath, he sprang forward, brandishing his spade.

Clifford met him half-way.

The fiendish wrong which had been, as he thought, meditated against him for the sake of a few paltry pounds of gum had turned the young man's blood to fire; the strength of his indignation was a measure of the strength of his moral nature. The encounter was desperate, but brief. Whether the resolution displayed by Clifford in again advancing on him instead of putting himself in a posture of defence, cowed his opponent, or for some other reason, he gained no advantage by his possession of a weapon. Rather the reverse, for while Clifford was able to avoid any severe blow from the spade, his assailant had no arm wherewith to defend himself from the swift, heavy blows which loosened his teeth and threatened to break his jaw. In a few moments he dropped his weapon and sheered off. Clifford instantly seized the spade and swung it to a distance across the scrub, then he pointed with his finger in the direction in which it had gone. "Go!" he said.

"You'll 'ear more about this, my fine feller," said the man.

"Go!" repeated Clifford, again advancing on him.

"Look 'ere," said the other, with a change of tone and slowly drawing back. "What's the row? What 'ave I done to you, any'ow? You struck me, but I never did nothin' to you."

"Don't talk to me," said Clifford fiercely. "Do as I tell you. Go!"

"But you're so damned onreasonable. Can't you say what I've done?"

"I'm not going to argue with you. Go!"

"Did you ever see me before to-day?" persisted the man. "Not you; you never seen me. Then I arsks you what 'ave I done?"

"Are you going?" demanded Clifford, with a white-hot quietness.

The man grumbled, commenced a further expostulation, but thought better of it, as Clifford showed symptoms of moving, and retired, looking about for his spade. When he had found it, he stood for some time looking back at Clifford, who was busying himself in bagging the remainder of his gum. "I'll be even with you, you —," he cried at length.

The contemptuous strength of silence displayed by the young man maddened the grosser nature of the defeated scoundrel. He looked about for stones, and finding none, commenced to pelt his enemy with clods of earth.

Clifford moved about, apparently unconscious of the cannonade to which he was subjected, till a missile, better directed than the rest, struck him sharply on the cheek. Then he instantly dropped everything and bounded across the scrub.

The man seeing him approach, turned and fled, and Clifford, who had no idea of catching him, suffered him to gain on him till he was lost to view in the gathering night.

This occurred about five days before Christmas. A few days later the field was almost entirely deserted, even his Maori neighbours having packed up their chattels and ridden off on a number of weedy-looking horses to their settlement beyond the field.

Clifford continued to work on as before.

Three days after Christmas Day there befell him a singular and romantic adventure.

CHAPTER VIII

DURING this time Clifford had not revisited the "Scarlet Man," nor had he seen anything of Upmore since the day he first set up his tent on the field. This particular evening, however, feeling a desire for society, he walked across to the inn, which lay at a distance of rather more than a mile from the spot where he was himself encamped.

A busy scene met his eye. From the doorway and the lamp above the door a patch of light was thrown across the verandah on to the road, where its edges were absorbed in the intense darkness of the moonless night. Through this glare moved a constant succession of figures—male and female, children and adults. In the roadway before the inn were a number of horses, twenty or more being gathered with their noses over the verandah, while their native owners, squatted in all positions in and outside the house, kept up a perfect babel of talk.

Clifford made his way between the heels of the horses and through the groups on the verandah into the crowded bar. Contrary to his expectation, very little drinking was going on, the natives being from some settlement in Hokianga, where temperance in the matter of liquor was more prevalent than elsewhere. Mixed and mysterious sounds from the region of the dead-house, however, convinced Clifford that that necessary adjunct to the bush pub was in requisition.

Upmore was in his shirt-sleeves, moving about as though he were busy, and from him Clifford learned the destination of the travellers to be a racecourse about fifteen miles distant, where some races were to come off the following day.

For the next quarter of an hour Clifford amused himself in watching the motley groups, who in their turn were not slow to bestow a curious regard on him. The Maoris were all in European costume, the men being clothed in the ordinary slop tweeds of the local stores, while the women and girls were robed in prints and other cheap and generally gaudy fabrics. A few of the older women had babies on their backs, closely enveloped in plaid shawls, while a number of older children ran in and out among the legs of the crowd. They had probably left some settlement among the bush-clad mountains of Hokianga well-nigh deserted of its inhabitants.

Presently there was a cry to horse, and the crowd began to troop off, the hubbub of their voices dying gradually out as horse after horse scampered away at full gallop into the night. In a few minutes the place was deserted, and the ordinary quiet of the gumfield had again settled upon the lonely inn.

Clifford stayed a little longer to recount his recent experiences, then made off in the direction of his tent.

It was now eight o'clock, and an intensely dark night. For the first time since his arrival on the field heavy clouds had arisen from the northward and completely obscured the sky. Instead of returning across the field by the way he had come, Clifford determined for the greater comfort of the walk to proceed along the road to a point a hundred yards from his camp and thence strike directly across. The way was a trifle longer, but the smoother nature of the ground more than compensated for the extra distance.

He had covered the greater part of the road, and turned off on to the rough ground of the field, when he heard the sound of a horse trotting steadily towards him from the direction whence he had come. For some reason he was never subsequently able to explain, he stood still where he was and waited for the rider to come up. From the sound made by the horse's hoofs, now loud and clinking, now dull and scarcely audible, he gathered two things: the horse was shod, and therefore in all probability the rider was a European; he was riding partly on the road and partly on the mossy margin to one side. It occurred to Clifford as he came to the latter conclusion that this was a dangerous thing to do. He had himself put his foot into more than one hole, which some careless digger had allowed to remain open, and though to a foot-passenger this might be merely a source of annoyance, the case was likely to be very different with a person mounted on horseback. Almost at the moment this reflection crossed his mind he heard the horse stumble, and a few seconds later the sound of its hoofs was again audible, this time advancing at a terrific pace towards the spot where he stood. Clifford ran forward on to the road in time to turn the frightened creature into the tea tree, where, after a loud rustling of leaves and cracking of branches, it apparently came to a standstill; he then moved hurriedly back in search of the rider.

About twenty yards along the road he thought he could discern some dark object in a semi-recumbent attitude by the side of the way. The sound of a voice, apparently that of a young woman, saying, "What shall I do now?" caused him to hurry to the spot.

"Here is help," he said cheerfully, as he came up.

The person on the road made some reply which he did not catch. He struck a light. The air was singularly calm, the flame of the wax vesta barely flickering as it burned. Before him, half kneeling, half sitting, was a young girl of nineteen or twenty in a close-fitting blue serge riding-habit. Her face was white and drawn, as if with pain; she looked dazed and frightened.

"Are you hurt?" he asked.

"My foot—but I have lost my horse."

"I might be able to catch the horse for you," said Clifford; "but are you sure you have no other injury?"

"Only my foot," she repeated. "But oh, if you could catch my horse! I don't know what I shall do if he is not caught. Will you try?"

"Certainly," said he. "I will leave my match-box with you. Call out if you want help."

Clifford went off, listening carefully for any rustle that might betray the presence of the animal, but not a sound was to be heard.

After a fruitless search of a quarter of an hour he returned and reported his non-success. The girl was in great distress, and for a moment Clifford was in agonies lest she should cry.

"Whatever shall I do?" she ejaculated.

"Try if you can walk," he suggested. "Let me assist you to rise."

She offered no objection, and he raised her to her feet; but no sooner was she standing erect than she uttered a sharp cry of pain, and would have fallen.

"I am afraid my foot is badly hurt," she said tearfully. "I cannot set it down without extreme pain."

"Throw all your weight on me," he said gently— "unless you would let me carry you."

"Where to?" she asked. "Of course, I would not let you do anything of the kind; but where is there to go to?"

"Nowhere but the hotel," said Clifford.

"Upmore's?" she asked, with a shiver. "I would sooner stay here than go to that place. Oh, dear, this is dreadful! If I only had my horse!"

"He is probably half-way home by this time," said Clifford. "But you cannot stay here, it will be raining heavily in a few minutes, and you have no protection; besides, your foot may be severely injured, and should be seen to at once. Why should you not let me carry you to the hotel? It is barely a mile distant."

"No, no," she said hurriedly; "let me lean on your arm, and I will try to walk. It is a shame of me to cause you so much trouble."

This was the first indication she had given that she did not demand and accept his services as a right, and the sweet tones increased the natural delight of the young man in his task.

"Think how I can be of use to you," he said, as they prepared to start.

But after moving a few yards it became clear that the girl would be totally unable to accomplish the distance to the inn, the intense pain rendering her breathless with every step she took.

"Look here," said Clifford suddenly, "I have a tent close by; if it were daylight you could see it from where we stand. Let me take you there, and then I will run off and find Mrs. Brandy, or Brandon, or whatever her name is, at the hotel. Will you do that? See, it is already beginning to rain; if we stay here another ten minutes we shall be drenched through."

The girl hesitated, peering about in the gloom.

"No," she said at last despairingly "Leave me here; I can wait here till the morning."

"Nonsense!" said Clifford brusquely. "I have thought of a good plan, and you must fall in with it. If you are silly enough to stop here in the rain, I am not so foolish as to permit you to do so. This is no time for ceremony; you must do as you are told."

"I shall stay here," the girl repeated coldly.

Clifford was at a loss. "If you were my sister—," he began.

"Well?" she asked.

"I should pick you up and carry you whether you would or no."

There was a pause.

"Is your tent far from here?" came her voice presently.

"Not a hundred yards," said he persuasively. "Come."

He again raised her from the earth, and they moved on to the rough ground of the gumfield. But if she had found hardship in walking on the comparatively smooth road, this was a hundred times worse. Clifford, supporting her as well as he was able, heard her uttering little pitiful "Oh's!" under her breath, until, no longer able to endure the thought of her suffering, he lifted her suddenly into his arms and set off with an amount of resolution that gave no heed to her cry of offended dignity.

Beyond this exclamation she suffered herself to be borne away in silence.

"Put your arms round my neck," said Clifford, after moving for some distance through the scrub.

She laid her right arm across his shoulder.

"Now the other," he said masterfully.

She obeyed, her two arms lightly encircling his neck.

This, however, was not at all what the young man had intended, which was to transfer her weight from his left arm; accordingly he gradually loosened the support he was giving her, and she, feeling herself slipping, was obliged to cling to him with some energy. His left arm could now be used in grasping the bushes when from any cause he found himself in danger of falling. In this manner he bore her to his tent, and laid her down on the couch of fern. As he did so he was surprised and alarmed to feel her head droop suddenly across his wrist, and her whole body to become limp in his hands.

Clifford hastily lit a candle and found, as he had conjectured, that the girl had fainted. Once on a previous occasion it had fallen to the lot of our young man to carry a swooning woman from a place of entertainment, and he was not therefore so terribly frightened as he might have been had the event found him totally inexperienced. He at once set about restoring her to consciousness. With trembling fingers he undid the heavy diamond brooch at her throat, and loosening the collar of her dress, sprinkled her face and neck with water, but still there was no sign of returning consciousness. He felt that whatever course of action might be demanded of him by the proprieties, he could not leave her in this condition. He had a shrewd suspicion that the fainting-fit was not so much of a hysterical character as induced by intense pain, and that immediate steps should be taken to alleviate her suffering.

The position was a difficult one. To a right-minded man there is a sacredness in the body of a woman which even in her own interest he finds it difficult to overcome. Clifford asked himself if he had the courage to release her foot from the boot in which it was confined. He grew indignant with himself as he felt the blood mantling in his cheeks, and this indignation finally nerved him to the act. As he unbuttoned and carefully drew off the long slim boot the girl sighed and moved. He at once returned to his restoratives, and in a few moments had the satisfaction of seeing her restored to consciousness.

Her eyes were deep and dark with pain as she turned them on him with a gaze of momentary wonder.

"You had fainted," he said. "I hardly dare leave you even yet."

"It is my boot," she said, with a catch of her breath; "it is killing me."

"I have taken the boot off," he replied. "I thought you would

58

never come to."

"Is my foot broken?" she asked.

"I hardly dared," stammered Clifford, "without your permission—though I know something of injuries. Perhaps, if you would remove—then we could put some cold-water bandages—"

"Yes," she said, with a composure born probably of his nervousness. She raised herself, and putting her hands under the rug, in a few moments a white foot was peeping from beneath the long skirt of her habit. As she leant back her face was again of snowy whiteness and her eyes dimmed and dreamy.

"Don't," he said anxiously, suspecting another faint.

"No," she replied resolutely, with a faint smile that ended with a pitiful drooping of the mouth at the corners. "Is it broken, do you think?"

Clifford took the small white foot tenderly in his hand. Over the instep was a villainous contusion, divided by a heavy purple line, where the steel of the stirrup had indented itself on the flesh. The whole of the ankle was more or less swollen and inflamed.

"There is a bad sprain," said Clifford, "but I do not think any of the bones are broken. Will you let me bandage it for you before I go up to the hotel?"

"If you will," she replied simply.

Clifford procured some handkerchiefs from his wardrobe, and having obtained a bucket of water from the creek, proceeded with the operation of bandaging the wounded member.

At the first touch of the cold water she breathed a sigh of relief.

"It is delightful just not to feel pain," she said, smiling. Clifford smiled in sympathy, and having completed his task, rose to his feet.

"Now," he said, "I will go for Mrs. Brandon."

As he ceased speaking there was a rushing sound audible in the still air, and the rain, loosened from the sky, smote the tent-roof in a perfect deluge.

CHAPTER IX

CLIFFORD hesitated, then buttoned his coat across his chest, and prepared to start.

"Are you going?" she asked hesitatingly.

"I shall not be very long," he replied.

"But in this rain?"

"Well, it is rather heavy," he admitted. "If you don't mind I will wait a few minutes."

"I could not think of letting you get wet through on my account," she said. "I have already sufficiently inconvenienced you."

"Not at all," said Clifford.

The fire, which must otherwise have been extinguished by the rain, was protected by a small fly of palm leaves, which the natives had given to Clifford for that purpose. He now occupied himself in piling on fuel, and thus flooded the tent with a cheerful blaze of cherry-coloured light. Then, with a feeling of disgust at his own large proportions, he sat down in a corner of the tent and looked respectfully at his patient.

"Are you feeling easier now?" he asked.

"Yes, thank you," she responded.

"Because there is plenty more cold water when your foot begins to get painful again."

"Yes."

"How did the accident occur?" he asked.

"I am afraid I was very careless," she replied. "My mind was occupied with other things, and I left everything to the horse. Then he stumbled and threw me. I could not immediately get my foot from the stirrup, and he dragged me a few yards before I got loose."

"It is a very dark night for riding," said Clifford.

"Let me tell you all about it," said the young lady. "My name is Esther Hamilton; I am a daughter of Dr. Hamilton, of Parawai. My father and I were to attend the races to-morrow, and at five o'clock this evening we were preparing to start. Then a message came for my father from a settler about half a mile from the village, and he told me to ride slowly on, and he would overtake me. I had just made up my mind to turn back, and, indeed, had pulled the rein with that purpose when the accident occurred."

"Then your father might pass by at any moment?" said Clifford.

"He might," she assented, "but I do not think so, because there was a chance the case he was called to might be serious, and he told me if he did not overtake me in a couple of hours either to turn back or press on as quickly as possible."

"It is very unfortunate," said Clifford. "There were some native women a short distance down the creek until a few days ago, but now the field is almost deserted. Do you know anything of Mrs. Brandon?"

"No," replied Esther slowly, with a slight change of manner,

"Because she might possibly object to come out such a night as this, though I hardly think it likely under the circumstances."

"She might," assented Esther, looking troubled.

"Is there anything else you can suggest?" he asked. "I might borrow a horse from Upmore and ride over for your father, but that would necessitate leaving you alone for a number of hours. I do not say it would be unsafe, but still—" He hesitated and looked out across the fire into the rain.

"Why?" she asked, as he remained silent.

"Well," he replied, "the field is nearly deserted, but there are still a few undesirable characters remaining. I do not believe any harm would befall you, but I have often had visitors of all kinds in the evening, and were you to be bothered by them in my absence, your friends would naturally blame me for leaving you unprotected."

"Yes!" she said hurriedly, a new fear dawning in her eyes, "do not leave me alone. Could I not go with you?"

"In this rain? You would get your death."

"But when it leaves off. It does not seem quite so heavy now."

Clifford listened. It was true the downpour had abated something of its first fury, but at this period of the year what are known as the Christmas rains might be expected to keep up more or less continuously for three or four days together. He conjectured it was hardly likely they could travel any distance that night without getting drenched to the skin.

"Are you afraid to remain alone while I run up to the hotel?" he asked.

"How long will you be?" she inquired anxiously.

"Possibly three-quarters of an hour—less, of course, if Mrs. Brandon does not return with me."

Her face fell.

Suddenly a thought struck him, and going to his knapsack he produced a small glittering object from the bottom.

"Can you use a pistol?" he asked.

"I never have, but I daresay I could."

Clifford withdrew the cartridges and showed her how to manage the weapon; then, reloading it, he placed it in her hand.

"Be very careful," he advised. "If anyone should come don't be too ready, but when there is a necessity cover your man. He will probably run away, but if he advances on you fire at his chest. Try and kill him, you understand. You must kill a man of that sort, for if you only wound him he will probably kill you. But don't be alarmed; it is getting on for nine o'clock, and not a night to induce anyone to be out. It is the unlikeliest thing in the world that you will be disturbed."

Esther placed the pistol under the rug within reach of her hand. Then Clifford buttoned his coat, threw a gum sack across his shoulders, and stepped out into the rain.

"Good-bye," he said cheerfully.

"Good-bye," she replied in scarcely audible tones.

After his departure Esther lay quiet, listening to the sound of the rain on the tent-roof; but about ten minutes later the downpour ceased as suddenly as it had begun, and was followed by a stillness broken only by the subdued singing of the creek beneath the bank.

In some way the sound of the rain had given her a sense of companionship which now on its cessation gave place to a feeling of intense loneliness. She drew herself into a sitting posture with her back against one of the supports of the tent, and wrapped the rugs more closely around her. She was feeling cold and at the same time feverishly excited. The pain in her foot had also again begun to assert itself with a gnawing, irritating persistence. All kinds of unhappy visions crossed her mind. She would be lame for life; her foot was so severely injured as to necessitate amputation. Such ideas were, however, too dreadful to brood over, and she dismissed them with a shiver to the background of her mind, where they hung like a thundercloud, casting a blacker shadow across her thoughts. There was another side, to the affair. Supposing Mrs. Brandon refused to come—and perhaps in any case—might there not be a scandal? People were so ready to attribute ill. Might it not even be said her foot had received no injury at all? Esther writhed at the thought like a wounded deer; probably she knew the scandal hunger of the district. From her father she doubted if she would get implicit credence, but how about someone else? He was not always very considerate. Perhaps he was just a little—a very little—suspicious. In any case he would be angry and say unpleasant things.

What a predicament! Alone in a gum-digger's tent at the mercy of a man of whom she knew nothing! Was ever girl so unfortunate? But was he a gum-digger, after all? He had not the appearance of the men she had seen round the stores of the settlement; and then he had been so gentle and considerate it was a shame to distrust him. He had been the first, if not to see, at any rate to suggest, the necessity for another woman's presence. No, she did not distrust him. It was the world she doubted and feared. Besides, there was the pistol. He would not have given her that if he contemplated any action which might necessitate her using it against himself.

How lonely it was here by herself, and how she longed for his return!—yes, though he came alone. Could she use the pistol in case anyone should come? Esther put her hand beneath the rug to ascertain the whereabouts of the weapon. As her hand touched the hilt she started and listened intently, her whole being concentrated in the sense of hearing.

There had been a faint rustling sound as of something moving in the wet bushes without.

The sound did not recur, but she was now alarmed almost to a state of frenzy. The possibility of some ruffian lurking in the vicinity, perhaps even watching her from the blackness beyond the fire, had the effect of increasing her trust in Clifford. The young man assumed in her mind the character of an invincible defender, of a tried and lifelong friend.

"Oh, come back, come back!" she whispered unconsciously, straining her eyes into the gloom.

In a few minutes she became calmer and relaxed the intensity of her gaze. Probably the sound that had frightened her was due to some motion of the atmosphere, though the night hitherto had been phenomenally calm and free from wind. She glanced round the tent, thinking if it were possible for anyone to enter save by the doorway. At one side the rain had left a broad dark mark on the canvas, and this set her wondering whether in the event of more rain falling the place was entirely waterproof. Her gaze passed across the dry roof and down the other side—no rain had entered so far.

Then again an event occurred which sent the blood in a tumultuous wave to her heart. She was now convinced that she was no longer alone. One of the tent walls had suddenly moved a few inches inward as though pressed upon by some object outside. It regained its place on the instant, and again everything was as silent and motionless as before.

In the deathly stillness Esther heard the quick, muffled beating of her heart. Some terrible danger threatened, and still there was no sound of her protector's return.

Again her eyes were fixed on the darkness without, and slowly the pitiful hunted look they wore was intensified to one of terror. Crouched behind the fire, his face rendered uncertain by the quivering flame and smoke, was a man who gazed fixedly into the tent.

In spite of herself, Esther uttered a startled cry, and the man, seeing himself discovered, rose, came round the fire, and bent himself through the doorway. He was a tall man, massively framed, and as he stooped beneath the canvas it seemed to the distressed girl that he filled the whole tent.

The intruder looked round, then pulled off his cap with mock reverence.

"'D evenin', miss," he said. "Boss not at home?"

Esther felt her mouth and lips to have become suddenly dry, but she was surprised at the steadiness of her voice as she replied in the negative.

"Then take the liberty of settin' down till he comes," said the man, suiting the action to the word.

"I expect him every minute," said Esther, moistening her lips.

The man cocked his head and listened intently for a moment, then he settled himself comfortably, favoured her with a long, cool stare, and said, "Do you, now? How very nice!"

As this did not appear to call for any reply, Esther remained silent.

"Me an' your mate," said the man, after a pause, "had a bit of a barney some days ago. I thought I'd just step round and bury the hatchet." He grinned, showing a mouthful of ragged teeth. "Yes, 'tain't the square thing to be on the cross-cut at Christmas-time; so I'm on the buryin' lay—that's my lay to-night. Here's the hatchet."

He pulled a tomahawk from his belt, and bending forward, held it in the face of the frightened girl. Then he laughed, and struck it deep into the earth floor of the tent.

"That's my lay," he repeated, "buryin' of it."

The idea appeared to cause him exquisite amusement, for he laughed again; then, suddenly checking himself, listened with the same intentness as before. Greatly to Esther's relief, he had drawn the axe from the ground and restored it to his belt before he again addressed her. This time his remark took a more personal tone.

"You'll be his fancy girl," he said, with a leering look of admiration. "My! if some men don't get all the luck."

"You are mistaken," said Esther, with a 'nervous quiet. "I

know nothing of him. I was thrown from my horse and hurt my foot. I never saw him before in my life till to-night."

"So I was thinking," returned the man stolidly. "You'll have met him mostly where there was no light to see him by. You're a sly one, you know, but we're all friends. There was a mate o' mine once had a girl on the field—Sandy George his name were—but, lor' bless you, he couldn't keep 'er; she just passed round, you know. You'll be thinking of givin' your mate the chuck by-an'-by."

"I am Dr. Hamilton's daughter," said Esther. "What I have told you is true. I am here as the result of an accident."

"Of course," said the man, with a sneer; "accident's the word. I've been there before. Bless you, I'm not so green as I'm cabbage-looking, though, dang me, if ever I saw quite such a pretty style on the field. But look 'ere, missy," he broke off, regarding her with a dreadful admiration, which seemed to the girl to affect her like the wound of a sword; "I'm not goin' to get you into no scrape with your mate, so give us a kiss and I'll sheer off right away. Come," he went on as she remained silent, "you look pretty snug and temptin' among them rugs. Don't carry it too high, or I may be asking you for a share. Give us a kiss, and I'll be off right away."

"Hark!" exclaimed Esther, with the cunning of desperation, "I hear him coming."

The man half started to his feet and listened. Save the purr of the water, not a sound was audible.

"You made a fool of me that time," said the ruffian, with a grin. "Hanged if I don't love you for your pluck; but I'll pay you out all the same. It was a kiss before, but the price has gone up now. What'll you give to get rid of me?"

"Everything I have," exclaimed Esther, a new hope dawning in her eyes. Feeling in her pocket, she produced a new Russia leather purse which she threw across to him.

"There," she said, "it is all I have; now leave me."

The man unstrapped the purse and poured the contents into his hand; then he sought for and removed one or two notes which had remained in one of the divisions.

"Four poun' three and sixpence," he remarked, transferring that amount to a pocket in the breast of his coat. "You're a generous little dear, but that ain't quite what I meant. Lord, I've made as much as four poun' ten in a day, but I ain't seen a girl like you in more'n a year. Come," he concluded, with an ugly smile, "what are you goin' to do?"

"I have given you all I have," replied Esther.

Her throat, tongue, and lips were now so parched by fear that the words seemed to suffocate her as she uttered them. All this time her hand had remained convulsively clasped on the hilt of the pistol beneath the rug. Her brain was working at an exhausting speed, and every one of her senses was sharpened to an abnormal degree by terror. In spite of all this not a muscle of her body trembled; she was possessed by that intense nervous calm which is the resource of timid natures driven to desperation.

The man turned over the empty purse and threw it into a corner of the tent. "Those things get a chap into trouble," he remarked. "There might be people to say it was stolen, whereas it was given to me by a sweet little critter of a girl when her fancy joker was out of the road. Now, missy," he broke off, extending a hand as if to touch her, "how are we goin' to get this square? Time's valuable."

"Do not touch me," she said clearly. "I am not defenceless, and it may cost you your life. I have given you all the money I possess, but if you go away at once I will promise any sum you like to ask for. My father will pay it, and I will say nothing against you."

"It won't work," said the man shortly. He listened a moment, then drew himself slightly nearer to her. "The boss is off for the night," he said hoarsely, with deadly intent in his eyes.

Esther's temptation to use the pistol had all this while been an intense drag on her will, but still she refrained. Nevertheless Clifford's terrible warning— "You must kill a man of that sort, for if you only wound him he will probably kill you"—repeated itself persistently in her mind, and she was fully determined, if the need arose, to aim at his head or his heart. As the ruffian approached the temptation became well-nigh irresistible.

"Remember," she cried wildly, scarcely conscious of what she said, "I have told you who I am and the reason I am here. If you dare to come nearer—Perhaps," she broke off, struck by a new possibility, "you have an enmity with the owner of this tent and think to harm him by injuring me, but believe me when I assure you he is a perfect stranger. I am here because my horse threw me and I have injured my foot."

"Oh, stow all that!" said the man brutally. "What the devil do I care who you are! Let's have a look at this foot."

As he spoke he moved suddenly forward and laid his hand on the rug above her knee.

No sooner was the action performed than he found himself looking down the barrel of a pistol.

The next instant there was a loud report and the tent became filled with smoke.

CHAPTER X

WHEN Hugh Clifford left the tent he struck across the gumfield in the direction of the " Scarlet "Man." The rain was still falling with sufficient heaviness to wet him through, but even had it not been so every leaf of the scrub was a tiny reservoir, which discharged its contents on his person as he brushed by. The night was so dark that he had to trust to his sense of locality to guide him until he had surmounted the hillock from which the lights of the inn were visible. From this cause, as well as the difficult nature of the ground, fully twenty minutes elapsed before he set foot in the inn.

Upmore came from the back of the house at the sound of his step, and listened with evident astonishment to his tale.

"Miss Hamilton!" he exclaimed. "Why, the doctor has gone through not half an hour ago. He called me out to ask if I had seen anything of her."

"Had you?" asked Hugh.

"The doctor went off pretty fast. I expect he will be half-way there by this time. What's to be done?"

"I might catch him," said Hugh, "if your horse is of any account."

"He's of no account to-night," replied Upmore, "because he is not here. I lent him to a man a quarter of an hour ago and he has taken him to the races."

"Hang the races!" said Hugh peevishly. "Well, of course, you will let Mrs. Brandon go down and look after her. If only for the girl's peace of mind, there should be a woman there as soon as possible."

"I'll ask her," said Upmore; "it concerns her, and not me. If she is willing to go, there is no more to be said."

Upmore then left him, and was absent for nearly ten minutes, Hugh in the meantime moving impatiently in and out the house,

When Upmore at length returned he notified that Mrs. Brandon was willing to visit the tent after ten o'clock, and that he, Upmore, would accompany her.

Hugh nodded his concurrence, and having purchased a small flask of brandy, set off at a run down the road. He regretted now not having sought the inn by the same route, in which event probably five or ten minutes might have been saved, running on the rough surface of a gumfield being, at any rate on a dark night, next door to an impossibility.

The exertion of a mile's spin through the close, heavy atmosphere rendered him unpleasantly warm, and when he reached the point of the road where he should turn off he paused for a few seconds to wipe the perspiration from his forehead. As he was on the point of resuming his journey an audible motion in the scrub a few yards lower down the road attracted his attention, and thinking it might be due to the escaped horse, he moved cautiously forward to reconnoitre. Hugh found his conjecture correct in one particular, but incorrect in another. A horse was among the tea tree, but it was securely tied by the reins, and though by passing his hand across its back he discovered it to be saddled, he made the further discovery that the saddle was a man's.

His attention, however, was too much engrossed by the young girl under his charge for him to bestow more than a momentary wonder on the presence of the animal in such a spot and at such an hour. He turned off the road and moved rapidly forward in the direction of the tent, the glare from the fire now being visible.

As he approached the spot he was startled to hear a murmur of voices, and a moment later the sound of a pistol-shot broke the intense stillness of the night.

With a loud cry of encouragement Hugh sprang forward, but scarcely had he moved a few yards when, stumbling against some clods of earth, he fell heavily to the ground. To spring to his feet was the work of an instant, but the delay had been sufficient to enable some person to dash past him and run at full speed through the tea tree.

Hugh started in pursuit. For some time the sound of a person stumbling and breaking through the scrub was to be heard in front of him; then there came a silence. As he stood

71

still listening and wondering there flashed on his recollection the lonely horse tethered in the tea tree, and again he darted forward, making straight for the spot where he had observed the animal.

The scrub in this direction was thick and strong, impeding his progress and occasionally bringing him to the ground; but barely conscious of these hindrances in the fierce anger that possessed him, the young man broke his way through by brute force, heedless of the rents inflicted on his garments and his skin, and in a few minutes bounded on to the hard road. Rapid, however, as had been his progress, the pursued man had managed to keep his original advantage, and at the moment Hugh reached the road he tumbled hastily into the saddle, set spurs to his steed, and with a hoarse, mocking laugh galloped away into the darkness.

Any attempt to follow him Hugh recognised to be hopeless, and choking down his anger, he set off for the tent as rapidly as his breathless state permitted him. What sight would meet his eyes on the spot where he had left the beautiful, peaceful figure of the girl? The pistol had been fired, but by whom? The man was apparently uninjured, but how about her? These questions, and a dozen like them, surged through his mind before he reached the tent and lifted the canvas to enter.

A pungent odour of exploded gunpowder greeted his nostrils. There, with her back against one of the supports of the tent, sat Esther, the pistol in her hand, her eyes wide open and turned towards him.

A passionate pity smote the heart of the young man as he looked at her, and scarcely conscious of what he was saying, he uttered a few words of tender endearment and sorrow. Then her face, like a still lake suddenly smitten by the breeze, broke and trembled, lines drooped from the corners of her mouth, her eyes smiled and the lids fell down and concealed them, her face blanched slowly to the whiteness of paper, and with a long, quivering breath she fell sideways in a dead faint on the couch of fern.

Hugh's first act was to remove the pistol from her hand

and examine it. One shot only had been fired, and as the weapon remained in her possession it was evident that no worse disaster than a severe fright had befallen her. Anxious as he felt as to the result on her health of the nervous strain to which she had been subjected, he almost smiled with delight as he reflected on the fortunate afterthought which had led to the pistol being placed in her possession.

He found this faint more obstinate than had been the previous one. It was not until as a last resource he had raised the tent walls so as to admit a fresh current of air and poured a spoonful of brandy between her lips that she showed signs of returning consciousness. Kneeling beside her, he struck her hands gently between his own, and continued to do so till her eyes were fully open and she was looking with a sort of puzzled curiosity into his face. Then, anxious to show the respect in which he held her unprotected position, he desisted and suffered her hands to fall to the rug. But no sooner were they out of his possession than she started violently and again held them out to him.

"Don't leave me," she said huskily. "I have no one but you."

"No, no," he said, gently stroking the soft white palms; "I will not leave you till I leave you in your father's hands."

She seemed satisfied and returned to her old puzzled look, never removing her eyes from his face.

"What is it?" he asked presently.

"I was wondering who you were," she replied readily.

"My name is Hugh Clifford," answered Hugh.

"Hugh," she murmured reflectively. The young man thought he had never observed such beauty of sound in the name before. "I had a brother Hugh, but he is dead."

"Have you no other brothers?" he asked, humouring her.

"No," she replied; "no brothers and no sisters. My name is Esther. Do you mind my holding your hands?"

"How is it possible I should mind that? I wish for your sake they were not so roughened by labour."

"They are the hands of a true man," she said in dreamy tones; "one to whom I owe—everything." Suddenly her bosom

73

began to heave violently. "Why does God suffer such men to be alive?" she exclaimed wildly.

"Don't think of that now," he urged soothingly. "You are safe with me."

"It is good to feel safe," she murmured, with half-shut lids.

"Are you feeling any pain in your foot?" asked Hugh.

"Ah, I had forgotten that!" she said, opening her eyes and slowly closing them until there remained but a narrow brilliant slit. "No, I feel nothing now; only that I am safe."

"Try and sleep," suggested Hugh. "Mrs. Brandon will be here soon and then you will feel quite contented."

"Do not leave me alone with Mrs. Brandon," she said suddenly, her hands tightening on his.

"No," he replied encouragingly, "you belong to me until your father comes, and I will leave you alone with nobody."

She smiled contentedly, and her eyes closed.

For five minutes there was silence, then her face took a tense look and she muttered, "For if you only wound him he will probably kill you."

Hugh pressed her hands and she opened her eyes. "Can you not sleep?" he asked.

"Oh," she said, "you don't know. I have been so frightened—so terrified; it has nearly killed me. Was it not cruel? And for so long—it seemed hours. I was praying all the time, deep down under my breath in my soul. Why do you look like that? I heard you run after him. Did you kill him?"

"He got away," said Clifford. "He had a horse waiting for him. But never mind him now," he added checking himself. "Try and sleep."

"Would you have killed him?" she asked curiously. "He ought to be killed."

"I might," said Clifford, "or he me; I am violent sometimes. But there—go to sleep, or I will leave you. You shall tell me about him in the morning."

She shut her eyes obediently and said softly, "Good-night"—then after a pause, "Hugh."

"Good-night," he replied, but though he had her christian

74

name on his tongue, he did not venture to pronounce it.

A quarter of an hour passed, half an hour. She had fallen into a deep, dreamless sleep of utter exhaustion and never moved. Clifford sat still holding her hands and looking into her face, hardly daring, or indeed desiring, to change his position.

It seemed to the young man that he would willingly sit there for ever, watching the rise and fall of her bosom, the snowy curve of her throat, the exquisite pallor of her face with its long, black lashes, its delicately curled nostrils, its slightly parted lips, its crown of dark auburn hair, and the innocent repose and trustfulness of the whole sleeping figure.

"Poor little girl!" he said softly. "Who would harm so tender and fair a creature?"

He laid her hands softly down and drew the rug across her shoulders, then rose to his feet.

There is something in the charge of the helpless, possibly a feeling of proprietorship, which induces love. Those things which are for a time ours are dear to us on that account, quite irrespective of their value, and so it may be with the love which so frequently arises between nurse and patient.

So far Hugh had not regarded himself as a susceptible subject. He had lived a good deal in the society of women, without feeling even a passing fancy for any of them. But whether it were that absence from their society and the loneliness of the life he was leading had turned the current of his inclinations, certain it is that the first sound of Esther Hamilton's voice in the darkness of the road had aroused a hitherto unknown sensation of the beauty that exists in life. The subsequent sight of her face, together with the tender ministrations, as of a brother or father, he had been compelled by the exigency of the circumstances to perform for her had increased the delight he took in her presence; and finally, whatever curb he may have been inclined to put on the rapidly increasing rush of his fancy towards the deep waters of love was forgotten in the affectionate recognition of his services accorded to him by the physically and mentally exhausted girl when she fell asleep with her hands trustfully clasped in his.

Nevertheless, as he rose to his feet and stretched his limbs, stiffened by their long motionlessness and the drenching to which he had been subjected, there was something of bitterness in his thoughts. Instinctively the young man knew that with the closing of the girl's eyes the door of sweet communion was closed also. Like the peri, he had been suffered to peep into paradise, but the gates were shut, and the windy world with its social exactions blew remorselessly in his face. She had pressed his fingers with her own; she had looked into his eyes with a trust and affection that bordered closely on love; she had delighted him with words of admiration in tones as mellifluous as the speech of birds; she had done that sweet thing which from the right lips entirely steals away a man's heart—she had called him by his christian name. But it was finished. Esther, his girl friend, had fallen asleep: she would awake Miss Hamilton and a stranger. There would be no more calling the gum-digger by his first name; no more holding of hands; no more entreaties that he would not desert her.

CHAPTER XI

HUGH heaped some more sticks on the fire and sat down in the doorway of the tent to await the advent of Mrs. Brandon and Upmore.

They arrived about half-past ten, the woman with a shawl over her head and shoulders, and the man carrying a small basket of provisions. Hugh met them outside the tent, enjoining caution. He and Upmore subsequently walked up and down before the tent, while Mrs. Brandon took up a position beside the sleeping girl.

The sky had cleared somewhat since earlier in the night, but heavy cloud masses were rising slowly to the northward, promising a renewal of the late rain-storm.

"They will not have much of a day for the races," said Upmore, after Hugh had told his surmises of what had taken place during his absence from the tent. "If I know anything at all, it is going to rain heavily all day to-morrow."

"It is very unfortunate," said Hugh, assenting; "a tent is not a cheerful place in such circumstances."

"Well, if I were you," said Upmore, "I'd start right away, and save a drenching. You are a good walker, and should reach the course in four hours. You can then find Dr. Hamilton, get a buggy or trap of some kind, and be back here before eight. Its likely we shall not have heavy rain before low water—let me see—nine o'clock to-morrow morning; that will give her a chance of reaching Parawai without any worse adventure."

Hugh hesitated. The scheme commended itself to him, but he was bound to adhere to the promise he had made not to lose sight of Esther till she was under her father's protection. The girl had extracted the promise while suffering from the effects of fright; possibly in her unstrung state she was not entirely conscious of or responsible for her words and acts, but of this there was no proof. He knew nothing of the reasons—if reasons there were—for her apparent dislike of Mrs. Brandon, sufficient for him that the distrust existed. He must obey the instructions he had received until the divinity saw fit to countermand her orders.

As a result of these reflections Hugh remained silent.

"What do you think?" inquired Upmore.

"It will be best to wait till she wakes," replied Hugh. "She knows her father's probable movements. How if the doctor should be gone?"

"Such a waste of time," objected Upmore, "and with heavy rain coming on—"

"Why not go yourself?" interjected Hugh.

"And leave the hotel shut up, possibly for a whole day, at the best season of the year! It's likely, isn't it?"

"Mrs. Brandon could keep the place going, I suppose, if that is the only objection," suggested Hugh.

"My dear fellow," said Upmore sardonically, "if you wanted a clear field with the girl, what the devil did you drag me down here for? We didn't want to interfere with you."

Hugh frowned and then laughed. "I forgot that," he said. "Well, we will wait till she wakes."

"As for that," said Upmore doubtfully, "I don't know. I might wait half an hour." The innkeeper, far from sharing the interest of his companion, evidently regarded the whole business in the light of a nuisance.

"There is no necessity for you to wait," said Hugh, "if you wish to go back. In fact, it would be as well for you to be at the hotel in order to intercept anyone who may be making for the racecourse in the morning."

To this Upmore assented, and shortly before midnight made his way back to the inn.

Meanwhile Esther slept soundly. Once only did she slightly change her position, drawing one hand from beneath the rug and murmuring a few unintelligible words.

Mrs. Brandon sat apparently buried in thought, her eyes occasionally wandering round the tent, but for the most part bent on the face of the sleeping girl. As the hand came from beneath the rug and fell carelessly down beside her, she leant forward and looked curiously at a ring—a broad band of gold set with turquoises—encircling one of the small white fingers.

The sight of this object appeared to arouse some new thought in the mind of the watcher. Keeping her eyes fixed on the tent-opening, she cautiously stole forth her hand, and taking the ring between her fingers, worked it softly over the knuckle and thence into her palm.

At this moment Hugh came to the tent and glanced in. "Not awake yet?" he asked in a whisper.

The deaf woman, guessing the subject of inquiry, shook her head, and after a moment he again retired.

Freed from observation, Mrs. Brandon lifted the ring from the rug, where she had hurriedly placed it, and turning it to the light, sought for and quickly deciphered a brief inscription on the inner surface, "A. R. to E. H." She then sat with an air of hesitation weighing the ring in the palm of her hand. Once or twice the hand closed and moved irresolutely towards the pocket of her dress, but finally she endeavoured to restore it to its original position. This, however, proved more difficult than the initial process of drawing it off, the girl closing her hand tightly together at the first touch of the woman's fingers. After several attempts Mrs. Brandon was compelled to desist and placed the ring on the rug, where it lay glittering and continually forcing itself on her attention. For a quarter of an hour it remained in the same place, catching and emitting the soft beams of the fire—then it disappeared.

Shortly after one o'clock Esther awoke. Her face was turned toward Mrs. Brandon, and for a few moments the two regarded one another in silence. Esther's face wore at first a puzzled expression, as though she were endeavouring to remember how she came to be in the society of the older woman; then this gave place to a look of anxiety, and she glanced quickly round the tent. Presently she smiled, though still somewhat anxiously.

"It is very good of you to come," she said, speaking slowly and clearly. "I am afraid I must have caused you a good deal of inconvenience."

The deaf woman appeared to make out her meaning, and nodded.

Esther again glanced round the tent. "Is Mr.—I forget the young gentleman's name—is he here?" she asked.

"Clifford?" asked Mrs. Brandon, following the direction of the girl's gaze. "Yes, he is outside. Did you wish to see him?"

"Oh, it is of no consequence," replied Esther, apparently losing interest, though her face assumed a more cheerful expression. "I was merely wondering if he had gone to Parawai as he proposed."

"We wished him to go," explained Mrs. Brandon, "but for some reason he desired to remain till you awoke. If you would like him to go now, I think he will."

"No, no!" said Esther quickly, "at least not until it is light."

"I am ready to go when you please, Miss Hamilton," said Clifford, who, hearing voices, had drawn near the tent and was now looking in.

"It is very good of you," she replied, just suffering her eyes to rest on his face and again turning them towards the woman.

"I hope you feel refreshed after your sleep," said Hugh. "We were uncertain what to do till you awoke."

Esther inquired how long she had slept. "Won't you come inside?" she asked presently, as he remained standing in the doorway.

Hugh assented readily enough and took his place in the corner of the tent. He was beginning to feel that wandering aimlessly about all night after a hard day's work was not a desirable occupation.

"I have found your horse," he said, as he sat down. "He had got himself tied up among the tea tree about a stone's-throw from the tent. I have the saddle drying by the fire."

"I don't know what I should have done without you," said Esther gratefully. "Though I shall not be able to ride, it is nice to know the animal is safe."

"Your father must bring a trap for you," said Hugh. "There are bound to be a few on the course, and in a case of such necessity he will no doubt get the loan of one easily enough. Perhaps Roller will be there with his."

The words were uttered at random, but they brought a

look of anxious reflection into the girl's eyes. The fingers of one hand sought the fingers of the other, then she uttered an exclamation of surprise.

"What is it?" asked Hugh, with solicitude.

"My ring," she replied, "it is gone."

"You will probably find it among the rugs. By the way, I pinned your brooch to the tent just above your head; it must have fallen."

"Have you lost something?" asked Mrs. Brandon in a dull, monotonous voice, her face a blank.

"My ring and my brooch," replied Esther, hunting among the rugs.

"Here is a purse," said Hugh, "but it appears to be empty."

Esther explained how it came to be in that condition, but added, "I did not see him take the brooch, and I don't know how he could have taken the ring from my finger without my knowing it. Besides"—then she paused and became of a sudden very thoughtful.

"What was the appearance of this man?" inquired Hugh, his indignation aroused less by what he heard than by what he suspected.

Esther gave as minute a description as she was able, awaking an unpleasant conviction in Hugh's mind that he and her assailant had met not many days previously.

"Did he give any reason for corning at that time and in such weather?" he asked.

"He did; he said that you and he had quarrelled, and that he was desirous of burying the hatchet—that was the very form of words he used."

"He wished to make friends?" asked Hugh in surprise.

"No," said Esther, "that was not the impression I received."

"I see," said Clifford slowly, with a laugh. "Really I have no fancy for a humourist of that kind."

"How can you jest about it?" asked Esther seriously. "I would not stop here another day."

"Your experience has not been so pleasant that I should like to think of you doing so," replied Hugh politely.

"But I mean if I were you I would not stay," explained Esther. "He might have murdered you in your sleep. Supposing I had not been here you would probably have been sound asleep, and what chance would you have had against such a man?"

"Just so," said Hugh, with more interest; "it is quite possible I owe you my life." The young man was perfectly willing to be in her debt even to that extent.

"That is nonsense," said Esther, smiling; "but it is quite certain I owe you mine."

The young man was delighted. Never in his life had he met a creature so frank, so fair, and so charming. The liquid glances of her dark eyes, hurriedly given, and followed by a fall of the heavily lashed lids; the brief, flickering smiles, like sudden flashes of sunlight breaking on the prevailing anxious pose of the lips; the soft, sweetly modulated voice, the innocent trust and comradeship of her manner towards himself—all these things played havoc with his heart and drew him deeper and deeper into the gulf.

"It is very curious," said Esther, after a renewed search for the missing articles. "He might possibly have taken the brooch, but I cannot understand about the ring."

"It must be somewhere," said Hugh. "By-the-by," he added suddenly, "he could not have taken the ring because it was there when I was holding your—"

A swift glance of reproach from the girl caused him to check himself, and he concluded, "when I came back from the hotel."

"I know it was," said Esther decisively.

"Perhaps it has rolled away beneath the tent," suggested Hugh; "it will be useless to look for it till the morning. As for the brooch and the money, we will have the police on his tracks before he is many hours older."

Mrs. Brandon meanwhile had been diligently searching for the missing property, but now at Esther's request she desisted, and something was said about refreshments. Esther confessed to being both hungry and thirsty, and in a few minutes the billy was boiling, tea was made, and the strangely assembled trio partook of a light supper from the contents of the basket which Upmore had brought down from the hotel.

During the meal Hugh explained that the innkeeper had promised to come over first thing in the morning and acquaint him with the steps he had taken to communicate with Dr. Hamilton. It was considered certain that some persons, either native or European, would be on the road to the racecourse shortly after daylight.

Neither Esther, who had been refreshed by her nap of two or three hours, nor Hugh, who was kept up by the excitement attendant on the presence of his fair visitor, felt any call to sleep; but Mrs. Brandon, whose share in the conversation was limited to such words and parts of words as found their way through her obscured organs of hearing, soon exhibited symptoms of sleepiness and yawned in a manner painful to witness. Finally Esther proposed that she should share her couch, and this arrangement was agrees to.

"What will you do, Mr. Clifford?" Esther asked remorsefully.

"I will lie across the doorway, if you ladies will permit me," said Hugh.

"But you will be so cold," objected the girl.

"I can warm one side at a time, you know," said Hugh cheerfully, laying down his haversack to form a pillow.

"Of course, you must have something," said Esther. "We will give you two of our blankets, because you are nearest the open air; one will be plenty for us."

"I won't listen to anything of the kind," said Hugh, beginning to stretch himself on the ground.

"Well, one then," she pleaded. "You have been wet through, and I am sure you will have rheumatism or something if you are so careless."

She rapidly rolled the rug up and pushed it towards him.

Hugh waited till the girl was comfortably curled up beside the older woman, then wrapping his blanket around him, extinguished the light and lay down across the doorway before the glowing embers of the fire.

"Good-night, Miss Hamilton," he said in a tone that was almost a caress.

There was a silence of some moments, and he was beginning to think she was already asleep, or had not heard him, when she replied, "Good night, Mr. Clifford."

Was it merely fancy, or had there been something in the "Mr. Clifford" which made it sound even dearer than "Hugh?"

CHAPTER XII

SHORTLY after six o'clock the innkeeper came down with the news that he had intercepted a large party of natives, who had promised to seek out Dr. Hamilton immediately on their arrival on the course. He had also taken the additional precaution of forwarding a note by one of the party. Nothing in consequence remained to be done until the arrival of the doctor.

With the first streak of light a wind had arisen, and now blew gustily across the gumfield from the north. Occasional heavy showers added to the unpleasantness of the day, while the sky was entirely obscured by large masses of dark cloud, shifting rapidly to the southward. Owing to the dampness of his fuel, Hugh found the greatest difficulty in keeping up a cheerful fire, clouds of sour smoke rolling with every puff of wind into the tent, greatly to the discomfort of its inhabitants. Without the bushes were dark and dripping, the ground sodden with moisture, and the creek below the bank was rising rapidly, momentarily increasing the depth and volume of its note.

At about eight o'clock Mrs. Brandon, who, having attended to the injured girl and assisted in the preparation of the morning meal, had become very fidgety, announced her intention of returning to the hotel, promising at the same time to come back should the doctor not arrive within the next two hours. Neither Hugh, nor, if the truth must be confessed, was Esther, particularly upset at her departure. The reason for Esther's apparent dislike was unknown to the young man, but personally he felt a sort of nervous objection to the woman's manner of watching each speaker's mouth in turn, He felt that during the last few hours he had been compelled to go through a number of exaggerated and unnatural performances with his lips purely on this account, and he was not sorry when those essentials to articulation had resumed their ordinary subjective relation to the workings of his mind.

Esther, probably from the effects of the pain in her foot, together with the smoke and the general unpleasantness, did not seem to the young man to be in quite such cheerful spirits as she had exhibited overnight. Her manner was still friendly, but it was unquestionably more reserved. This was only what he had anticipated, but he was not thereby prevented from feeling depressed by the circumstance. During the last few hours he had bestowed an exaggerated amount of reflection on a bunch of violets nestling against her bosom. The flowers had brushed against his lips as he carried her from the road, and they had since filled the tent with their delicate fragrance. The point for consideration had been whether he might dare to claim them as a reward for his services, but now he became more and more sure that such a request would be little short of audacious.

"Remember you're a gum-digger," he said to himself bitterly as he stood among the scrub looking out for the expected buggy.

The loss of the ring had also apparently caused the girl some uneasiness. Might it be that the trinket was a keepsake from someone—even a token of some prospective relationship nearer and dearer than that of a friend? He dismissed the thought with a sudden contraction of the brows. More than an hour had been devoted to a search for the missing jewellery, but neither ring nor brooch was forthcoming. Whatever might account for the loss of the latter, the absence of the former was all but inexplicable.

"I should not have cared much for the brooch," said Esther, "but the ring is different."

"Yes," said Hugh quietly.

Very little conversation passed between them. Hugh spent the greater part of the time among the scrub, seeking the tent only when the showers were unusually heavy. At length, a little before ten, he caught sight of a trap advancing rapidly towards the inn, and calling out the news to Esther, he made for the road.

The occupant of the trap, seeing him approach, pulled up and waited. He was an elderly man, probably sixty years of age, with a delicate and somewhat irritable appearance.

"Doctor Hamilton?" inquired Hugh breathlessly, as he drew near.

"That is my name," said the gentleman impatiently.

"Miss Hamilton is in the tent," said Hugh. "You have heard, no doubt, that she was thrown and hurt her ankle very badly."

"Where did it happen?" asked ,Doctor Hamilton, preparing to dismount.

Hugh pointed out a spot a few yards away.

"It is just like her," muttered the doctor crossly, "to choose some spot where assistance was not to be obtained."

This struck Hugh as highly unreasonable, but he said nothing.

"If you will hold my horse, young man," the doctor continued as he dismounted, "I will go over and see what is to be done. He is one of Roller's horses," he added, regarding the spirited-looking animal with a glance of no favour, "and his mouth is cast iron; keep an eye on him. There is someone with her, I suppose?"

"Not at present," said Hugh, anticipating an unpleasant time for the girl and wishing to mollify him as far as possible. "Mrs. Brandon was there until a short time ago, but she has now returned to the hotel."

Doctor Hamilton growled some response, and picked his way gingerly through the wet scrub in the direction of the tent.

Twenty minutes later he found his way back to the buggy, looking rather more irritated than before. He was leading Esther's horse, which he proceeded to tie up behind the vehicle.

"She can't walk," he said, as he came up, "and I'm sure I haven't the strength to carry a lump of a girl weighing over nine stone. You carried her there, she tells me, and I suppose there is nothing for it but for you to carry her back—that is if you have no objection," he added, with a desperate attempt at politeness.

"Not the least," said Hugh, with an indifference he was far from feeling. Whatever else came and went, the remembrance of two occasions when he had held her in his arms could not be taken from him.

He found Esther waiting in some embarrassment, and noticed as he bent towards her that her eyes were slightly red.

"I am such a bother to you, Mr. Clifford," she said, her colour rising.

Hugh did not immediately reply, but took her up carefully in his strong young arms. When he did speak it was to say, "The place will seem very dull when you are gone. Do you know, I think your visit has disorganised my life?"

Whether or not she were conscious of the deep ring of earnestness which underlay the superficial levity of his tone, she made no reply but a smile, and he bore her out into the open air.

"It was not your fault," he said presently, in the tone of one petting a young child.

"No," she said, immediately understanding him—probably because her thoughts ran in the same channel. "I could not arrange where I should meet with an accident."

Nothing more was said on this subject. Esther was the next to speak. "I want to ask you," she said, "if you find my ring and brooch to send them to me at once. Will you do so?"

"I will," he replied. "Shall I send them or bring them?"

"As you please," she answered; then, after a pause, "bring them if you will. I hope you will come to see us. You have been very kind."

They were now close to the buggy and almost within the doctor's hearing.

"Your violets are withered now," said Hugh suddenly. "May I have them?"

Whatever might have been the outcome of the request, its fate was determined by the fact of the doctor looking towards them as though in impatience at the delay. He had made a sort of rest for the girl's foot in the fore part of the buggy. She was soon comfortably ensconced among the rugs with a waterproof cape drawn well up about her. Hugh handed in the reins, and with a curt nod the doctor prepared to start.

So far Esther had not looked at Hugh since the moment he

had mustered sufficient temerity to ask for her flowers, but as the horse got into motion she turned suddenly towards him and, reading in his eyes an unmistakable look of reproach, leant forward and said something in an undertone to her father.

"Oh, ah—yes," said the latter half unwillingly, at the same time checking the animal. "Miss Hamilton reminds me that I have not thanked you for your services to her at a time when she was—er—dependent on them. If you will let me know—"

The fact that the person he addressed had suddenly become rigid, while the face of the girl beside him had at the same instant flushed scarlet, warned the doctor that it was possible to make a mistake, and he concluded somewhat lamely, "I am much obliged to you."

"There is no need for thanks," said Hugh. "I hope you will soon be quite recovered, Miss Hamilton."

"And Mr. Clifford has promised to come and see us, father," said Esther, wishing to atone for her father's meditated offence.

"Just so," said the doctor, in non-committal tones. "Well, we shall have to dash between the showers."

"And you will come, Mr. Clifford?" said Esther, as they moved off.

Hugh bowed, but made no reply. Something very like anger burned in his heart.

The girl seemed to read the meaning of his silence, for she laid her hand on her father's arm and again the doctor brought the carriage to a standstill. "Do you promise?" she asked, looking back.

"Yes," he replied, disarmed by this evidence of her sincerity.

"Good-bye, then," she cried, waving her hand.

Doctor Hamilton gave the horse a sharp cut, causing the animal to rear and then break away swiftly along the road. Hugh watched it till it was out of sight and a sudden splash of rain drove him reluctantly back to the tent.

How dark, dismal, and disordered seemed that abode where

but twenty-four hours ago he had dwelt in nearly perfect contentment! Was it not an absolute truth that her visit had, as he had told her, disorganised his life? To rise with the lark, to be entirely absorbed in the vicissitudes of his daily work; to rest in the evening, thinking and smoking beneath the tranquil stars; to sleep dreamlessly, until the increasing light awakened him to a new day: how pleasant it had all seemed, but now how narrow and unsatisfactory! What a waste of existence! Absolutely, on such terms of solitude and persistent labour, life was not worth living. Here was the spot where she had twice lain in a dead swoon; where she had held his hands and looked confidingly into his face. Almost he could smell now the scent of the violets in her dress; could watch the droop of her eyelids, the sudden sunlight of her smiles; could catch the dovelike tones of her voice.

He tried to set the tent in order, but desisted from sheer disgust. He tried to scrape gum, but the mechanical nature of the occupation sickened him. Had the day been fine, like its predecessors, he might have deadened thought by hard, muscular effort, but here in the tent, with the showers falling heavily at shorter and shorter intervals, there was no employment which could check the miserable; delightful whirl of imagination. Finally he stretched himself on his couch, and lay looking with wide, absent eyes into the rain-dimmed sky. The thought of the girl had flooded his being and pulsed in every fibre of his brain. His blood brought pictures of her from his heart, and built them up in his eyes. Her very exquisiteness seemed to make her impossible of attainment. It was not reasonable that such a creature could ever be his, for it was quite certain that no man could look at her without love; then what chance had he—a stranger—against those with whom she was in daily communion?

Would Clifford have felt any happier had he heard what passed between Esther and her father immediately they left him?

The doctor cut savagely at the horse as though displeased with something that had occurred, and a few yards further down the road he broke out with, "What the deuce is the meaning of all this?"

"Of what?" asked the girl.

"Of your good-byes and your promises," replied the doctor, fuming; "and asking him to the house."

"He has been very considerate," said Esther, "but I will tell you by-and-by."

"A gum-digger!" said the doctor scornfully. "You should have more sense."

"I don't care," said Esther rebelliously. "I like him."

CHAPTER XIII

THE spot where the annual race-meeting of the district was held lay about fifteen miles from the "Scarlet Man" and half that distance from the chief port on the coast.

With the exception of a single house of accommodation, there was no settlement in the vicinity, though a number of farms were scattered about the surrounding district.

In ordinary circumstances a large gathering of both sexes might be expected to fill the natural amphitheatre in which the races were held, but on this occasion the threatening aspect of the weather had considerably lessened the number of male attendants, and saving a few enthusiasts who had probably ridden a long distance, and were in consequence not inclined to be balked of their pleasure, the ladies were conspicuous by their absence.

It would have been difficult for a casual visitor, whose soul was not concerned with the respective merits of Briseis (colloquially "Breezes ") and the Digger, or any other of the favourites whose names were in the mouths of all, to conceive that a scene of such squalor and apparent misery represented a high percentage of individual enjoyment; yet cheerful faces and sounds of laughter prevailed. The allusions to the weather were frequent, but they consisted mainly of such good-natured badinage as "Call this a climate? Why, it would knock the old country out in one round!" "Breezes? Yes, but can the beggar swim? I'll lay five to four against her, anyway."

"I'll tell you what, the climate's bankrupt, like everyone else. There goes Roller! What's this they're saying about Miss Hamilton going off with a gum-digger?"

"What nonsense!" said another speaker. " 'They Say' was a liar from his birth up."

"Never smoke without fire," said the first speaker. "Look here! Who wants to back Roller's brute? I'll lay the Digger."

He raised his voice intentionally, and Roller, who was standing a short distance away, overheard him and came across.

"How much will you lay, Johnson?" he asked.

"Thirty to ten," said Johnson.

"I'll take you," said Roller. "Make it sixty."

"Thirty to twelve now," said the other.

"I'll take that too," said Roller, after a pause. "What an awful day!" he added, after he had booked the wager. "The course will be knee-deep in mud before we're finished."

"The course?" said Johnson. "Where the dickens is the course? Why the mischief does the committee let the gorse grow up like this? They ought to put up a notice board, "First to the right, second to the left," just to give people an idea."

"I suppose the jockeys know where it is," said Roller. "It is to be hoped so, at any rate."

"Here, James," called out Johnson to a person pushing hurriedly through the throng, "you're a committeeman—where's the course?"

"Blowed if I know," said James. "I'm weigher in. You'd better ask Dixon."

"Course?" said Dixon on being appealed to. "Why, you're standing on it; and I wish you chappies would keep over the other side. We had it all flagged yesterday, but the wind has blown most of them over. I've got a man tying calico on the bushes at the difficult places."

"Oh, so long as it isn't mislaid, you know," said Johnson drily.

Just then a burly native in a red jersey, who had stood an interested witness of the booking of the wagers between Roller and Johnson, approached the latter and looked him carefully over with his brown eyes. A crowd of native women and men followed him and formed quite a large group on the track.

"How much you lay Wikitoria?" the native asked.

"Victoria?" said Johnson. "Not bookmaker me, you know. No money about him."

"You tink Wikitoria good fella? She very good horse, I tink?"

"Very fair, I should say, by her breeding," Johnson replied.

"She bloody horse, I suppose so? "

Johnson turned the question over with his tongue in his

cheek for some time before its exact significance occurred to him. "Blood horse? Oh yes; she's a thoroughbred all right."

"I back him," said the native. "How much you lay?"

Johnson signalled to a bookmaker on the other side of the track. "Here, Davis," he said, "they want to back Victoria. What's the odds?"

"Four to one," said Davis, turning to the natives. "How much?"

"Kapai, five to one," said the native. "Wikitoria no good, p'raps so. You lay five to one?"

"Give us hold, then. Five to one Wikitoria! Five to one Wikitoria! I'll lay Wikitoria!"

The challenge drew the Maoris, who flocked in from all sides, struggling with one another to secure the bookmaker's tickets in exchange for their money. So persistent were they that after a while Davis got frightened.

"What is this Victoria?" he asked *sotto voce* of Johnson,

"Well bred enough," said Johnson, "but—" He elevated his eyebrows.

"There must be something to make them come at me like this," Davis opined.

"Don't you catch on?" asked Johnson, grinning. "It's the name—Victoria. This is merely an outburst of patriotism, my boy; and it's up to you to foster it."

Davis whistled and his face cleared. "Here you are," he shouted. "I'll lay Wikitoria! Four to one Wikitoria! Four to— Eight bob to two Wikitoria—take your ticket. Pound to a crown Wikitoria. I'll lay Wikitoria!"

At this juncture a native with an ugly but good-natured face forced his way to the front of the crowd.

"Hullo, Pine!" * said Red Jersey. "How you feel?"

"Oh, half," said Pine nonchalantly.

"You back Wikitoiria?"

"I back a few poun'," replied Pine. "The ol' lady, Mrs. Moses, like to back him some now." He stepped aside and disclosed an extremely old woman, who had followed him through the crowd and was now squatting in the mud in front of Davis.

* Pronounced "Pinney."

94

"The ol' lady want to know what price Wikitoria? Pine asked.

"Four to one," said Davis.

Pine turned and communicated the information to the old dame, and an animated discussion ensued between the pair in their own language, frequent explanatory notes being supplied by the bystanders. Finally, Mrs. Moses seemed satisfied, and producing a handkerchief from her skirt, she undid a knot in one corner and took out a two-shilling piece.

"Na, he Wikitoria," she said.

"Eight bob to two Wikitoria," said Davis, pocketing the money.

The old woman examined the ticket from all points of view, felt it over carefully with her thumb, and at last stored it away in a separate corner of the handkerchief. Then she produced a pound note and handed it up to Davis.

"Na, he Wikitoria," she said again.

The natives, who evidently knew the old dame's style of doing business, nudged one another and watched Davis with sly delight as he wrote out a fresh ticket and handed it down.

Again the old lady examined her purchase, had the figures explained to her by Pine, felt it over with her thumb, and stowed it away. And again she took a pound note from the knot in her handkerchief.

"Na, he Wikitoria," she said stolidly.

A burst of laughter greeted the demand, and Pine and Red Jersey stamped their feet delightedly on the ground.

"Rum go this," said Davis doubtfully, as he wrote out a second ticket for five pounds.

There was a dead and expectant silence while Mrs. Moses assured herself of the authenticity of the document. Everything proving satisfactory, she again turned to the knot and produced yet another pound.

"Na, he Wikitoria," she said, to the intense delight of the bystanders.

Davis scratched his ear as he looked down on the impassive old body, with her sphinx-like countenance and bright eyes.

"Don't let her break you," said Johnson, highly amused, and the bookmaker stretched out his hand for the money.

There were a few moments of keen expectation, during which every eye was riveted on the little wrinkled old creature inspecting her ticket. Would she or would she not? Carefully and methodically she at last knotted it with the others, and carefully and methodically she untied her money and produced still another note.

"Na, he Wikitoria," she said inevitably.

But this was altogether too much for the natives. Frantic with delight, they slapped their bodies and shook hands with and hugged one another. Pine, however, who had become aware that the performance was reflecting considerable glory on himself, saw fit to control his emotions.

"Ol' lady very good form to-day, Mr. Shonson," he said, with fluent ease.

"Go on," urged Johnson, as Davis showed signs of backing down. "Never say die."

Thus encouraged, the bookmaker entered up the fifth wager. "What's wanted?" he asked desperately.

The little wooden old woman, who grew only more deliberate with each transaction, made her customary examination of the ticket, and replied to his question by stonily passing up still another pound.

"Na," she said, "he Wikitoria."

"Not me," said Davis, drawing back amid the frantic delight of the assemblage. "Two to one him." And two to one Victoria remained from that moment.

To the natives the victory of Mrs. Moses over the bookmaker seemed a certain precursor of the triumph of Victoria over her equine rivals, and thereafter they backed that animal at any price for all they were worth. In the saddling inclosure they surrounded the mare, praising her good points and congratulating themselves on their prospective winnings. Blucher and Merry Boy they regarded with contempt; Briseis was but little noticed, and even the Digger with his magnificent quarters was comparatively neglected. The idea of the horse named after the great, remote, ever-victorious Queen had caught the warm fancy of her devoted subjects, and a horse of far less merit than Victoria might equally, so named, have carried their money to the post.

But if the Maoris were assured of the virtue that lay in the name of their Sovereign, the gum-diggers were none the less certain of the splendid qualities concentrated in their namesake the Digger, and the betting ultimately developed into a fight between these two for the position of first favourite. The real horsey fraternity, however, including the men from Auckland and the bookmakers, to whom gambling was a matter not of sentiment, but of business, looked upon Briseis as a certain winner on the strength of previous performances, and thus the three horses continued almost upon an equality—the price of the two former being sustained by the public, and that of the latter by the disinclination of the bookmakers to lay.

Meanwhile a few events had been decided with more or less success, a certain amount of money had changed hands, a few men—natives and Europeans—had got drunk, and one or two had become violent. In these cases the constable in attendance, acting on the principle that discretion is the better part of valour, watched his men until they were sufficiently far gone to offer but an impotent resistance, when he arrested them and roped them to the nearest fence until he was ready to go home. Some of them escaped, or were released by their mates and went off with the county rope as a perquisite; but one or two, falling asleep, escaped the attention of the crowd and were duly removed to durance vile.

The rain had now set in heavily and all prospect of the weather clearing before the close of the day was at an end. Many, especially such as were from remote districts, had begun to lose interest in the events still to come, and a good deal was heard of floods, bridges, and the possibility of fording creeks which lay between the pleasure-seekers and their various homes. Round the skirts of the inclosure parties could constantly be seen mounting their horses and riding rapidly away into the mist and rain.

Of all there assembled the Maoris appeared to be least affected by the inclemency of the weather. Wet to the skin, and with rheumatism, consumption, and death staring them in the face, they yet entered with childish enjoyment into the amusements provided for them by the superior devilry of the pakeha. On the now slippery course a number of natives, intoxicated with excitement and liquor, were driving their famished horses down the narrow grass alleys, no little to the danger of the crowd, which occasionally surged across the track in the neighbourhood of the booths. At length it became known that with the chief race of the day the meeting would be abandoned, and as this was the next event on the card a more cheerful spirit diffused itself throughout the assemblage.

Roller made his way to the drinking-booth and obtained a glass of spirits. He had backed his horse, the Digger, for a considerable amount, though the comparative poverty of the district did not allow him to involve himself financially, in the event of that horse failing to win. He stood smoking and listening to those around him, occasionally exchanging a few words with a friend. He gathered from the hubbub—for the tent was full to overflowing—that Briseis still stood slightly in advance of the field, and that a third horse was backed on equal terms with his own. He said nothing, but confined himself to quietly taking the odds from everyone who offered, and the effect of this was that shortly before the starter's bell rang it was difficult to say which horse held the premier position.

Standing with his back to the bar, Roller commanded a view of the entrance to the tent. As he was on the point of moving a sound of raised voices and scuffling immediately outside the canvas attracted his attention, and turning from the person with whom he was at the moment conversing, he was in time to see the tent invaded by a tall, small-headed person, evidently under the influence of liquor. A momentary silence followed the advent of the stranger, who glared fiercely around him until his gaze fell and was fixed on the face of the prosperous storekeeper.

"There's that—Roller," he observed, apparently for his own

information.

There is a tendency in human nature to delight in the humiliation of a successful man, and it would not be too much to say that a pleasurable feeling ran through the crowd as they waited in silence for the further development of the scene. After the first start of surprise at the sound of his name Roller remained quietly sucking his cigar and apparently endeavouring to remember where he had previously encountered the ill-looking person before him. Suddenly a light of recollection gleamed in his eyes, and he said something in a low voice to the person beside him, who immediately left the booth.

"Gen'l'men all," said the man thickly, "and a damned nice crew you air," he broke off suddenly, with a scowl for those nearest to him; "as drunk a lot as ever I see."

This raised a laugh, in which the fellow joined, almost instantly resuming his ferocious look as his eye again fell on the storekeeper.

"There's two men," he remarked, with elaborate distinctness, "for which I'd sooner swing 'n drink beer, and that—'s one of 'em. Roller's 'is name and garden roller's 'is nature. He'd crush you like worms. There's many a — gum-digger 'as felt the weight of 'is thumb. The diggers 'as made 'im what 'e is; they're 'is slaves, you see, a bloomin' lot o' white slaves. He takes 'is profit out o' their gum, and 'e takes 'is profit out o' the food they eat and the clothes they put on their backs, and if 'e was to meet one on 'em dyin' on the road to-morrer 'e'd pass 'im by. That's Roller, that is. Some folks call 'irn *Mister* Roller—I don't; Roller's good enough for me, the blasted little fat devil."

During this harangue Roller's face had darkened till it wore a look nearly as ferocious as that of the person who denounced him, but he neither spoke nor moved.

"Come, this is too much," said a gentleman in the crowd, and a murmur of approval greeted the words. "If you have any grievance against Mr. Roller, take it where it can be heard and redressed."

"He's a gambler," went on the man, taking no heed of the interruption, "and 'e bets with men poorer than 'isself. He's got more money than all the rest of you put together, and 'e uses it to ruin you every way 'e knows 'ow."

This assertion was so much like truth that it aroused the indignation of the whole assemblage. Cries of "Hit him!" "Chuck him out!" arose on all sides, and several even moved forward with the idea of putting these suggestions in practice.

At this moment the blue-coated figure of the local constable forced its way through the crowd at the door.

"What's all this?" he demanded, with the amazed indignation peculiar to his class.

"Take that man in charge, Howell," said Roller in a high voice, "for drunkenness and using abusive language. Here are plenty of witnesses."

"Very good, sir," said Howell, for Roller was a local J.P., and he touched the man on the shoulder.

The latter seemed astonished at this conclusion to the episode, and demanded in a dazed manner whether or no he lived in a free country.

"Too free," responded the constable, "while men like you are allowed to be at large. I know you!"

This was deliberately untrue, because, as a matter of fact, the constable did not know him from Adam. However, he slipped the handcuffs on as he spoke and endeavoured to lead his prisoner from the booth. The latter, who seemed to have become sobered by the predicament in which he found himself, at first offered no resistance, but when they reached the tent door he turned suddenly and looked the storekeeper steadily in the face.

"My God," he said, "you've done a bad day's work?"

"Now, none of that," said the constable, shaking him roughly by the arm. "Come along out of it."

"A damned bad day's work, Roller," repeated the man, unmoved, "and as long as you live you'll never do a worse." Then he suffered Howell to lead him quietly away.

The awkward silence which followed his disappearance was

broken by the sound of the starter's bell, and the whole party, Roller among the rest, immediately made for the stand.

It is unpleasant to be called names, and however little one may feel oneself to merit it, abuse—as well as arousing suspicion in those who hear it—has a disastrous effect on a man's self-esteem.

The prosperous man, whose spine has assumed the rigidity of a steel poker—one of the most general outward and visible signs of social prosperity—is frequently by his exposed position in danger of such attacks, and he usually feels them the more severely in that his vertebral column has lost that flexibility which is the chief capital of a man who has yet to make his mark in the world.

Roller, as he ascended the stand, felt both sore and angry. The fact that no one had seen fit to allude to the scene subsequently to its occurrence was an additional offence, arguing as it did a feeling of delicacy among the auditors which could only be explained on the supposition that in their minds the necessity for such a feeling existed. An argument of this sort must not be thought too subtle for an egoist, who is apt when wounded to sound some of the least explored depths of the human mind. It mattered little that the person who had so freely spoken his mind was not a respectable character; for if it be, as we are told, a sin against society to be found out, then it must be equally a sin to have one's credit shaken with the world, though the charges which effect that result be without foundation or only partly true. The man's allusion to the truck system in dealing with the diggers had hit Roller hard, for he was aware of certain transactions in the past which, were they known, might call forth the indignation of civilised beings. But the sorest insult to his pride was the likening him to a shark among minnows.

It would be too much to say that his interest in the forthcoming race was gone, but there had certainly been a large leakage of animal spirits, so that now he was inclined to be wrathful with the men who, standing up on the seats, clamoured and shoved around him, and with the rain, which, dripping from the brim of his hat, ran in a continual stream down the bridge of his nose.

When, however, the dip of the starter's flag liberated the horses from the post all thought of the insult he had received vanished in the excitement of the race.

The start was said to be a good one, and when the five horses engaged passed the post on the first round there was little to choose between them. After this there was a short interval, during which an occasional jacket might be seen to flash through an opening between two furze bushes on the other side of the course.

"By Jove!" exclaimed Johnson, who had never previously attended a country meeting, "this is the most exciting thing ever I was at. Can you see the horses anywhere?"

James, the committee-man, who was standing on the seat uttering frantic bellows—intended for the encouragement of the steed he had backed—desisted on being roughly shaken. "I tell you the last horse will win," he said excitedly.

"Even that wouldn't surprise me," said Johnson. "Only don't break the drum of my ear."

Three horses shot suddenly out of the gorse and passed the stand in a bunch, amid vociferous cheering. The other two had evidently run into a *cul-de-sac*, as the caps of the jockeys could be seen as they galloped hither and thither in the centre of the plain seeking
an exit.

Johnson hugged himself delightedly. "I would not have missed this for a hundred pounds," he said.

"It's a great race," declared James, boiling over with excitement; "the best that has ever been run on this course. Isn't Blucher running a great horse? Did you notice him?" And without waiting for a reply, he again lifted up his voice and howled.

His faith in Blucher proved to be well placed, for he was the first horse to finish. The Digger, however, ran him very close, and but for the fact that his jockey mistook the track at the last moment, he would quite possibly have won.

As for Victoria, she was hopelessly out of it from the start, and not even the patriotic cheers of her numerous supporters sufficed to shift her, even momentarily, from her position of dead last.

CHAPTER XIV

ROLLER bore his loss with equanimity, and none of those who expressed condolence with him in the result of the race were able to decipher in his countenance any other expression than good-tempered indifference. It was probably some consolation to a man who had been denounced as a shark to prove in his own case that the minnows occasionally have the advantage.

Leaving information with those around him that he would be found at the accommodation house, and was prepared to settle all claims immediately, he left the course and seated himself before his cheque-book in the house parlour. To such as presented themselves he showed himself at once cheerful and business-like, and, not to be balked in his determination to immediately discharge all claims against him, he wrote and posted cheques to the few who, from feelings of generosity, refrained from putting in an immediate appearance. These duties concluded, he began to reflect on his next course of action.

To pass the night in the squalid little house in which he sat was, in his then state of mind, highly distasteful; to ride twenty-five miles to Parawai in the rain hardly less so. He would have liked to see Esther and learn full particulars of the accident, if only for the reason that his apparent callousness in allowing her father to go unaccompanied had probably not raised him in her esteem.

For a man to be without fear of rivals is a bad thing both for himself and the other party concerned, because, while it degrades the latter from the queenly position which is hers by right of her attractiveness, it can never be consistent with passionate love on the part of the former. The capability for jealousy is implanted in the nature of every man and woman, doubtless with a wise and beneficent object, and the strength of its outbreak is in proportion to the security that preceded it. On this score for a man to be without fear of rivals is a bad thing for himself, and such was Roller's position with regard to Esther Hamilton.

Their engagement had come about in the commonplace fashion which characterises the majority of matches. They had seen and heard of one another daily; he was fairly good-looking, wealthy, the leading man of the district; she was young and charming. They danced together, picnicked together, rode together. No other man interfered, no other woman. Then he proposed and was accepted.

Yet though it never entered Roller's head to doubt the entire satisfaction of the girl in the prospect of marriage with a person of his importance, or to question the genuineness of her affection, this was, perhaps, rather due to the fact that she had hitherto given him no cause, for in other affairs of life he had sometimes shown a suspicious and overbearing disposition. A little more doubt, and it is probable the attractions of the racecourse would have had a slighter hold on his mind. One grain of jealousy, and the open flood-gates of heaven might have been powerless to keep him from her. As it was, he determined to ride the nine miles to the township on the coast, where it would be possible to pass the night in comfort and amid congenial society. Another reason existed in the charge he had laid against the man who had attacked him in the booth, whose name he now recollected to be Brice. If he were to proceed further against him—and in this he was quite determined—then his presence would be required in the court-house on the following morning.

Thus it happened that several days elapsed before he again saw Esther.

Brice was fined forty shillings, which, no little to the surprise of the court, he paid. The man's manner was quiet and respectful. For the abusive language he pleaded a drop too much, and for the drop too much the season of the year and the excitement attendant on the particular occasion of the races. He neither looked at nor addressed Roller during the progress of the case, and on being released immediately quitted the township.

Esther, meanwhile, had had an unpleasant time with her father. On hearing a full account of her adventure, the doctor's wrath knew no bounds. Had the whole been the result of a deliberate plan, he could not have shown greater irritation than he now displayed. Unable to formulate any distinct charge of misconduct, he returned again and again to the subject from different sides, vacating his position whenever the girl's protestations rendered it no longer tenable.

This kind of harassing warfare, which while it is the hardest to overcome is also the severest to endure, had a wearing effect on the nerves of the invalided girl. She began to long for some call on her father which would take him for a few days from his home, and thus give him a chance of forgetting the incident which at present entirely engrossed his thoughts.

"The most extraordinary adventure that ever happened to a respectable girl," he said once.

"Perhaps I am not respectable," she said, closing her eyes in weariness.

"Good heavens! what can you mean by that?"

"Just that you make me doubt it," she said in the same tone.

"It is your incredible folly—" began the doctor.

"In what?" she interrupted, straining her attention to discover the exact nature of her offence.

"In what!" repeated her father in tones of exasperation. "Do you hear of other girls involving themselves in such an intolerable mess?"

"If you would let me feel that your anger is just, father," she said quietly, "it would be better for us both."

But this was exactly what the doctor was unable to accomplish.

Nor did affairs improve greatly with the arrival of Roller. This gentleman had, on learning the facts, neither reprimand nor reproach; he slew with the subtler and far more deadly weapon of silence. The incident was something to be buried at once and beyond resurrection. He asked no questions either as to the name and whereabouts of the gum-digger or with regard to the second man who had played a part in the affair. He even went so far as to defend Esther when in private conversation with the doctor the latter revealed the irritation under which he laboured; but he was distinctly and dreadfully cold. Like an iceberg, Esther told herself in the rebellious mood to which she was fast being driven.

Rendered helpless by the injury she had received, subject on the one hand to the volcanic outbursts of her father and on the other to the frozen silence and arctic countenance of her lover, while she herself, seeking in vain to discover a rational reason for the attitude of either, writhed under a sense of injustice, blended with a not to be subdued feeling of discredit in the eyes of the world—was it to be wondered at that her thoughts constantly turned to the young man who had so chivalrously defended her? Or that once, lying between sleeping and waking, she fancied for a moment she beheld him kneeling beside her, his eyes full of solicitude for her suffering, and that she felt again the clasp of the strong hands that had held her safe from harm? A sense of intolerable shame followed the tender fancy; shame both in that she had been so far overcome as to permit the action and in that the bare recollection of the scene increased the beating of her heart. She wondered at and accused herself momentarily, inflicting sharper blows than any that reached her from outside; yet the difference between the gentle treatment she had received from the young Samaritan who had found her wounded by the side of the way and the harsh upbraiding and icy politeness of her father and lover exercised a persistent fascination for her thoughts, and was not to be overpowered either by a sense of shame or of the fealty she owed to her betrothed husband.

Nor was Esther happy in the thought of the promise she had exacted from the young man to call at the house. For the first few days the sound of a horse on the road or a rap at any of the doors filled her with alarm, and sent the blood in a rush to her cheeks; but as day followed day and still he made no appearance, this feeling gave place to one of surprise, not entirely unmixed with disappointment. It had seemed to her during the period of her alarm that her invitation had been rash, even bold; but as the days passed, and it appeared that the young man did not intend to call, she began to think that in common gratitude and politeness she could have done no less than she did.

This was the state of Esther's mind when one day the girl of the house handed her a wire couched in the following terms: —

"Down on Tuesday for a month.—Wilfrid Hamilton."

From that moment her face lost its troubled expression, and her injured ankle, which had hitherto puzzled and added to the irritation of the doctor, commenced to mend rapidly.

As for Hugh Clifford, he had returned to his old manner of life, and was fast becoming a proficient in the art of gum-digging. The old spirit of enjoyment in the speculative nature of his pursuit was, however, dead, and though he worked no less indefatigably than before, anyone sufficiently interested to observe him might have read distaste and weariness in his eyes. Why had be made no attempt to see Esther Hamilton? He had.

On the day that witnessed Esther's departure for her home the rain, as we have seen, fell heavily, and it continued to fall with almost unabated violence for two days following. During this time, digging being an impossibility, Hugh devoted himself to collecting firewood from the creek, which, swollen almost to the level of the bank, bore down on its turbulent waters the long-accumulated debris of the woods. Stripped to the skin, the young and vigorous man entered with the athlete's delight into a fierce conflict with the flood, fighting desperately for the coveted prey as it was whirled by in the arms of the roaring stream. He had provided himself with a tomahawk, to which was attached a strong line, and with this implement he enticed to the shore logs of considerable magnitude. None came to interfere with him. With the exception of a solitary figure, which on the third day of the rain appeared on the summit of the hill and remained there for a quarter of an hour with its face turned the other way, not a soul did he see. The gumfield might have been, and not improbably was, entirely deserted. As for the figure, no doubt it was that of the innkeeper, who seemed to entertain a special liking for that elevation, where he might be seen, tall and lean against the sky and not unlike a native hawk in appearance, two or even three times a day.

At one time, towards the close of the third day, it seemed to Hugh likely, on account of the continued rise of the creek, that he would be compelled to shift his tent to a point higher up the bank, though everything inside that structure was already well-nigh as damp as it could be. But shortly after nightfall the wind, which since the commencement of the rain had continued to blow steadily from the north-east, shifted to southward, and in a few hours the oppressive damp heat had yielded to a cool breath from the pole, and the glorious southern skies were again lit up with all their wonted brilliance of star and constellation.

The following day Hugh found plenty to do in pulling down his tent and thoroughly drying everything it contained. The next day he was once more at work with his spade.

All through the hot, arduous hours his mind was occupied with his prospective visit to Dr. Hamilton's. Five days had elapsed since the day of the accident, and the question to be decided was whether the visit ought not now to be paid. To this question he could find no reply. The intense interest he felt in the result of these deliberations militated against any result being arrived at. Indifferent towards the girl he had assisted, he might have called the following day and regarded it as a politeness to do so; deeply concerned as he was, the point to be considered was whether a delay of five days was not altogether too brief.

That evening, as he sat scraping his gum, he noticed that the rapid increase of his wealth was beginning to cramp him for room. He thought over this, and scraped rather more rapidly than before. A little later he made the discovery that certain of his stores were running low, and would shortly need to be replaced.

When he blew out his candle that evening he had determined to walk to Parawai the following day. He would get Wilson to pack out his stores and take back the gum. If he found time he might call and inquire after Miss Hamilton. It is curious when one reflects on the persistency with which every man tries to deceive himself as to his motives that no man has ever succeeded in the attempt. Who can explain why a fraction of the mind should wilfully endeavour to stultify the whole?

Hugh adhered to his determination, reaching the settlement about eleven o'clock the following morning. Wilson expressed pleasure in seeing him, remarked chaffingiy on his stylish get up, and inquired if he were making a fortune. Then without giving him time to reply, immediately broached the subject of Miss Hamilton and her adventure.

"I suppose you were at the races, like everyone else?" he remarked. "The funny thing is no one seems to know the gum-digger's name."

"No?" asked Hugh.

"No. Not that it's of any account, you know, because the whole thing was as straight as it could be. I'd like to hear anyone say anything to the contrary."

"So would I," said Hugh slowly. Then he added, "for that matter."

"Just so," said Wilson, glancing over his shoulder; "but I'll tell you what—the boss has looked as black as thunder ever since."

"The boss?" inquired Clifford, with a prophetic stilling of the blood.

"Roller," explained Wilson, with a wink and a nod. "They're going to run in double harness. Didn't you know? Yes; the marriage is to come off in two or three months' time. He's a daisy, you know," continued the youth, "and if she knew as much about him as I do she'd stand off. He'll lead her the very deuce. But, I say, what's up? You're looking pretty sick on it. I guess you've been working too hard for this gum. How much did you say there was?"

"Two tons," replied Hugh, with a desperate wrench at his

whirling brain.

"Two tons!" exclaimed Wilson in astonishment. "Pounds you mean?"

"No, hundredweight. Did I say tons? Two hundredweight."

"You look queer," said Wilson solicitously. "You don't think it's sunstroke?" he asked. "There have been several cases this summer already, and to-day is as hot a day as we have had. I wonder how you could walk at all in such a sun."

"It's nothing," said Hugh; "perhaps I did overwalk myself. Well, I'll be off back. You won't forget those stores?"

"No," said Wilson, with a puzzled look, "I'm not likely to, for this is the first I've heard of them."

"Well, send them as soon as you can," said Hugh, making for the door. The point was to get somewhere where he could think without being bothered.

"Hold hard!" shouted Wilson; "let me know what it is I have to send."

What was the man talking about? Hugh gave another wrench and remembered that the paper was still in his pocket. He would forget his head next, he said, with a contortion of the face intended for a smile.

Wilson watched him depart in some doubt as to whether he should allow him to go, but seeing how erectly and steadily he moved along the road, concluded it was all right and dismissed the matter from his thoughts.

As for Hugh, he was astonished when he found himself entering his tent, because it seemed he had only that instant left the store. Certainly he had not had time to reflect on the piece of news he had just heard.

CHAPTER XV

ESTHER and Wilfrid Hamilton, having been brought up together, regarded themselves as brother and sister, though their relationship was that of first cousins.

Wilfrid was an orphan, the only son of the doctor's dead brother. From his father he had inherited a small fortune of between two and three hundred pounds a year, which until he reached maturity had been paid to his uncle to be expended on his account. During the last four or five years the cousins had seen but littles of one another, Wilfrid having spent the greater part of that time in the study and practice of medicine in England. He had returned about eighteen months ago a full-fledged M.D. and was now on the point of starting a practice in Napier. He was Esther's senior by several years. Since his return Wilfrid had become engaged to the daughter of a wealthy sheep owner in the provincial district of Hawke's Bay, and but for a circumstance with which the reader will shortly be made acquainted the marriage would already have taken place.

Wilfrid was one of those long-headed, superior young persons, the product of the latter quarter of the nineteenth century, who are fast getting the reins of the world into their hands. In disposition generous, good-tempered, considerate, he was yet thoroughly fitted by nature to safeguard the interests of Number One, and without implying discredit, it may be said that the interests of that gentleman were thoroughly well safeguarded. As Wilfrid himself might have observed, if a man is not capable of looking after himself, can he be trusted to protect the interests of anyone else? And a decided negative would seem to be the sole possible reply.

Putting aside the lady of his affections, with whom these pages are not concerned, there was no one for whom Wilfrid entertained such fondness as his young cousin. The sisterly love and admiration with which that young lady had followed a rather brilliant educational career may have been in part responsible for this regard, but its depth and genuineness were beyond question.

Esther's engagement to Roller had not entirely pleased the autocratic young democrat—singular paradox. Not but that the man was sufficiently personable and well to do, but from what he had seen of him Wilfrid had a strong suspicion that he was a cad—whatever precise collection of undesirable attributes that denomination might imply. His letter in response to Esther's brief note—"You will remember Mr. Roller," and so on—which announced the engagement, was equally short and rather ambiguous. He had hoped she would defer any arrangements of that kind until he was himself a widower. It was his duty to congratulate her. Roller's credit was considered pretty good in town; he was really a desirable connection in several respects. Hoped she would be happy and was her affectionate brother, Wilfrid. It showed something of the state of mind in which the young girl entered on her engagement that a perusal of the carefully worded note brought a smile to her lips.

True to his announcement, Wilfrid presented himself at the doctor's house on the Tuesday evening. In person he was tall and slim, gracefully attired, though without foppishness. His face, in its quick look of intelligent mastery, was probably more pleasing to women than to men. His features were too irregular for beauty and too vivacious for plainness. The dominant weapon in his natural accoutrement, and to which his success in life was probably due, was a strong fund of resolution cloaked by an unruffled placidity of manner.

Wilfrid was considerably disgusted at Esther's condition. "Only a sprained ankle!" he exclaimed, with affectionate roughness; "why, you look half dead!" Nevertheless in a few days' time the girl was moving about the house with the assistance of a stick, and a week later had discarded even this support to her steps.

"I had fully expected," he said one evening, as he sat on the verandah smoking his cigar and carefully nursing one foot across his knee—"I had fully expected after the arduous professional employments of the last twelve months to obtain a little well-merited amusement."

113

"And how are your expectations disappointed?" asked Esther from the dark corner in which she sat.

"Can you ask?" he inquired, with mock reproach. "Here have I been in the district ten days—or is it eleven? However, I have been left entirely to my own resources."

"I am dreadfully sorry you have found them so inadequate," said Esther. "Pray, am I to consider myself to blame?"

"Certainly you are," returned Wilfrid. "When a man revisits the home of his fathers or his uncles, he naturally expects to be made much of. I don't know if you are aware that my health is in a very precarious condition."

"Poor boy," said Esther. "Is it heart disease?"

""There is not much the matter with yours, at any rate," retorted Wilfrid swiftly.

"You expected me to amuse you, I suppose," said Esther, disregarding the interjection.

"Why else should a man have a sister?" inquired he in matter-of-fact tones.

"Really? You confine us in very narrow limits—unless it is someone else's sister you mean."

"Now I arm at a loss to understand that apparently deep observation," said her cousin emphatically after a pause of reflection.

"Ah, Wilf," she said, laughing, "you are spoiled. To amuse yourself will be a beneficial change, for I am sure you are called upon to do so seldom enough."

However Wilfrid might eomplain of lack of amusement, his time seemed to be fully occupied. A day or two after his arrival he had hired a couple of horses, and immediately after breakfast every morning he disappeared, frequently not returning till nine o'clock at night, and then usually in a condition of ravenous hunger. To all inquiries as to where he had been he gave invariably the same reply, "Riding about the gumfields," which for a man of his stamp seemed a form of amusement singular enough.

"Are you thinking of abandoning the medical profession and turning gum-digger?" asked Esther one evening, when he had been with them rather more than a fortnight.

"Well, not exactly," he replied, laughing, and with a slight embarrassment. "The fact is I am looking for someone."

"Looking for someone on the gumfield!" exclaimed Esther, fairly astonished.

But Wilfrid had become somewhat absent-minded of late, and apparently unconscious of her presence, and with a far-off look in his eyes left the room. Thinking he did not desire to be questioned, Esther did not again allude to the subject.

But one afternoon, a day or two later, while she was occupied with her flowers in the beautiful garden which completely surrounded the house, she saw her cousin ride by on his road to the stables, having returned from his mysterious quest rather earlier than was his wont. A few minutes later he entered the garden and, instead of proceeding immediately into the house, came over to her side and stood looking down on her labour, tapping his boot with his riding-whip. Esther noticed that he was covered with dust and that there was a bored look in his eyes.

"One might as well hunt for a needle in a pottle of hay," he observed presently.

"You have not found him, then?" Esther asked quietly, without looking up.

He replied in the negative, tapped his boot a few minutes longer, and wandered away into the house,

Esther's curiosity was aroused. For whom could he possibly be searching on the gumfield of all places in the world? On reflection, also, she could not determine whether he desired to keep the matter secret or was willing to converse with her about it. The whole thing was an enigma, but, being a sensible girl, she determined to hold her tongue and ask no questions, save such as he himself forced her to employ.

After the evening meal, when in response to his request she had dutifully brought him a light for his cigar, he opened his lips to say, "Little sister mine, are we never to have a ride together?"

"Why not?" asked Esther.

"Bravo!" he said, looking pleased. "Is our foot perfectly well and strong?"

"I hardly remember whether it was the right foot or the left," replied Esther.

"Good; then it shall be so. Prepare yourself for to-morrow."

"Where are we going?" asked Esther, settling herself comfortably in a lounge among the brilliant bougainvillea blossoms of the verandah.

"Where you will," he replied, looking critically at her from between his half-closed lids. "Do you know you are rather a handsome creature?" he interrupted himself to inquire.

"Thank you," said Esther, laughing and colouring. "Even with the qualification, I suppose I ought to consider myself extremely flattered"; then she added, "coming from such an authority."

"What's-his-name ought to consider himself deucedly lucky," he remarked after a pause.

"Oh, Wilfrid," she said, with sudden seriousness, "I wanted to ask you. You don't seem to like Mr. Roller. Can't you for my sake make a point of remembering his name, dear, when you speak to him?"

"I might try," said her cousin slowly, "on the understanding it was for your sake. Yes; surely the offence was unintentional." But he felt a terrible inclination to laugh.

"I don't ask you to call him Albert," said Esther, "though I am not sure—"

"But I am," broke in Wilfrid, with an expression of horror; "I am quite certain I never could. I would die for you, Esther, to-morrow, or even as soon as I have finished this cigar, but I cannot call him Albert. No, no; that is beyond my strength."

Esther retained her serious look till the intensity of the strain brought tears to her eyes, then she broke into a laugh like a peal of fairy bells.

"What an absurd creature you are, Wilfrid!" she exclaimed, her eyes dancing wickedly.

But it was his turn now to be serious. He pulled his chair up until he sat facing her, then he placed his cigar on the rail of the verandah and took her hand.

"Esther," he said, "I have laid a trap for you, and I have caught you. Ever since the day I came here I have waited to catch you tripping, but you were wary and until this moment eluded my snare, but I have you now and you cannot escape. Do you know what I mean?"

"No," she said unblushingly.

"Esther!"

"Well, I do; but let me hear what you have to say."

"You do not love this man," he said sternly. "It is impossible you should."

"I am engaged to him," Esther replied evasively.

"You do not love him. Had you loved him, could you have endured his being turned into ridicule by another man?"

"It was not himself," stammered the girl, "but his name."

"Esther, you prevaricate," he said relentlessly. "You do not love him. Confess the truth, for I mean to have it."

"Well?"

"That means you assen; you admit that you do not love him?"

"Yes—I suppose so."

"And yet you will marry him?"

"And yet I will marry him."

"Why?"

"What does it matter why? I have given my promise."

Wilfrid released her hand, took up his cigar, and placing it between his lips, leant back in his chair in silence.

"Well?" she asked curiously.

"I have no more to say," he replied calmly.

She was silent for several minutes, swinging a vine of the bougainvillea backwards and forwards and tapping one foot nervously on the floor.

"I suppose you are angry with me," she said presently, with a slight change in her voice.

"No, no," he said indifferently; "let us talk of something else. What a lovely night, and how delightful is the scent of your flowers!"

These things, however, had now no interest for Esther, who remained silent for so long that at length he leant forward and murmured "Sulky?" in interrogative tones. Then he noticed that the eyes turned up to his were wet and shining and the long lashes heavily gemmed with tears. "Well," he said after a moment, "have your own way. I suppose you will punish me for this, and I must take my ride alone as usual."

"I will come if you want me, Wilfrid," she replied.

He seemed on the point of saying something further on the subject of their dispute, then with a movement of irritation threw away his cigar and changed his tone to one of business-like cheerfulness.

"Then the point is where shall we go? Have you any preference?"

"N—o," she said slowly.

"Why such a dubious negative? But if you really do not mind where we go, what do you say to the direction of the 'Scarlet Man'?"

"If you like," she said quietly; "the roads are very good."

He appeared relieved by her answer.

"I have almost confined myself to the westward so far," he observed, "and I think I have explored pretty well every field in that direction. Perhaps a change to the east and your society will bring me better fortune."

"Then you intend to combine business with pleasure," she said in the same low voice in which she had hitherto spoken.

"To a certain extent, yes, but it will not interfere with my attendance on you. I shall merely take advantage of such opportunities as occur on the way."

Then it was arranged that they should start immediately after breakfast, ride as far as a certain native settlement in the bush, lunch there on provisions taken with them, and return some time before nightfall.

Doctor Hamilton, who since Wilfrid's arrival had been on his best behaviour, even going so far as to treat his daughter as a rational being, whose opinions might occasionally be worth consideration, offered no objection to the scheme. Esther was looking pale from a too rigid confinement to the house. A ride, not too prolonged, would certainly do her good.

Nor did Roller, who usually spent a part of each evening with his betrothed, see cause to interfere with the arrangement. In common with everyone else in Parawai, he regarded Wilfrid as Esther's brother, and in no case would it have entered his head to suppose that the girl could be attracted by so ridiculous a person as the natty young doctor appeared in his eyes. He privately expressed his sorrow to Esther that an appointment with some natives — who were coming to discuss an important matter of business on the morrow—prevented him from joining the party.

As she retired to bed that night, Esther could have torn herself for the duplicity of her smiling reply of regret. But how else could she have received his apology?

CHAPTER XVI

SOON after breakfast the following morning Esther retired to her room to prepare herself for the ride.

This was the first occasion since the accident that she had donned her riding habit, and her attention was arrested by a withered bunch of violets attached to the breast of her jacket. Her first impulse was to remove the flowers, but before the pin was half withdrawn she hesitated and thrust it back into its place. Standing before the glass, her face wore a doubtful, partly guilty expression, and as she proceeded with her toilet it was evident by the look in her eyes that her thoughts were far away. Finally, before pinning her hat with its long streamers of white, shimmering veil to her thick masses of hair, she did remove the flowers, but instead of throwing them away laid them on the toilet table. Then she ran downstairs into the garden.

Esther was passionately fond of violets. Her name in the minds of those who knew her was associated with the delicate scent of these flowers. In order to gratify her love for these delicate children of the earth, she had reserved a well-shaded corner of the garden to their sole use, and from this spot she was in the habit of picking the blossoms long after they had ceased to be found elsewhere. The season, however, was very late, and as Esther made her way to the spot where they grew, it was with small hope of finding sufficient for the purpose that had taken possession of her mind. She was consequently highly delighted to discover that the recent rains had enabled her favourites to put forth a last display, and to these she helped herself so liberally that when she rose to her feet not one remained on the bed.

"Vision of, splendour!" exclaimed Wilfrid, who had come up unperceived and now regarded her with admiring eyes. "How thoughtful of you; but won't you keep some for yourself?"

"These are all for myself," said Esther, laughing, and holding the flowers behind her back. "You may have roses or mignonette, or what you will."

"Violets or nothing," he said resolutely.

"Then nothing," she replied.

He laughed, but she read curiosity in his eyes, and with a faint increase of colour left him and ran up to her room.

Here she proceeded to tie up the bunch, but before the task was half completed her eye caught sight of the withered nosegay on the table and she paused, looking rather more guilty than before. Presently she unwound the thread, and speading, the bunch open in her hand, laid the withered flowers in the centre. When this was done she again tied them up, and holding the bunch against her breast, looked at the reflected image in the glass. The result appeared to be unsatisfactory, for again she unwound the thread, and this time placed the withered violets to one side, subsequently pinning that side against her bosom; and with this, though her eyes had not lost their guilty expression, she seemed more pleased. Then she gathered together her whip and gloves and moved slowly, half irresolutely to the gate, where the horses were already waiting.

Wilfrid, helping her to the saddle, looked for and discovered the violets. He himself sported a very large and ragged cactus blossom, measuring between two and three feet in circumference, which he had found growing on the rockery beside the stable. In reply to her laughing remonstrance, he said he was prepared to effect an exchange, but would not part with his flower on any other terms.

"People will think we are going to be married," she said thoughtlessly, as they rode away.

"No such luck," was the unexpected though scarcely unmerited reply.

They rode gaily forward, Esther delighting in the rush of fresh air after her perfunctory confinement to the house. As they neared the "Scarlet Man" her manner became thoughtful and somewhat absent. Wilfrid noticed with his habitual quickness of observation that her eyes continually roamed across the wide, sunlit expanses on either side of the road, as though in search of someone or something, but he was careful to let his knowledge of her manoeuvres remain unseen. After they had passed the inn her manner became more than ever distrait and her replies to his remarks were monosyllabic and less and less apposite. He was thinking whether or no to rally her on some very in-consequential reply to which she had just given utterance, when she surprised him by saying, "That is the first sign of human life, with the exception of the inn, we have seen since we started."

Following the direction of her gaze, Wilfrid discovered the roof of a tent rising above the scrub about a hundred yards from the road. Fixing his eye reflectively on this object, he brought his horse to a standstill.

"Would you mind my riding over there?" he asked presently, turning towards her.

"I would rather you did not," she replied.

"No?" he inquired, with a glance of astonishment.

"You could call as we return."

"Very well," he said quietly.

Wilfrid was a person remarkably skilful in putting two and two together. He had determined on some association between the tent and the bunch of violets, and the idea made him increasingly watchful.

"I have something to tell you about that tent, Wilfrid," Esther said as they moved forward.

He was a trifle staggered at this evidence of his discernment, but no emotion was visible in his face as he replied encouragingly, "Tell away."

"You remember the accident to my foot," she began.

"I have reason to, for I have been the chief sufferer."

"But you have never heard the whole truth," she went on. "It is true that I was thrown, but it was at night-time and within a few yards of this spot. My horse escaped; I was left alone by the side of the road."

"I had not heard that," he said, seeing that she paused.

"A gentleman came to my assistance," continued Esther, a trifle breathlessly. "I was unable to walk, and suffering extreme pain. I hardly knew what I did. I let him carry me—in his arms."

"Where did this 'gentleman' spring from?" he asked, as she again came to a stop.

"He lives in the tent we have just passed; he carried me there."

"I see," said Wilfrid, with a thoughtful contraction of the brows. "Well?"

"I remained there all night."

"To be sure. Could you have remained on the road?"

"*Should* I have remained on the road?"

"What nonsense!" said Wilfrid uneasily. "Who has been putting that notion into your head?"

"Well, I remained in the tent. Mrs. Brandon was there the greater part of the night, but not all."

"Mrs. Brandon is the gentleman's wife, I suppose?"

"His wife!" exclaimed Esther. "His mother you mean! No, she is Upmore's housekeeper at the 'Scarlet Man.' When the gentleman left me to fetch Mrs. Brandon he gave me a pistol to protect myself in case anyone should come during his absence—you see?" Her face was aglow with vivid recollection as she spoke. "And someone did come—a man. He came into—"

"Stay a moment!" exclaimed Wilfrid. "Was this the gentleman, or merely a man?"

Esther looked indignant. "It was a man," she said, "but"—resuming her earnest manner—"oh, such a man! He wanted to kiss me—"

"So does everyone, for that matter."

"He tried to," continued Esther, waving away this flippancy; "he took all my money, my brooch, my ring—"

"The devil!" exclaimed her cousin, with a slow flush.

"Then," she continued brokenly, "I put my pistol in his eye and shot him."

"You what!" asked the astonished Wilfrid.

"I put my pistol in his eye and fired," repeated Esther. "I think it must have frightened him; I know it made a dreadful noise."

"Let me understand this. You say you put your pistol in his' eye and fired; what became of him after that?"

"He went away," said Esther, opening her eyes. "Did you expect him to remain when he knew that there were five more shots ready for him?"

"Well, I did," confessed Wilfrid. "I expected him to remain for the reason that, as a general thing, if you put a loaded revolver in a man's eye and fire, he—well, he does remain."

"That may be the case with people who know how to shoot straight," admitted Esther; "but, you see, I had never used a pistol before."

"No, no," said Wilfrid, "of course not. Well, what happened next?"

Esther related the remainder of her adventure.

"How is it I have heard nothing of this before?" asked Wilfrid not unnaturally when she had finished.

"Mr. Roller did not wish it to be spoken about, and though I had made up my mind to tell you everything, I have waited till I could do so without fear of interruption. I was afraid of speaking in my father's presence lest you should take up his impression of the affair."

"And what kind of impression is that?"

"Well, that too little cannot be said about it. He said it was an extraordinary adventure for a respectable, girl, or something to that effect."

Wilfrid looked as though he did not know whether to be annoyed or amused. Both expressions were blended in his face as he said, "That is the doctor all over; you must not take it to heart,"

"No," said Esther, without looking at him; "but I should like to have shown him that I was grateful. I do not think that every man would have been so considerate; and he met with something that was very like insult from my father. I know he was hurt and surprised."

"You are alluding to the gum-digger?"

Esther was silent a moment. "Yes," she said presently, "a gum-digger, but none the less a gentleman."

"We might reverse the terms of that proposition," said

Wilfrid quietly, "and say a gentleman, but none the less a gum-digger."

"Very well," said Esther, with a slight cooling of her tone; "I am content to bow to the opinion of the gentlemen of my own family. They must, of course, know what is right. I had supposed that a kindness merited acknowledgment, no matter by whom or in what circumstances it was conferred."

"I am far from disputing the correctness of that supposition; my doubt is concerned with the exact form of the acknowledgment and in how far you are a fit and proper person to express it."

"It will never come from either my father or Mr. Roller," Esther said, with a slight rise of colour.

"It is a duty I am disposed to take upon myself," said Wilfrid. Then, not wishing to commit himself immediately to any line of action, he fell into a silent mood, and the next few miles were covered without a word being spoken.

At length, as they arrived at a country where the increased size and luxuriance of the fern and scrub gave signs that the gumfield was drawing to an end, he roused himself from his reverie to say, "Esther, I will call on this person on one condition—that you will be perfectly frank with me."

"I will try," she answered, her manner betraying a slight uneasiness.

"For whom are those violets?" he asked, looking straight into her eyes.

Esther had nerved herself for almost any question but this. She was aware of her cousin's extraordinary penetration and had steeled herself against it, but the insight displayed by his question seemed to border on the supernatural, and it shook her.

"Violets?" she said to gain time.

"Do you deny they were intended for someone?"

"For someone? For myself. I am accustomed to wear flowers in my dress."

"Are you perfectly frank with me?"

She was silent.

"Because it was on that condition I offered you my assistance."

"Wilfrid—if they were for him, is there any harm in it?"

"Esther, you have made me think so."

"Just a few violets!"

"The importance is not in the number of them nor in the nature of the gift, but in that you denied it. What must I think was intended by a gift which you thought it so necessary to conceal?"

"Not so necessary," she said, "since I have not concealed it from you."

"True."

He rode forward in silence, his brows contracted, his face full of thought. This was infinitely worse than the entanglement with Roller. Confound it! It behoved him to be careful to keep the girl in her present obedient mood. She could be managed now with gentle and careful usage. Yes, but none knew so well as he the strength and daring of her nature. Once put himself in angry opposition, once let her feel he was ever so slightly unjust, and his hold over her was gone. After all, the prevarication had not been bad, and it was natural enough in the circumstances. Had she lied him down, though he would have been none the less certain of the correctness of his surmise, he must have been completely silenced.

Wilfrid had not the least doubt that his cousin entertained a kind of romantic fancy for her gentleman gum-digger, and his fear was lest by any injudicious action on his part this vague sentiment should be fanned into flame. On the one hand, such intercourse as he had had with the species gum-digger led him to believe that her mind could be best disillusioned by complete freedom of intercourse with the object of her thoughts; but on the other, was her emphatic statement that the man was a gentleman, and he was bound to give her credit for sufficient discernment to pronounce upon the point.

At this stage of his mental soliloquy a sudden thought illuminated his brain; so unexpected and abrupt that a half-uttered question leapt to his lips.

Esther looked interrogation.

"We will call at the tent as we come back," said Wilfrid, though that was not what he had been on the point of saying.

"I do not know that I particularly wish to see him," Esther replied, after a pause.

"Very well," said Wilfrid cheerfully;" then I will undertake your commission. By the way, what is his name?"

"Hugh Clifford. He has a second name, which is either Hilton or Hinton."

"Probably Hilton," said Wilfrid, with an odd look in his eyes. ,

CHAPTER XVII

THEY had now left the main road, which, it will be remembered, led on in the direction of the racecourse and the sea coast, and were riding through a country which increased momentarily in interest and beauty.

As they left behind them the wide, sun-bathed plains of the gumfield, the manuka, rejoicing in a richer soil, sprang up to a height of twenty or thirty feet. Other and statelier specimens of the vegetable world began also to mingle their foliage with the minute-leafed tea tree. On every branch, almost on every twig, sat the evil-looking but harmless cicada, their assembled multitudes shaking the air with a deafening whir of voices, as of innumerable tiny grindstones among the foliage.

As they moved deeper and deeper into the warm, moist depths, the tea tree thinned and vanished, a hundred different varieties of trees now contending for mastery of the soil and mingling their varied foliage against the sky. In the heavily shadowed recesses glanced the foliage of the shapely native palm, standing in clumps or mingled with tree ferns, and fringing the banks of loud-sounding, yet invisible creeks. It would seem that gloom could go no further, but it was not so.

There had now begun to appear among the other members of the forest an occasional symmetrical pillar, which, rising in stately grandeur from the earth, broke without branching through the leafy cover of the woods. Rare at first, these majestic beings became increasingly numerous. Beneath them the remainder of the forest was suddenly dwarfed and of no account, They were marked by another significant fact. In the ordinary mixed forest the trees lived on equal terms; they grew side by side; they jostled one another for a sight of the sun; they leaned sometimes in one another's arms: the bush was entirely republican. But with these fawn-coloured giants came a different order of things. They built for themselves mounds, and stood there, and nothing ventured within the sacred circle. No tree jostled them, no vine cast its arms about their feet or attempted to scale their sides; the demon parasite, on his way as a grain of dust through the air, shunned them and sought other prey.

"It is like riding through a cathedral," said Esther, looking upward to the great branches with their cloud on cloud of foliage. "Strange that such a temple should be without a single worshipper."

"This is the Holy of Holies," said Wilfrid. "The parson-bird has his service of song without the gates in the sun-warmed outer woods, where also food is to be found. He may sing sometimes of the tranquil majesty of the abode of the gods, but, like the rest of us, he prefers the certainty of a ripe berry and a cosy bough."

"I love these kauris," said Esther, scarcely heeding him, and suffering her eyes to roam among the mighty boles. "They are so silent, so enduring, so strong."

"I should expect a woman to admire them on those grounds," said Wilfrid.

"On the principle that we love best those qualities we possess least, I suppose."

Wilfrid laughed. "You are too caustic," he remarked. "My intention was more innocent. You might love them for the reason that those qualities are in themselves admirable."

"And not because I am myself talkative, fickle, and weak," continued Esther, with more seriousness than the occasion seemed to warrant.

"You are not talkative," said Wilfrid thoughtfully; "I should not have described you as weak; and as for fickleness, I have no means of judging."

"You are very literal," said Esther, with a suspicion of a pout, "and not very complimentary. I do not like being analysed in that matter-of-fact way."

"To which of my remarks do you take exception?" Wilfrid asked easily.

"To all of them. In the first place, the implication is that I am secretive; in the second, that I am—headstrong; and in the third, that I am not certainly faithful."

"I object to an argument on these terms," said Wilfrid,

laughing. "I protest against your expounding my views as well as your own."

"Hark!" exclaimed. Esther, suddenly holding up her hand.

The road, which was here very rough and little more than a horse track, had continued to ascend gradually for the last two or three miles; but by an increase of light in the forest ahead it was evident that they had now nearly reached the summit of the elevation. The sound which had arrested Esther's attention appeared to come from a point immediately over the brow of the hill, and as the cousins paused to listen, it was repeated over and over again at regular intervals—the hollow ring of an axe. As they moved forward the sound of a second axe broke on the silence of the woods, then of a third and fourth, until the loud echoes blended with and destroyed one another. Drawing still nearer, several new sounds were added to and mingled with the ring of the axes—the rhythmic swing of the cross-cut saw, the clanking of heavy bullock chains, the occasional sighing groan of tired or angry oxen, the cries of their drivers, the voices of the workers talking or shouting to one another in their soft native tongue. These and similar sounds prepared them for the busy scene which met their eyes on surmounting the hill.

Below them, fifteen miles away on the horizon, glittered the sea. Then came a rolling tract of fern and scrub land, streaked and blotted with occasional patches of bush. To the left the broad, shining arm of a tidal river ran through an avenue of mangroves. To the right a dense and interminable forest lay black as night in the beams of the midday sun. Immediately beneath them, at the foot of the steep, tree-denuded hill, stretched a green valley dotted with huts, with here and there a shingle-roofed weatherboard cottage standing in its orchard of peaches and figs. The road led in a downward curve round the Side of the hill, being broken at one point where a shoot had been constructed for the purpose of sliding the logs into the valley.

On the summit of the hill itself was assembled a large party of natives—some employed in crosscutting or squaring with the broad axe the logs already sawn; others in yoking up the team of bullocks, whose duty it was to draw the squared timber to the mouth of the shoot; others, again, were engaged in the dangerous task of jacking and rolling the huge logs from the spots where they had been felled and cut; while a number, at least as great as those who were actively engaged, lay or sat about in small groups, enjoying that extreme luxury of laziness, which is the possession of idleness in the midst of toil.

To the rear, slightly in advance of the standing bush, stood an enormous tree, close on three hundred feet in height. He stood alone, erect, his branches evenly distributed on every side, his foliage darkening the sky. Like a massive piece of masonry, clean, solid, absolutely without flaw, he stood, where he had probably stood for a thousand years, and where, uninjured, he might have stood for another thousand. But in the clean sound wood of his side the American steel axe had bitten deep, and his life blood ran from the gaping scarf. On a platform behind the tree four men were engaged in laying in the long cross-cut saw which was to complete the work of demolition.

The advent of the riders was the signal for an immediate cessation of toil, each one of the natives coming forward, as is their custom, to shake hands with the new-comers. Esther was acquainted with most of those present, and greeted them by their names. Then, in response to the request of a fine-looking man of about sixty years of age, she and Wilfrid dismounted and seated themselves, the Maoris squatting on their heels in a half-circle before them. After a few remarks had been interchanged, the old man addressed Esther in a low, musical voice, and continued speaking for some time to a chorus of "Ae" (yes), "pono" (true), from those around him.

"What is the matter?" asked Wilfrid, whose knowledge of the language was insufficient to enable him to follow the speaker.

"They think we have come here on account of some disagreement between themselves and Mr. Roller," replied

Esther. "They say they have sent to him to-day to endeavour to come to an understanding as to a fine which Mr. Roller appears to have imposed, and which they consider to be exorbitant."

"The sooner you disabuse their minds of that notion the better," said Wilfrid. "We have nothing whatever to do with Roller or his business methods."

Esther explained this to the natives, who received the statement with polite incredulity. "Mita Rora," said the chief, addressing Wilfrid in broken English, "very good man in some tings, I s'pose so; but to the Maori, no good. Ehoa (friend), sometimes ago we make contrac' with Rora; he say I buy so many tausand feet, I pay you so muttee. He say you bring so many every week; if you no bring, I make you pay all the same the fine. We say, 'Kapai' (very good). Two weeks, tree weeks, four weeks—oh, very good, all the same the swim. Then one week, no logs; nex' week, no logs; nex' week, too few; but af!r nex' week, all same's before. But Rora very angry man; he too hard altogether; he say, 'Pay up fine.' Then the Maoris tell, 'Too many dead body at our 'place that times.' Rora, he say, 'Damn urn dead body—where my logs?' Then the Maori very cross man too; he say, 'Go to—.' "

"I say! steady on," expostulated Wilfrid. "Don't mention the exact spot on a sultry day like this."

The Maoris have a keen perception of the humorous, even where it tells against themselves; and Wilfrid's shocked air had the effect of converting their eager, attentive faces into laughing ones.

"Taihoa" (wait), continued the old chief, when he had had his laugh out. "Rora say, 'Kapai, we make new contrac'. You buy your toa (stores) from me—ah, very good, no fine. You bring logs; I pay half toa, half money.' Then the Maoris say, 'No gooru that way; your place too far. Too many the utu (price) your toa. Kapai, all same's before.' Rora say, 'No.' " He waved his hand to denote that such was the condition of affairs at the present moment, and a chorus of approving "aes" greeted this lucid exposition of the case.

"We can't interfere in this," said Wilfrid in a low voice to Esther. "Timber has gone down in value, and I expect the real fact is that Roller is anxious to get out of the contract."

Conversation on the same subject continued in a desultory fashion for the next quarter of an hour, the Maoris endeavouring in vain to get an expression of opinion from Esther, of whose prospective connection with Roller they were well aware. Then Wilfrid suggested that they should proceed on their descent into the valley, which was to form the termination of their ride. But to this the old chief objected. The great kauri tree, one of the largest in the whole forest, was to fall within half an hour. He wished the pakehas to remain and see a sight which they might never again have a chance of witnessing; the direction of the fall was perfectly assured, and it could thus be watched in entire safety. Esther readily gave her assent to the proposal, and at the old chief's direction she and Wilfrid seated themselves to the rear and to one side of the tree. The workers then ascended the platform, and the saw, which was already buried in the wood, was again got in motion. As the instrument swung backwards and forwards on its deadly work, its path followed and assured by the levering powers of the steel wedge, the immense tree began a slow and imperceptible descent towards the earth. Now and then, and with increasing frequency as the saw neared the apex of the deep scarf, an ominous crack, as of the rending of some titanic heart-string, spoke of the terrific force which, in response to the puny efforts of man, was now bringing this ponderous mass of timber to the ground.

None save those who have engaged in bush-falling, or have witnessed the descent of some such monarch of the woods, can conceive the intensity of the excitement which attends the process. Unable to remain seated, Esther moved close to the platform, nervously holding Wilfrid's arm, her whole soul absorbed in the event. The loud cracking noises from the heart of the tree now came at brief intervals, and the maul for driving the wedges home was in momentary requisition. At length, when but a few inches of the bole remained unsevered, the saw, was withdrawn. A few blows on the wedges completed the work. Moving with increasing impetus across the sky, with groans and sharp rending sounds, and the roar of its foliage as it swept the air, the great giant of the woods fell forward and, leaping from his severed bole, came with a deafening crash to the earth.

Subsequently as Wilfrid and Esther, having mounted their horses, rode by on their way to the settlement, they found that the huge barrel of the prostrate tree still rose above their heads.

The old chief accompanied them down the hillside to one of the weatherboard cottages in the valley. Here they found a spot which, with a little greater regard for cleanliness and order, would have been little short of a paradise. A beautiful clear stream, sheltered by the thick branches of titoki trees, flowed close by the house; all around were groves of fig trees, heavy with unripe fruit, their branches overrun and tangled with grape vines. Further out came the splendid green of maize and potatoes, the latter ready for digging. Beyond again were other paddocks, sprinkled with horses and cattle, after which came the hilly ramparts of the vale, clothed in tall white tea tree or the more sombre grandeur of the interminable forest. Disorder and a wasteful luxuriance of growth characterised the scene, and would have sufficed without other indication to announce the fact of its Maori ownership. The fences were patched and unsightly, the orchard choked with weeds, the buildings warped and black from want of paint. Such of the windows as remained unbroken were crusted with dirt, and spiders and mason bees had stretched their webs and built their mud pits on the frames and sashes undisturbed. Nor was the interior of the house more attractive. The paper was falling in strips from the walls and ceilings, the uncarpeted floors were rough with dry dirt, and such furniture as the place contained was mostly in a dilapidated condition. The old bare-footed chief, who marshalled his visitors through the rooms with an importance that did full justice to the palatial splendour he mistakenly saw in his surroundings, explained that he and his family never used the building, except occasionally on Sundays. Personally he could not afford to live in such state. The house was reserved for European visitors, who could be trusted to make no improper use of the good things it contained. He had at one time, on the occasion of the marriage of his eldest son, suffered the place to be occupied, but—he almost blushed to mention it—when he, the chief, went to see them, he invariably found the young couple seated on the floor. He had also a suspicion that they did not occupy the best bed, but made their couch under the kitchen table. In short, he had felt compelled to eject them, and since then the house had remained tenantless.

It was with some difficulty Esther managed to convince the old man that they would prefer to take their lunch and their rest under the trees in the open air. He was astonished at this, because it seemed to show a similarity of tastes to his own. He loved the open himself; being a Maori, he said with humility, it was only natural he should; but it was evident that he was somewhat lifted up in self-esteem by the discovery of this unexpected bond between himself and the white man. Yet given the existence of such tastes, it was curious that the pakeha took such infinite pains to confine himself between four walls; but this was only another of his many puzzling characteristics which the Maori could never hope to comprehend.

The native hut, with its rush walls and palm-thatched roof, to which the chief next conducted them, presented a far more homely and comfortable appearance than was afforded by the house reserved for Europeans. It is true there was neither floor nor chimney, neither chair nor bedstead, but it possessed that air of being in constant use, that indefinable impress which speaks of contact with humanity, and without which the palace of an emperor is but a dreary and uninviting abode. Here it was again found necessary to go through the process of handshaking with the women and girls of the village, who, having descried their visitors afar off, had hastened to the fires on hospitable thoughts intent.

The afternoon passed pleasantly in excursions about the

valley and through the orchard, and at four o'clock the cousins remounted their horses and made the ascent of the hill.

On their way back through the forest Wilfrid, who throughout the afternoon had been subject to fits of abstraction, seemed little inclined to enter into conversation. His manner was that of a man engaged in thinking out arguments for and against a scheme on which he is already half determined. Beyond mechanically adjusting his horse to the motion of Esther's, he appeared almost unconscious of her companionship. This, however, was in appearance only, for presently, when they reached a point on the road near to which was a broken culvert, he recalled the fact to her memory, thus showing himself to be perfectly alive to his surroundings.

In due time the neighbourhood of the tent was reached. Esther, who since her conversation in the morning had found her thoughts constantly returning to the one subject, wondered if in his present mood he would pass the spot unregarded, and she was consequently startled when, without glancing in the direction of the tent, he reined in his horse and suggested that she should accompany him.

Esther shook her head. "I'd rather not," she said.

Wilfrid was silent a moment. "Shall I give him any message?" he asked next.

"No; you may remember me to him."

"Miss Hamilton begs to be remembered?"

"Don't be so ridiculously particular; give him my kind regards—anything. What does it matter?"

"I wished to avoid mistakes. He may think it singular, being so near, that you do not consider it worth while to deliver your message in person."

"He may," replied Esther, who was in a doubtful and suspicious mood.

"Anything else?" asked Wilfrid after a pause.

Esther shook her head. "Just my kind regards. But, Wilfrid," she added, with sudden compunction, "you will remember he is a gentleman, and not—" "Not what?"

"Not offer him money."

"The violets will be a sufficient offering on the shrine of gratitude," he said drily; "at any rate, for the present."

His hand was extended towards her as though the gift of the flowers were a matter of course, and Esther, falling into the snare, removed them from her dress and gave them to him. She regretted the act and her colour rose when, after a glance at the nosegay, he dropped it into his pocket. Whatever unusual he may have noticed, his face gave no sign as he turned his horse and rode off in the direction of the tent.

For five minutes Esther sat still, watching the tent, half fearing, half hoping, and fully expecting to see the figure of Clifford emerge and move towards her across the gumfield. Finally, however, Wilfrid came out alone, and remounting his horse, moved slowly back on to the road.

"Well?" asked Esther as he drew near.

"He is not there," he said. "We might have known that he was not likely to be there at this time of the day. I have left a message for him. I have asked him to come to the house."

The message he had left was as follows: —

"Come, like a good fellow, and let us talk things over. I am staying at Doctor Hamilton's, where I shall remain at home for the rest of the week in expectation of your visit. After a search extending over a fortnight, I discovered you rather singularly through the instrumentality of my cousin, Miss Hamilton, who sends you her kind remembrances. I have said nothing of our relations.

"Yours,
"WILFRID HAMILTON."

CHAPTER XVIII

ONE afternoon, a few days later, Hugh lifted the latch of Doctor Hamilton's gate and found Esther busy among the flowers. Esther greeted her visitor with a fine blush which was reflected in Hugh's countenance, and though the meeting meant much to both of them, or perhaps because it meant much, they shook hands in silence.

"I know you have not forgotten me," the young man said, when he was master of the excitement that possessed him; "your flowers told me as much as that."

Esther tried to look puzzled, but with indifferent success. "The violets?" she asked innocently at length. "Oh yes, I remembered you asked me for them. My cousin thought it would be an act of kindness to send you some token of remembrance."

"Then it was Wilfrid who was responsible for the nosegay?" commented Hugh, with a shade of disappointment in his tones.

Esther caught at the christian name and wondered. "Would you like to see my cousin?" she asked.

"Yes," he answered, "presently—when you have answered my question."

Esther picked a few spent flowers from a rose bush. "Ask me no questions," she said, "and I will tell you no—fibs. I wonder what you thought of me?" she added, with sudden impatience.

"I wish I dared tell you," he replied.

"Ah, then don't," said the girl slowly. "Shall I take you to my cousin?"

"I did not send you to anyone else when you came to me," remarked Hugh.

"I am not sending you away; I am asking if you would like to go of your own accord."

There was a short silence.

"Are you fond of flowers?" Esther asked. "Come, and I will show you my garden." She led him along the paths, pointing out the various plants and naming them rapidly, punctuating her remarks with shy silences, until they reached the bush-house.

"This is truly refreshing after the gumfield," said Hugh as they passed into the cool shadow of the passion vines. "You must give your garden a great deal of attention."

Contrasted with the thoughts and memories of their last meeting, both of them were conscious of an astonishing emptiness and strain in the conversation.

After moving round the house they returned to the doorway. Here, for some inexplicable reason, their eyes met, and they looked steadily at one another for the first time.

"Are you quite recovered now, Miss Hamilton?" Hugh asked.

"Quite," she replied, "but I shall never lose the memory of that terrible night; it lives with me like some impossible nightmare."

"Was it all terrible?" he asked. "How differently can the same facts be regarded by different minds!"

"I am thinking of that man," said Esther. "I did not know there could be such a difference in human nature; he did not seem to be human at all."

"No," said Hugh, "I can understand how such an experience might shake your faith in humanity. That," he added, "was the only part of the night we did not share."

"Have you ever seen him since?" she asked.

"Not from that day to this, though I have heard he is on the field. I still hope to come across him."

"Why?"

He was silent awhile. They were moving along a narrow path under the shadow of cabbage trees and tree ferns towards a small gate that opened from the garden into the orchard.

"If you have not forgotten," he said at last, "neither have I. There are some cases where the law is powerless or resort to it impossible; this is one of them. Should a scoundrel like that go scot free?"

"What could be done to him?" the girl asked as she stopped to unlatch the gate.

"He could lose some more teeth, to begin with," said Hugh in lighter tones; "then I am not altogether pleased with his expression, and I think there is room for improvement there."

But Esther had become grave and anxious. "If it were the last favour I had to ask of you, Mr. Clifford," she said, "it would be that you leave that man alone and never interfere with him."

"I should have said nothing about it," said Hugh.

"I am glad you did, however, because I can now ask you to promise me."

"Of course, you have my promise," he replied. "I think these sort of accounts ought to be settled, but you shall command me."

"I suppose there are numbers of accounts that never get settled in this world," said Esther, "and after a little one ceases to wish that they should be. I wonder if it is an admirable thing to be always of the same mind; to cherish our hatreds and loves unalterably, or to be always forgiving and forgetting."

"We are told to forgive our enemies, but there are no instructions about ceasing to love our friends."

"I was wondering," mused Esther, "whether it is contemptible in us to change our minds or whether it is only 'sweet reasonableness.' There does seem something great in lighting a fire in our hearts and never suffering it to die out. One would like to be like that in preference."

"We may make mistakes," suggested Hugh, "and is there to be no effort to retrieve them? At any rate, one cannot keep a fire going without fuel. Do you recollect saying to me that that man ought to be killed? It was true when you said it; it is none the less true now that a certain number of weeks have elapsed and given you time to forget. The fire has died out for want of something to feed on."

"I remember how you looked when you came back," Esther said. "There was something that made me just a little afraid of you, and that was chiefly why I spoke. You must recognise how unpleasant it would be for me were any part of my adventure made more public than it already is. I should like to forget it entirely."

"I am sorry that I also should have inspired you with fear," Hugh said.

Esther looked unhappy. "You are only pretending to misunderstand me," he said. "It was not for myself I feared, but—well, let us, forget all about it and start our—friendship here."

"It is a lovely spot in which to make a beginning. For my part," he added presently, "I do not want to forget anything, and this for me must always be chapter two."

"You must have thought me a very extraordinary creature," she said curiously, harking back to the topic she had herself forbidden.

"You were thrillingly interesting," he averred.

She laughed merrily, and it seemed that the restraint that had hitherto possessed her vanished with the laugh. "What a complete change I must have been for you!" she said mockingly.

"Yes," replied Hugh, "I have never been the same since. All the world has been differently coloured since then."

"But that is really surprising, you know," said Esther, with mock amazement. "You really ought to communicate with a doctor in a case of such seriousness."

"Doctor Hamilton, for instance," the young man suggested daringly.

"You *ought* to take something for it," said Esther, looking innocently up into the heavily laden peach tree beneath which they stood, "and I will give you a kitful when you go away," she added.

"A kitful of what?" he asked.

"Peaches," she said, opening her eyes; "of what else are we talking?"

"I am sure I don't know," said Hugh. "It is only my thoughts I am certain about, and it is not conventional to speak one's thoughts."

"How curious!" she said lightly. "Haven't I heard or read somewhere of a club where all the members are sworn to speak what is in their thoughts regardless of consequences? What a barbarous idea!"

"It could never come to anything," Hugh thought; "in the end, if not in the beginning, it would resolve itself into the subtlest form of flattery. It is only at some great crisis in life that we take off the mask, and we are generally in pain while it is off, and get it on again as rapidly as possible."

Esther looked at him musingly. "That explains everything," she said, "except why we should be ashamed of ourselves afterwards."

"I suppose convention is a sort of mental clothing," he said; "it has its fashions, like our coats, and is continually on the change, but we always wear it in some form or other. It is only under the influence of strong emotions that we throw it aside and become completely natural."

"My mind is easier now," Esther declared. "If you can regard my extravagances as wholly natural, we should have no difficulty in forgetting them."

"None," he said, "unless it might be a desire not to forget."

They had now completed the circuit of the orchard and again approached the gate into the garden. A figure crossing the other end of the path attracted Esther's attention, and she paused with her hand on the latch.

"Do you know Mr. Roller?" she asked in a low voice.

"By sight, not otherwise."

"Would you like me to introduce you to him?" she asked hesitatingly.

"I leave it to you," he replied. "I am not an ambitious man."

"What do you mean by that?" she asked in the same low, reflective tone as they moved down the path.

"I suppose I meant to be funny," he replied, with compunction, "but I believe I was merely rude. Forgive me if it seemed so to you. Is he—is he a friend of yours?"

It was a long while before she answered, and the reply when it came was produced with difficulty. "We are engaged to be married," she said.

"I had heard that," Hugh said presently. "I did not know

whether it were true or not; so many things you hear are not true—or had better not have been." The last words appeared to be wrung from him, and he bit them off sharply and concluded almost inaudibly.

Esther chose not to hear, and they emerged from the path on to the walk in front of the verandah. Roller, who was on the point of quitting the garden, saw them and turned back, Esther standing still until he came up.

"I have been looking all over the place for you, Esther," said the storekeeper.

"Let me introduce you to Mr. Clifford," was Esther's reply. "Mr. Roller, Mr. Clifford."

"How do you do, Mr. Clifford?" said Roller affably.

Clifford raised his hat, and there was a short pause.

"Mr. Clifford is the gentleman who assisted me so generously at the time of my accident," Esther explained.

"Oh, indeed," said Roller, scanning Clifford slowly from head to foot. "You are gum-digging out there, I believe, Clifford?"

Hugh nodded a careless assent, and snapping off a rosebud, drew the stalk with elaborate care through his buttonhole, then he turned to Esther.

"Is your cousin to be seen now, Miss Hamilton?" he inquired.

"Yes," she said. "Shall I tell him you are here—or will you come in with me now?" There was even an exaggerated deference in her tones.

"I will go with you," he replied in a manner that was purposely meant to imply that he would follow her to the end of the earth.

Roller whistled and strolled a few yards away from the verandah, while Esther led her visitor into the house.

"There is some mystery about this," Esther said. "May we hope some day to be enlightened as to its meaning?"

"It is rather a prosaic mystery," said Hugh uneasily, "and it is remarkable you haven't guessed the secret. I will tell Wilfrid to communicate the facts to you."

Esther led him through the house to a side verandah where Wilfrid was sitting. The latter, on seeing them approach, threw away the paper he had been reading, and rising hurriedly to his feet, came forward with both hands extended.

"Well, Hugh, old fellow, here you are," Esther heard him say as she stepped down off the verandah and made her way round to the front of the house.

Roller was waiting for her on the steps and looked impatient. "I came to see if you would come for a ride, Esther," he began.

"I can't to-day," she replied; "Mr. Clifford will be here to dinner."

"Clifford!" he said, with thinly veiled contempt. "What, that gum-digger fellow?"

"Yes," she said, "that gum-digger fellow."

"Oh, well," said Roller in a huff, "if you prefer his company to mine—"

"It is not what I might prefer, Albert," explained Esther," it is a matter of hospitality. I could not leave them all to the mercy of the girl."

"Well," he said, "come round to the bush-house, I want to talk to you."

Esther, after a momentary hesitation, moved in the direction indicated, and they seated themselves together on a rustic seat among the ferns.

"I can't stay very long," Esther said, "because Maria is no good when she is left to herself. She seizes every moment I am away to try on my clothes in front of the looking-glass."

"Oh, well, never mind her, I want to have a talk with you. Don't you think it's about time we were getting married?" he asked abruptly.

"Married?" said Esther slowly.

Roller laughed, but a little uneasily. "The idea seems to be a new one to you," he said presently.

"No, no," she said, "only—" and then she fell silent.

"Only what?" he asked.

"I did not think of getting married quite just yet."

"Well, not to-day or to-morrow or the next day, but

reasonably soon. Why not next month?"

"Next month?" she repeated.

"I do not know why you should repeat my words like that," he said crossly. "I suppose we are to be married some time."

"I do not want to get married quite just yet," Esther said again.

"So you told me before, but now I want to know what 'quite just yet' means—if it has any meaning."

"I should like a little more time," she said, with a momentary tremble in her voice. "I should like to be certain of myself."

He was silent a long while. "Certain of yourself," he said at length. "Is that what you said? But surely you were certain of yourself when you told me six months ago that you would marry me?"

Esther was silent.

"Because if you were not your conduct was outrageous."

"What was the date you wished to fix?" Esther asked when this remark had sunk in.

"Certainly not later than the end of March," he replied.

"Well," she said, after a pause of reflection, "I will let you know in a fortnight's time—a fortnight from to-day," and she rose to her feet.

"Stay a moment," said Roller. "Do I understand you to say that you will fix the date in a fortnight's time?"

Esther nodded assent without looking at him. "I will give you my answer then," she said.

He did not seem entirely satisfied, and there was a look of reflection on his face as he followed her into the open air and to the door of the house.

"Will you come back to dinner?" she turned to ask as she left him.

He made a motion of assent, and quitting the garden, crossed the road to the store. Though he was barely conscious of it, the last few minutes had implanted in his mind a seed of doubt, which was destined before many days to expand and darken his life with its growth.

CHAPTER XIX

IT was not until the gong sounded for dinner that Hugh and Wilfrid again became visible to the other members of the household. Esther, looking curiously at them as they entered the dining-room, thought that Hugh's mouth had that stubborn, set look she remembered seeing on it once before, while Wilfrid appeared discouraged and seemed inclined to be argumentative.

"It is not nearly as warm as yesterday," he said, in opposition to the doctor's complaint of the heat of the weather; "nothing like as warm. By the way, uncle, you have not met Mr. Clifford, I think? Son of the Honourable Clifford, of Hawke's Bay, and my prospective brother-in-law."

"Oh, indeed," said the doctor. "I have met Mr. Clifford before, but he kept me in the dark as to the relationship."

"I was not aware of it at that time," said Hugh, glancing towards Esther, who stood listening in surprised silence. "I suppose Wilfrid must have told me about his people, but somehow I did not think of connecting them with you. The world is only a small place after all."

"I ought to have guessed it ages ago," said Esther, a bright spot of colour in her cheeks.

"I don't know that there is much to be surprised about," said Wilfrid, taking his seat at the table. "Apart from myself, the families have been no more than names to one another so far."

"Are we waiting for anyone, Esther?" asked her father.

"For Mr. Roller," she said; "that is his step now."

Roller came in briskly, greeted the whole company with a comprehensive nod, and dinner commenced.

Maria, a big, handsome half-caste, did the waiting, walking in a leisurely fashion round the table and occasionally joining in the conversation, usually to contradict someone. Esther, knowing her habits, watched her with anxiety, for Maria was a desperate flirt and always in danger of being attracted by fresh faces to an extent impossible to conceal.

"You have forgotten to give Mr. Clifford some vegetables, Maria," her mistress said.

Maria had not forgotten, but she now walked elegantly and with the utmost deliberation to the sideboard, removed the vegetable dishes, and brought them round to Hugh, slightly leaning against him as she proffered them one after the other. This accomplished, she strolled back to a point opposite and there by the exercise of all kinds of little stratagems endeavoured to attract the young man's attention,

Hugh, however, appeared to be totally unaware of these manoeuvres. His whole attention was absorbed by the girl, not in front of, but beside him, and in speculating on the depth of her attachment to Roller he found ample material to occupy his thoughts.

The storekeeper seemed in rough good spirits, and rattled away on the subject of the dispute between himself and the natives, addressing himself chiefly to Wilfrid, who responded crossly and in monosyllables.

"So," concluded Roller, "I told the old beggar I would have nothing more to do with them, and I told him personally that he was an old shuffler."

"H'm!" said Wilfrid.

"You told Rewi that?" asked Esther. "I am sorry you did that. I have always looked upon him as the soul of honour. I'm sure he would not cheat anyone consciously." She spoke with some fervour and then turned to Wilfrid. "You remember Rewi, Wilfrid," she said— "the old chief who took us round his house?"

"Yes," said Wilfrid; I was greatly struck with him, and am no less surprised than you at Mr. Roller's remarks."

"Ah," said Roller, "you don't know the natives; and as for Esther, she is always finding perfect gentlemen in the most unlikely places."

"That is not her invariable fortune," snapped Wilfrid, who observed the covert sneer and resented it.

"There is a good deal of difference in the natives," said Maria, speaking slowly and clippingly and gazing lustrously into Clifford's eyes. "Some are just like Europeans, while others are—"

"Still more like them," suggested Wilfrid as she paused. "That was remarkably brilliant of you, Maria."

"I was going to say no good at all," said Maria, who, failing generally to understand Wilfrid, was rather afraid of him.

"There is a lot of rubbish talked about the natives," said Roller aggressively. "They are a lazy, dirty lot, take them all round. I have never been able to find much good in them. A man has only to run through my ledger to discover what they are like."

"You would hardly set up your ledger as a criterion of the merits of the Maori race, I suppose," said Wilfrid. "For my part I am disposed to pay less and less attention to the cash book as a measure of human merit. I know that the dirtiest and laziest of your natives would cheerfully beggar himself in the cause of hospitality, and that the best of them have a hatred of the meanness and paltriness that is associated with so much of our civilised system of money-making."

Roller looked slightly chagrined. "They are always thought best of by those who know least about them," he said.

"And if so," said Wilfrid, "theirs is only the case of the majority of mankind. It would not be fair to judge them by a standard higher than is applicable to ourselves."

"There is a good deal to be said on both sides of the question," said Dr. Hamilton didactically. "The Maoris are universally admitted to be the most intelligent aboriginal race on the earth, but that intelligence does not go so far as to enable them to withstand the progressive movement of the European; they are doomed to disappear."

"Our discussion," said Wilfrid, "was as to whether the Maori were less honourable in business matters than the European."

"There was a Maori in the kitchen this morning," said Maria, "who picked up my thimble with his toes; if I hadn't seen him, he would have gone away with it."

Wilfrid laughed. "Obsessions like that," he said, "are common to humanity; but Maria has spiked my gun, and I shall say no more."

"Ah, well," said Roller, "I have given the natives best, and now I am going for Upmore. I always make a point of having a European to fall back upon in dealing with the natives."

"We'll see how you get on with the European, then," said Wilfrid. "I've met Upmore once or twice, and if I am any judge of character, you will fare still worse. How does he come into it?"

"I suppose he was making a commission," said Roller, "but that's no business of mine. I refused to bind myself to anything with Rewi until he brought the signature of a reputable European to back him, and Upmore's fist was the result."

"I knew that man before you came here, Albert," said the doctor. "There have been some singular circumstances connected with his tenure of the inn, and I would advise you to be cautious in your dealings with him."

"He can't get round me," said Roller in his overbearing way.

"I suppose you see a good deal of him, Mr. Clifford," said Esther.

"Upmore?" asked Hugh, with a start. "I see him pretty well every day at a distance. He doesn't attract me, and I should judge that Dr. Hamilton is right and he might be dangerous."

"He is a hateful man," said Esther, with a sudden flash. "He has some dreadful place there that the diggers call the dead-house."

"Yes," said Hugh, "I've seen it; where he puts his violent drunks."

Esther nodded. "Do you know a digger called Jess Olive?" she asked— "the one they call the King of the Diggers; a man with the most beautiful blue child's eyes?"

"Yes," said Hugh, "I know him very well."

"Upmore put that poor soul in the dead-house," she said, "and kept him there all night. Can you conceive what it meant?"

Roller laughed as though at some amusing recollection. "You should hear Johnson describe the scene," he said. "He was staying there at the time, and it appears there was a digger they call Bart there, and Olive came to try and get him away from the place—thought he was drinking too much or something. Bart was drunk, and there were three or four others as bad as he was. Upmore had been bothered by Olive before—the man is a sort of mad reformer or religious crank, something of the kind—anyhow, Upmore took and shut him up in the dead-house. What followed beggars description. Olive was on one side of the door, howling supplications, and Bart on the other reciting impromptu poetry—he is said to be rather good at that kind of thing—while the others sat round drinking raw rum and applauding. Upmore leant against the shelves behind the bar, watching his customers' faces and apparently indifferent to the uproar."

"Was Johnson indifferent too?" asked Esther, with cold disgust. "One would have thought the prayers of that poor mortal would have moved the very walls to fall down and release him. *You* can feel what it meant, Mr. Clifford," she continued, turning to Hugh. "You know his horror of darkness and can guess what he must have suffered. When they let him out he was like one stunned by a cruel blow; his childlike faith in mankind was gone, and it was months before he was himself again."

"Yes," said Hugh. "I can understand your antipathy to Upmore now. I am surprised, however, that Bart should have had a hand in it. I know him, and though he has many defects, I did not think brutality was one of them."

"He was probably too intoxicated to know what he was doing," said the doctor; "but he was most assiduous in his attentions afterwards; he became quite a nuisance tramping in here and begging permission to see him."

"Yes," said Esther, with a smile of recollection. "I like Bart. I must have heard him a dozen times asking Jess to forgive him. Jess's answer was always the same: 'You could not be expected to know; it is a strange weakness for a man to be afraid of the dark.' He never said anything else, and in time, I think, he forgot all about it; but one can never tell."

"How did he come to be here?" Hugh asked, interested.

"He always comes to me when he is in trouble," Esther said. "I remember him that morning and the shock his appearance gave me. His hands were cold and trembling as he held them out to me, and he stared about him as if in dread. 'It is always darkness now, Esther,' he told me. 'Nonsense, Jess,' I said; 'it is a beautiful sunny day.' And I took him right out on to the middle of the lawn. 'Darkness, Esther,' he repeated; 'why did God make the darkness to be a continual horror to His creatures?' What is the matter with you, Jess?' I asked. But it was not until Bart came that we learnt the reason for his disorder. We kept him doing little jobs in the garden for the next three months, until he was quite himself again and the voices of the gumfield called him away."

Hugh was touched by the little narrative and the tender eyes. "I know now what he meant," he said, "when he told me one day that angels still dwelt here and there on the earth."

After dinner Roller took his departure. He seemed loath to go, but it being, as he said, mail night, he had no alternative. Esther walked with him as far as the gate, and they stood there for a minute or two almost in silence.

"Is that—Clifford going to stop here all night?" he asked, after he had said good-bye and gone out on to the road.

"Yes," she said.

He stood a moment invisible in the darkness; then with another good-night crossed the road.

Esther remained where she was, slowly rubbing her cheek where his parting salute had fallen, until a step on the gravel caused her to turn.

"Is that you, Esther?" asked Wilfrid's voice. "The doctor is shdwing Hugh his collections, and we shall not be missed for an hour. I am in trouble, like Jess Olive, and I want to unburden my soul to you."

"What is it, dear?" she asked, linking her arm in his.

CHAPTER XX

THEY went out through the gate on to the road and along the grassy margin past the lights of the Post Office, where Roller could be seen in his shirt sleeves at work on the mail.

"He is a good business man," Wilfrid said absently as they passed. "Would you mind my smoking?"

"I like it," said Esther.

And Wilfrid got out a cigar.

"Esther," he said presently, "you may have noticed at your father's table, this evening a big, fair young man with grey eyes."

"Mr. Clifford?" Esther asked.

"The same," said Wilfrid. "He is a mule."

"I hope that has done you good," she said as he paused. "I could tell by your faces that you had disagreed."

"Yes," he said, "I talked till my jaw ached. I showed him the folly of his conduct from every point of view; and I might have been a cow lowing for all the effect my remarks had on him. That is the sort of young man he is."

They walked along the dim road in silence, Esther waiting patiently, yet with curiosity, for what was coming.

"Money, Esther," Wilfrid began at last, "is the root of all evil, and that is one of the two true sayings of the world. I am going to relate to you the story of a man who made a fortune many years ago in New South Wales. He was from England originally, and his name was Hilton. Yes, you see the connection; he was Hugh's grandfather. He was not an educated man, but he had a strong will and unlimited capacity for hard work, and he achieved success. He married and had a child, a daughter, who subsequently became Mrs. Clifford, and Hugh's mother. His wife died, and many years afterwards he married again, and this time he had a son, whom he christened Cuthbert. His daughter did not get on very well with her stepmother —who was a very young woman, and had been an actress, I think— and coming to stay with some friends in New Zealand, she married, as I have told you, and passed out of the old man's life. Do I make myself clear?"

"Perfectly," said Esther.

"Old Hilton," resumed Wilfrid, "was entirely taken up with his son and heir, and a lively young beggar he was, according to all accounts. Perhaps the crooked strain came in with the mother; perhaps the old man spoiled him: but he turned out bad, and became finally a continual trouble. You can guess the rest; it is in half the novels you read; it is as old as humanity. What the special act was is shrouded in mystery, but he left his father's house for good, and the old man took him out of his will. His story apparently closes there, for from that day to this he has not been heard of.

"As for old Hilton, he had one desire left, and one only —the desire to found a family. It had grown out of the reminiscences of his early life when he had been a peasant on a great estate. It seemed that this desire might be gratified in the person of his son, but when that hope failed him he bethought him of his daughter and her family, and he settled all he had on her eldest son Hugh. About a year before he died—and now we come to the crux of the whole matter—he had his will revised, and this was the result. After a number of comparatively unimportant legacies he left the whole of his estate entailed upon Hugh and his heirs for ever, but to remain in trust until Hugh was twenty-five: that was the first provision. Failing Hugh and his heirs, he harked back to the son who had disgraced him, and left everything to him: that was the second provision. Failing Hugh and Cuthbert and their heirs, he entailed everything on his eldest surviving male heir: and that was the third provision. Do you follow me yet?"

"I think so," said Esther.

"Now Hugh's mother had three children—Hugh, Grace, and Reginald; so that practically the order of entitlement to the old man's estate is divided in the middle of the Clifford family by the inclusion of their uncle, Cuthbert Hilton."

"And he has come back, I suppose?" said Esther.

"Not he; his story is still a blank."

"Then where does the trouble come in?" she asked.

"It is to be found in the second of the two true sayings of the world," replied Wilfrid —"*cherchez la femme.*" Old Hilton, you have seen, interested himself entirely in male heirs, but God made woman, and then the trouble began."

"And who is the woman?"

"Here is a convenient log," said Wilfrid, "let us sit down. The woman is Hugh's mother, and now my story dwindles off into that pettiness which is nevertheless responsible for half the tragedies in life. I wonder whether I can give you an idea of the sort of person she is without leading you to draw entirely erroneous conclusions as to her general character. She is not a strong-minded woman, but on the other hand she is no fool. Perhaps it would be safest to regard her attitude in this affair as an isolated aberration, which does not react on her general conduct. I like her, we all like her, but—Well, no doubt she loves her eldest son, but the weak spot in her heart is unquestionably for the other boy Reginald, and she has come to look on him in some curious way as a victim. She may not have meant much, possibly even she meant nothing at all, but there is no doubt Hugh was rendered wretched by her constant harping on the injustice which she considers was done to the younger boy by the terms of her father's will. It seemed nothing to her that Hugh was not responsible; that he didn't care twopence for the ten thousand a year that was to be his in a year or two; that he would split it up with his brother or anyone else to please her, if she so willed it; she just clung stolidly to the one fact, that Hugh was to get everything and Reginald nothing, and from that position nothing could shift her. Do I give you a dim idea of the sort of woman she is? Or have I failed and portrayed a monster?"

"Certainly not that, but let me hear the rest."

"Well, Hugh is a good fellow, but he is not very old or experienced, and at the beginning of life we are inclined to take little things seriously, and dropping water wears away stone, and constant nagging destroys the best tempers, and so the end came. There was no violent scene; it occurred one day at dinner, and it was all said and done in less than a minute.

Something she said touched him to the quick, and he got up and put his chair against the wall. 'Say no more, mother,' he said; 'I will never touch a penny of grandfather's money as long as I live.' The madness of her conduct came home to her then. I read it in her face, and though I was angry with her, I was sorry for her too. They found him an hour later packing his things, but they could not change his determination to go. Gracie tried him, Reggy tried him, I tried him, but it was no good. Then his father took him in hand and walked him up and down the lawn half the night, reasoning with him, expostulating, commanding—no effect. Hugh's father is one of those men—and, strangely enough, they are frequently, as in his case, men of great gifts—who are contented to take second place in their own households. He had never interfered between mother and son, I doubt if he was aware of half that took place even before his eyes, but he came out of his shell that night, and he fought the demon of temper in his boy as though his life depended on it. But no. The Hugh we knew was gone, and this was quite another creature. Nothing shifted him a hair's-breadth from his original determination, and when morning came he was gone."

Esther drew a long breath as Wilfrid concluded.

"Yes," he said, reading in the sound something of her feeling, "human nature is a strange thing. We are only on the world a short time, and we all alike desire to be happy, and we muddle our lives and are miserable. What do the great events matter? We rise to them with all our strength and pass them or perish. But the little things spring up all day long in our path and drive us here and there, and what should have been a broad, smooth river is frittered away into rivulets and stagnant pools. But let me bring my story to an end and show you how it affects myself. If I have succeeded in conveying a true picture of the Clifford family, you will understand that Hugh could not drop out of it without leaving a gap. Everyone liked him and needed him; Grace worshipped him, and his departure affected both her spirits and her health. Illogically enough—but conduct is always illogical—I became the chief sufferer. I had hoped before this to have been married and settled, but marriage until her brother returns she will not hear of. When I became assured that this resolve was unalterable I set out in search of Hugh; I traced him up here and I found him, or rather you found him for me. But I might as well have let him be. Time has made absolutely no difference in his resolution; the old stubborn temperament of the Hiltons has worked itself an outlet, and there's an end of it."

"Does he say nothing?" asked Esther.

"Practically nothing. He is polite, confoundedly polite. He refuses to lose his temper and he listens with the most admirable patience; finally he yawns, still with the utmost politeness, and there you have him."

Esther laughed. "Then what is to be done?" she asked.

"My only hope now," said Wilfrid, "is in you."

"In me?" said Esther, surprised. "What could I do?"

"Much," he replied, "if you chose."

"But, Wilfrid, he is nearly a stranger to me; this is only the second time I have met him."

"Friendship," replied her cousin, "does not depend on time, but on feeling. One may be intimate with some people in ten minutes, with others not in ten years."

"That is oracular, but hardly applicable. Two meetings do not make a friendship, and mere acquaintance would not warrant me in lecturing him on his private affairs."

"He has consented that the story should be told you; he has even expressed a desire that you should hear it. Probably he is afraid you might suspect worse; he cannot be surprised if you make it a subject for comment."

"What could I say?"

"You could show him the folly of his conduct."

"I am not certain that I see it," said Esther. "He may forgive his mother, possibly even his feeling is tenderer for her now than it was when they were together, but if that is so it is only an additional reason why he should remain away from her. I can understand such an idea influencing him."

"And yet you have only met him twice."

Esther was silent. "There is something," she said at length, "in what you said about ten minutes and ten years."

"There usually is something in my remarks," Wilfrid allowed.

Esther laughed absently. "The circumstances were so peculiar," she said; "it was like the walls between two houses falling down—one could see everything." She fell silent, and for a minute or two nothing was said.

"Of what are you thinking?" he asked at length.

"Of him," she replied readily; "of his resolution not to give in—isn't there something admirable in it?"

"Nothing that I can see," said Wilfrid. "The whole business is too childish, and it is inflicting pain on a number of very estimable people—myself among them."

"But as a principle," Esther urged, with a strange insistence, "it must be good to stand to one's guns—to promise a thing and hold fast to it at all cost; it must be good because—because—"

"Because?" he asked.

"Because it is so terribly difficult."

"I see," said Wilfrid, with sudden thoughtfulness. "Shall we go back, Esther?" he asked presently.

Esther rose, and he drew her hand through his arm and held it, but he said nothing.

"You have not told me exactly how I am to help you, Wilfrid," she said after a little.

"No," he replied slowly; "nor have you told me how I may help you. Do you think I don't understand? That in my selfish puzzling over my own concerns I have no thought for yours? What is this great principle you have asked me to applaud? That one should stand to one's promises, good or evil, at any cost? To that I answer no, a thousand times."

Her arm tightened against his, but she gave no other sign of comprehension.

"We have been as brother and sister," he resumed, "all our lives. Do you forget the old home on the beach of the Bay of Islands, where the whalers drew in close to the shore? Is the old life, the old comradeship nothing to you, that now I must stand by and see you walk alone into the darkness and have no right to hinder you?"

"Wilfrid," she said huskily at last, "if there were any reason, any excuse that might make my conduct appear less—outrageous (the word was a memory), who knows? But there is none, none. I have done this with my eyes open, and there is no escape."

"Good," he said cheerfully, as he stopped to unlatch the gate, "now we understand one another. It is enough for me that the wish to escape is there."

CHAPTER XXI

FINDING Hugh a patient and intelligent listener, the doctor took a fancy to him, and as a result he remained a guest at the house for over a week. There was nothing surprising in this, colonial up-country hospitality being built on such broad lines that the request for a glass of water from a passing stranger has been known to terminate in an invitation to stay a month.

The prolonged visit was entirely pleasing to Wilfrid, who was thus able to argue with and bully the young man to his heart's content. At first he spread his remarks with an impartial regularity over the whole day, just as they occurred to him, but after a day or two he came forward with the suggestion that they should devote an uninterrupted hour to the matter every day.

"It will give you time to work the thing up," Hugh said drily; "just as you please."

"What hour would be most convenient to you?" Wilfrid asked considerately.

"Get it over as early as you can," Hugh stipulated.

So immediately after breakfast every morning the two retired to the room on the side verandah, and there Esther, in passing frequently, heard Wilfrid's voice traversing the heights of argument, his speeches punctuated by growls from his victim. Punctually as the clock rang out the hour, Hugh opened the door and came out. There was no variation to this performance, and Esther got quite accustomed to seeing them emerge at the same moment daily, Hugh like a great schoolboy released from his lessons, and Wilfrid with an exasperated look in his eyes and a repressed smile—due to his sense of the humour of the situation—on his lips. Before this arrangement was agreed upon Esther had been a frequent witness to the discussions, but as she never interfered between them except occasionally to register her applause in a little peal of laughter, she came to be regarded as neutral, and later on her society was tacitly allowed to be neutral territory.

Except for the one hour the days belonged to the three,

and for two of them at least were wholly pleasant. They spent them in the orchard or in wandering in the bush on the outskirts of the settlement, or in cantering along the soft roads into the shadow of the great kauri bush, or among the interminable billows of the gumfield, where nothing was gay except the unceasing sunlight. Once, Hugh desiring to pay a visit to his abandoned tent, they rode past the "Scarlet Man," where they were surprised to see an alteration being effected to the building: a large room, thirty or forty feet long and twenty wide, had been thrown out from one side and was now approaching completion.

"What can that be for?" wondered Hugh.

"I expect Roller has started on the European," Wilfrid said, "and the European is building an opposition store to collar the trade of the field."

They found the tent apparently undisturbed, and Esther again looked with interest on the scene of her startling adventure. Every detail of the night came back to her as she gazed.

"Look, Wilfrid," she exclaimed; "here is where I was sitting when that horrible man came in."

"What, Hugh? No wonder you were alarmed."

"And the pistol—have you got the pistol, Mr. Clifford? Do show it to Wilfrid."

Hugh went obediently to his wardrobe and began turning out the things, as she remembered seeing him do on the night of the accident, but this time he went through them twice without result.

"Funny thing that," he said reflectively, and commenced tossing the rugs about and overhauling the tinware.

"It's gone," said Esther, with sudden conviction; "it is no good looking for it."

"Why should you think that?" he asked, surprised.

"Because there is something uncanny about this place," she said, with a shiver. "You have things one minute, and the next they are gone."

"You are thinking of your jewellery," said Clifford, "but I

never lost anything before then, or since, till now." And again he began searching among the contents of the haversack.

"It's no good," insisted Esther, with confidence. "Why did that man want to kill you?" she demanded, frowning. "What had you done to him?"

"Nothing, please, miss," he replied.

"Has he been quarrelling with someone else?" Wilfrid asked.

"All I know is," said Esther, "that that man stole in here armed with a tomahawk thinking to find him and found me instead. That was not done without cause."

"Out with it, Hugh," said Wilfrid. "What have you been up to?"

"There is nothing to conceal," said Hugh, giving up his search for the pistol and bundling his possessions back into their places. "It was one day on the gum-field; he came up behind me with a spade, and we had a bit of a scramble; that was all."

"Why did he come up behind you with a spade?"

"Don't know, unless he wanted my gum."

"But that's slightly mysterious, isn't it?" asked Wilfrid, "I suppose the diggers are not in the habit of murdering one another for the sake of a few pounds of gum. Was there nothing else?"

"Nothing so far as I was concerned," said Hugh. "I had never seen the man before to my knowledge."

He had been engaged while he spoke in opening a collection of tins and inspecting their contents, and he now turned to Esther. "Shall I "make you some tea?" he asked.

"Won't it take a long while?" she inquired.

"Only a couple of minutes to boil the water in the frying-pan."

"Whoever heard of such a thing?" exclaimed Esther, her eyes dancing with amusement. "Is that how you make your tea?"

Hugh nodded. "You can fry the water in half the time you can boil it," he explained.

Wilfrid became enthusiastic on the spot. "This has got to be done, Esther," he said. "Hugh is evidently a strategist of a very high order, and we cannot get fried tea every day."

The fire was soon alight and the tea made. "I am sorry I cannot offer you any milk," their host said, as he passed round the cups; "the only tin I had has gone sour."

"Never mind the milk," said Wilfrid; "it would spoil the flavour of the smoke. Get out the cake."

But the establishment contained nothing save cabin-bread, and after tasting this Esther declared that it looked better than it tasted. "Don't you ever have bread and butter?" she asked compassionately.

"Oh, yes," said Hugh, "but the butter has gone rancid, and I make the bread, you know, as I require it."

"I don't believe a word of it," said Wilfrid. "Get out the frying-pan again and let's see you."

"Do you make the bread in the frying-pan?" Esther asked, deeply interested.

"I make it in the camp oven when I have time," Hugh said; "but when I am in a hurry I just bake it in the ashes. Shall I make you some?"

"It would be a shame to put you to all that trouble," Esther replied longingly.

"It is no trouble at all," replied their host, procuring a tin basin from his stores and half filling it with flour. "It takes no time to make and not much longer to cook." He poured out some clean water from the billy and began to stir the mixture with an iron spoon.

"Don't you put any baking-powder in?" Esther asked.

"No," replied Hugh, with conviction.

"Nor any salt?"

"Yes," he admitted, pausing in his labours, "when you remember it you do," and he proceeded to remember it by shaking in a few coarse lumps from one of his tins.

"What do you do next?" Esther asked presently, as he stopped stirring, and looked with doubtful reflection at the spoon.

"I was trying to remember whether you do put baking-powder in after all," he admitted; "but I don't think you do, and anyway it doesn't matter."

"Not a ha'porth," said Wilfrid encouragingly; "the more things you leave out the less you are likely to regret it."

When the mixture had been sufficiently stirred, Hugh turned his attention to the fire. "It hasn't been burning quite long enough," he said, "but we'll risk it" ; and removing the flaming wood, he laid the dough among the embers and covered it over. After the lapse of twenty minutes or half an hour the expert proceeded to withdraw the damper from its bed of ashes.

"Oh, what a lovely smell!" said Esther.

"Yes," said Hugh, with a shade of misgiving, "that is sometimes the best part of it."

"Perhaps you had better consider you have had your share, Esther," Wilfrid suggested.

"It gets a bit cindery and ashy," their host allowed, as he deposited it on the box that served for a table, "but if you just brush it over, and if it is properly cooked inside, it is not so bad as you might suppose." He put a knife into it as he spoke, and immediately a pale substance of the consistency of treacle ran out of the interior.

"What a pity!" said Esther, who looked really disappointed. "If we had only let it bake a little longer!"

"The fire was not quite ready," explained Hugh; "but damper is generally like this, and you can usually eat the outside."

These culinary feats achieved, the party again took to the road. On their way back, some distance beyond the inn, they overtook Roller, who was returning in a bad temper from a stormy interview with Upmore. His smouldering gaze swept the party and dwelt with distaste on Hugh. Then he fell in between Wilfrid and Esther, and endeavoured to manoeuvre the latter into the rear.

"How are you getting on with the European?" Wilfrid asked, in the drily humorous manner that always jarred on the storekeeper.

"That is my business," was the blunt reply.

"Certainly," said Wilfrid, with the utmost smoothness. "And in order to assist me in a desire to know nothing of your business, pray do not in future intrude your private affairs on the mixed company of a dinner table."

With such smiling equanimity was this reply delivered that it was not until the lapse of some seconds that Roller recognised it as a gage of battle. He had not intended to be especially rude to Wilfrid; on the contrary, he desired, if anything, to propitiate him, seeing, as he could not avoid seeing, how high he stood in Esther's regard; and during the last week he had begun to think that he might have need of an ally if his engagement with Esther was to stand. His coarse-grained temperament was, in fact, not equal to grasping the offensiveness of the rebuff he had administered, and he was slightly nonplussed at its effect.

Ever since their interview in the garden, the storekeeper had thought a great deal about Esther, and if his love for her had not hitherto been passionate, it was now in a fair way to become so. Her manner towards him, he could not fail to notice, had undergone a subtle change, and at every fresh meeting their relations appeared to become more difficult. During the first months of their engagement none of this strain had existed; they met and parted daily with good-will, and the girl's manner, if lacking in lover-likeness, was always frank and affectionate and apparently without tinge of regret. She appeared to look forward to their marriage, not perhaps with eagerness, but at least with confidence. Now things were quite different, and he asked himself why. What had he done or what had occurred to render her, as she described it, uncertain of herself? To this plain questioning his mind, under the influence of his pride, gave but cloudy replies. If he admitted anything, it was that the beginning of the estrangement dated from the time of the races; but the upshot of all his meditations was a mortal antipathy to Hugh. What was the connection between "that gum-digger fellow" and the Hamilton family, that they invited him to the house and called him by his christian name? He might have been satisfied on this point simply by propounding the question, but he preferred to treat the matter with contempt and remain in ignorance. As a rule he ignored Hugh's presence altogether, but he was not above a contemptuous allusion to gum-diggers when the opportunity offered, and as the days went by a secret jealousy prompted him to the making of such occasions when they did not occur spontaneously.

"Where have you been, Esther?" he asked, gulping down the wrathful feelings aroused by Wilfrid's retort.

"As far as Mr. Clifford's tent," Esther replied. "Mr. Clifford has been giving us afternoon tea."

"It's, well to be a gum-digger," said Roller, sarcastically, "able to ride about the country as you please. What wages are you making, Clifford?"

"Sufficient," replied Hugh. "What is your weekly turnover?"

Roller smiled darkly. "I suppose," he said, "that is funny; but it strikes me as being impudent as well, and I do not allow people to be impudent to me."

"I take very little interest in what you allow," Hugh replied indifferently.

"What is the matter with you all?" Esther asked, reining in her horse and regarding the whole company with reproachful eyes.

We might have set it down to the effects of the damper," Wilfrid said, "but that Mr. Roller did not partake of it. Forgive us, and we will endeavour to mend our manners."

Very little, however, was said during the remainder of the ride, and as the storekeeper parted from them at Dr. Hamilton's gate there was a feeling in the hearts of all four that trouble was at hand.

CHAPTER XXII

NOR was the trouble long delayed.

That evening after dinner Hugh was out in the garden, smoking his pipe by the gate, when Roller crossed the road and came in. The storekeeper hesitated when he saw him and finally came to a standstill.

"I should like to speak to you, Clifford," he said, "if it is convenient."

"Perfectly," said Hugh, surprised. "What is it?"

"I have intended talking to you for some time," Roller began; "but it is not a very pleasant matter, and I wished to give you the opportunity of broaching the subject yourself."

"Just so," said Hugh, who scented battle in every word; "I haven't the remotest idea what you mean."

Roller laughed unbelievingly, and there was insult in the sound. "Of course you know very well," he said, "that I am alluding to Miss Hamilton's brooch and ring. Don't you think it would be better if they were found and returned?"

Hugh was completely staggered. "It is not possible that I can understand you aright," he said.

"Then let me put the thing quite plainly," said Roller, with brutal sarcasm. "The jewellery I speak of was of comparatively little value, but as the things were my gift to Miss Hamilton we are naturally concerned at losing them. You will probably not be able to sell them for half their cost, and sooner than run any risk I will write you a cheque for twice their value. Do you understand me now?"

"I do indeed," said Hugh. "You make yourself incredibly clear."

"Then what do you say?"

"I was wondering whether I should break every bone in your skin; but the imputation is too contemptibly ridiculous, and I refuse to be moved by it."

"You cannot carry the thing off in that high-handed manner," said the storekeeper in a white heat. "You seem to be acquainted with Miss Hamilton's cousin, and for that reason I have spared you; but unless the things are returned forthwith I shall certainly put the matter in the hands of the police."

"I have had a suspicion of you, Roller," said Hugh, disregarding all this, "and now it is confirmed. You are a confounded little cad."

"By God, I will stand that from no man!" exclaimed the storekeeper.

"Lower your voice," said Hugh, "and keep calm. If you want a thrashing I shall be glad to give it you, but not in this garden. You appear to have no sense of decency, and it is necessary, therefore, for me to think for us both. Don't make a row."

"You are here under false pretences," said Roller furiously. "I will ring up the police first thing in the morning, and have you put where you ought to be."

"Go away, and don't be absurd," said Hugh, resuming his pipe.

"I will speak to Miss Hamilton and the doctor about you, masquerading about the place as a gentleman and loafing on their hospitality,"

"I refuse to lose my temper with you," said Hugh, turning his back on him. "Go and do as you please."

The storekeeper stood a moment, then, turning sharply, went swiftly up the path into the house.

Standing alone, Hugh saw a shadow cross the lawn, and Wilfrid came up in his house slippers.

"What was all the noise I heard?" he asked.

"Noise," said Hugh. "What noise?"

"I thought I heard Roller's voice."

"Oh, talking, you mean. Yes, he has just gone inside."

"He seemed to be excited" persisted Wilfrid. "We heard it inside, and Esther turned quite pale. What was the matter?"

Hugh swore under his breath. "Have you any money, Wilf?" he asked suddenly.

"Yes," replied Wilfrid, surprised, "do you want some? How much is it?"

"I don't know," said Hugh, and walked a pace or two impatiently up and down the drive. "What do rings and brooches cost?" he asked.

"All kinds of prices," replied Wilfrid wonderingly, "from pounds to hundreds."

Hugh uttered an exclamation of impatience. "I'd give something to know what he paid for the ring and brooch he gave your cousin," he blurted out.

"So that's it. You had better make a clean breast of it and tell me what occurred."

"It's too absurd," said Hugh, with disgust. "They were lost in my tent, you know, and he pretends to think I've got them. Of course, what he thinks doesn't affect me a penny piece, but then, I *am* responsible for what happened, though the idea never suggested itself to me before, and I'd like to fix the thing up on the instant."

Wilfrid stood silent awhile. "Fancy her engaging herself to a cur of that description," he said bitterly at length; "it's almost beyond belief."

"Could she have been driven to it?" Hugh wondered, forgetting his grievance in the interest of the new topic.

"God knows!" said Wilfrid. "She was alone—a motherless girl in a God-forsaken land. What influenced her, who can tell? I expect she got precious little sympathy at home. She could not have loved him, or had the vaguest idea what marriage meant, poor little girl!"

Hugh moved about as though under the stress of great emotion, and at last gripped Wilfrid by the arm with a hand that shook.

"Wilfrid," he said, "I love her with all my heart and all my soul and all my strength. It sounds blasphemous, but it is God's truth."

"Do you, my boy?" said Wilfrid. "I wish you all the good luck in the world."

"You do?" exclaimed Hugh, with a catch of astonished delight.

Wilfrid laid a hand on his shoulder and wheeled him on to the lawn. "I don't know," he said, "what strict honour demands in these cases, but I do not value it one snap of the fingers if it is to be matched against her life's happiness."

"I should think not," said Hugh.

"She has made a mistake. Any girl as young and inexperienced might make such a mistake, but it shall not blast her whole life, if I—if we can prevent it."

"We will prevent it," said Hugh.

"It is, of course, unfortunate that the making of mistakes frequently inflicts pain on innocent persons. That, however, is an arrangement beyond human control, and it would be absurd to batter ourselves against destiny in an attempt to alter it."

"Perfectly absurd," Hugh considered.

Wilfrid wheeled him round and again escorted him across the lawn. "So much for the morality of the thing," he said. "Now Roller will get her as certain as we are here, if he only plays his cards properly and goes slow. She will trample on her heart sooner than cause suffering to anyone she respects. He has only to adopt the proper manner with her, and she will go like a lamb to the altar."

"But that is too horrible," said Hugh restively. "He is twice her age, to begin with."

"I don't look upon that as of great importance," Wilfrid replied. "Character is the only thing that matters, and there is exactly where we have him. He is a surly, ill-conditioned beggar without an ounce of refinement in his nature. His only interest is in making money, and I expect he is pretty ruthless in the methods he adopts to do it. Fancy Esther, with her tender heart and her glowing enthusiams, tied to a clown of that description! Can't you see him in your mind's eye trampling across her flower-beds?"

"Don't," said Hugh; "you make me sick."

"Yet," repeated Wilfrid, "he will get her if he has the cunning to treat her in the right way."

"What is to be done, then?" Hugh inquired, with a shade less confidence in his tones.

"Stand by," said Wilfrid, "and give him rope and trust that presently he will hang himself. Unless he develops the cunning of the old gentleman himself he will shortly come to grief. There is one thing Esther detests with every fibre of her being, and that is meanness. You may be weak, even wicked, and she will find excuses for you; but to be mean is to shut yourself out of her good graces for ever. I believe it is nothing but the way he has treated her friend Rewi that has alienated any affection she may once have felt for him. Just a little more of that, and her passive indifference will turn into active dislike, and out he goes. I don't say that she might not attempt to carry out her promise even then; but if we can once win her whole heart to our side she must surrender."

"And supposing he *has* the cunning of the devil?" suggested Hugh.

"We must hope for his own sake that he has nothing of the kind," said Wilfrid; "but if it should prove otherwise, there is nothing for it but to stir him up with a judicious administration of pin-pricks—just one here and there on the raw. This thing has got to be done, and I shall not scruple to do it merely because I have a feeling that I would rather not."

Meanwhile Esther and the storekeeper were seated in the dining-room, equally deep in conversation. Dr. Hamilton was away at the Bay, having been called over to a patient early in the morning; and with the exception of Maria, who was probably reading a novelette in her bedroom, the betrothed pair were alone in the house.

When he left Hugh, Roller was moved by an insane intention of attacking Hugh's character before Esther; but before he reached the house he had recognised the smallness of the foundation he had to build upon, and he entered the room where Esther was sitting, his mind a tumult of rage, seeking in vain for an outlet.

Esther, who was at work with her needle, started at his abrupt entry, and looked with a frightened curiosity at his face, which was of a patchy whiteness and twitched spasmodically.

"Are you unwell?" she asked, as he stood making faces which were the expression of an endeavour to smile at her.

"How can I be well," he asked, detecting his opportunity and controlling his emotion by a fierce effort of the will, "so long as I am in doubt of you? Esther, what have I done that you avoid me and remain silent except in reply to my questions?"

"Avoid you?"

"It is avoiding me, when you do not come to me as once you did. There is a change in you, and I have a right to know the reason. Upon my soul, one would think we were no longer lovers!"

"Tell me what you complain of," said Esther, "and if I have done wrong I will try to amend."

"It is your manner that wounds me, its lack of spontaneity. With me you are either grave or dejecte; with others I hear you—I heard you to-day while you were standing with that fellow Clifford on the lawn—talking and laughing freely, but with me you are silent. Is there no longer anything to talk of between us that we meet and part with hardly a word?"

"Is it my talking with Mr. Clifford on the lawn you object to?" Esther asked.

"Clifford! Hang Clifford! Why is he dragged into everything? Who in heaven's name is this man?" he demanded, with a gleam of fury.

"You mentioned him," said Esther coldly. "I merely desired to know definitely what your grievance was, that I might see if you were justified. There is no need to shout at me."

"No," he said apologetically. "I beg your pardon; but, Esther, you must see that I am greatly troubled over all this. There is a change, and you must know it; tell me what is the meaning of it. When I asked you a week or so ago to name the day of our marriage —and surely it was a natural question for me to put and for you to answer—you seemed surprised and dumb-foundered, and finally you appointed a day a fortnight distant on which to answer me. The day is nearly at hand, but in the meantime all your attention has been given to others, and for me you have had nothing but monosyllables. What was your meaning when you said you would answer me? Was it as to the day of our marriage? Or was there something else

171

in your mind?"

"If there were," Esther replied, without looking at him—"if I suggested that we should both reconsider our engagement, would—would it cause you—unhappiness?"

"So that is it," he said bitterly. "And you speak of unhappiness! Have you no notion of the serious nature of a contract of this kind?"

"It is for that very reason that I hesitate. It is so easy to do, so impossible to undo. And, Albert, if we are making a mistake, think of the consequences to us both."

"You should have thought of them at the time," he replied; "not now when my life's happiness is bound up in the fulfilment of your promise."

"Your life's happiness!" she repeated in awe-stricken tones. "Surely you exaggerate. Why should you feel the loss of a girl who did not know her own mind?"

"Because I know mine. I am older than you, Esther, and my mind, maybe, is not so easily made up; but on the other hand, the resolutions it arrives at are based not on impulses, but on judgment, and they stand. I had never before put to a woman the question I addressed to you. My proposal was deliberate, and the cost had been counted in every detail before it was spoken. I loved you, Esther, as strongly and sincerely as a man can love a woman, and I knew that there was no one else in the world for me. From the moment when the words of consent fell from your lips, from that moment I regarded you as mine, and since then every thought of the future has been connected with you."

Esther regarded him steadfastly with dilating eyes. "Why— oh why," she whispered, "have you never spoken like this to me before?"

His glance shifted under the steady gaze. "Because," he replied, "your manner has kept me silent."

"But," she said, with wondering simplicity, "if you had loved me like that, surely, surely I must have known. Can a great love, such as you describe, be concealed even when there is every incentive for it to display itself?"

"Blame yourself for that, Esther," was the reply, "not me."

"Myself? Yes, it is myself I blame for everything; but are we both to suffer for my mistake?"

"There can be no suffering for me, Esther, in a marriage with you." He crossed the room and seated himself beside her. "If I have seemed to be neglectful of you, dear, or if my love has not shown itself in the demonstrative fashion of other men, is it too late to alter? Surely you have not ceased to love me altogether."

For a while Esther sat motionless, looking straight before her with wide, absent eyes. The way of escape lay open—could she take it? She had never loved him, and now she felt that what he complained of was true. She did avoid him; his presence seemed to chill and restrain her, so that before him she became, as he had said, dejected and speechless. Latterly too there had grown up a physical shrinking, against which she wrestled in vain. Could she—*must* she—marry a man whose very touch was distasteful to her? She gave a little shiver, and rising to her feet, laid her work absently on the table.

He reached out his hand for one of hers and, after a movement of withdrawal, she bit her lip and allowed it to remain in his possession. Slowly the absent look died out of her eyes, and she stood gazing down on him with an expression he could not fathom.

"I have no love for you," she said mercilessly, "none."

He winced at the cruel little speech, but did not loose his gaze from hers.

"Understand," she went on, "that I have no heart in this marriage, absolutely none. I would sooner be free. I do not think I shall make you a suitable wife or add to your happiness. I shall not be happy myself." The sentences fell like knife-stabs, but the man, after the first stroke, took them unflinchingly. No doubt he saw whither they tended, and in the contemplation of the promised land the terrors of the way passed unheeded.

She moistened her lips, and her voice fell to a lower key. "I have told you the truth as I feel it, so that you may understand clearly what you are doing. I promised to marry you. I think now I was mad when I made that promise; but it is done, and only you can set me free."

"That I will never do," he said resolutely, with a smile.

She turned deathly pale. "Then," she said breathlessly, "take my answer now—I will marry you."

"When?"

"When you please."

Roller reflected a moment. In the strong exultation, masked by the smiling face, was no shadow of relenting. The interview should be final, and no loose thread should threaten its unravelling. "Then it shall be on the tenth of March," he said, and he attempted to draw her towards him.

With a gesture of unmistakable repulsion she tore herself free.

"No," she exclaimed, breathing quickly, "not that. Let it be when you will, but until then—" She spread her hands towards him and was silent.

He watched her with sullen eyes. "Have you no affection for me at all?" he asked in spite of himself.

Esther laughed mirthlessly. "Can you ask such a question of the girl who has consented to marry you? Surely in the circumstances it is the strangest question that a man ever put to a woman."

"Ah, well," he said, rising, "my love shall suffice for us both. With or without love, you are mine, and I will never let you go."

So, in spite of the conspirators still perambulating the lawn, the lover they sought to depose secured himself yet more firmly in his hold.

CHAPTER XXIII

IT was the evening of the following day. Dinner was over and all the house was still. The doctor had not yet returned from the Bay, and Wilfrid, who had undertaken to look after a few cases nearer at hand, had been absent since morning. Hugh had practically had the house to himself all day. He had employed his time in wandering about disconsolately, looking for Esther, who had been won't hitherto to spend a portion of her time among the flower-beds. This day, however, she too remained invisible. At lunch she sent a message by Maria, excusing herself from attendance, but offering no reason.

"Is Miss Hamilton unwell?" he asked.

"Esther may have a small headache," Maria opined, and she reported the inquiry to her mistress a moment later.

"How that young man loves you, Esther!" she said calmly.

Esther shrank as though from a blow. "How dare you say such things, Maria!" she exclaimed, with flashing eyes.

Maria, so far as was possible to one of her leisurely disposition, showed signs of astonishment. "What harm?" she said. "I wish he was half as fond of me. Shall I tell him your head is bad?"

But Esther peremptorily forbade her to again enter the dining-room, and Maria, who really respected and never wilfully disobliged her young mistress, yielded grumbling obedience.

At dinner, which was delayed in the vain hope of Wilfrid's arrival, Esther appeared, but her manner was silent and distrait, and nearly all the conversational embellishments were supplied by Maria.

But now dinner was over; the clatter of clearing away the dishes had ceased and silence reigned supreme. Hugh wandered again into the garden, now delightfully cool and dark after the heat and glare of the day, and seated himself in a basket-chair on the lawn. Across the road a single light burned in the office attached to the store, and he had learned that so long as this was visible Roller was not to be expected.

The light, therefore, though it had disagreeable associations, was welcome rather than otherwise, and the young man watched it with satisfaction. Away to the left a few scattered lights were visible from the village, but the native settlement behind was buried in profound darkness. Overhead the sky was full of flashing constellations, and the Southern Cross, like a diving kite, hung away to the southward of east. All through the slow sultry hours Hugh had pined for the night. At last it was with him, but where was she without whom it was valueless? Through all the days of his visit this had been their hour. While the light burned in the store and the stars waxed in the sky, they had wandered through the scented garden, absorbed in one another and dreading only the moment when the disappearance of the beacon should tear them apart. The supposed indifference of the other was the reliance of each, so perilous was the path they trod.

The precious minutes slipped by, the light burned steadily on, but no Esther appeared. Was it possible that to-night she would disappoint him? He rose and moved restlessly about the lawn and up to the verandah, where he could see through the open windows that the dining-room was tenantless. There was no light in the drawing-room, and, saving the gleam that fell through the drawn blinds of the kitchen, the whole house seemed in darkness.

Ten minutes went by. He had drawn the bush-house and found it a blank; he had returned again and again to the lawn, but still there was no sign of her; there remained only the orchard and the path that led to it. Hopeless of finding her, he turned into the narrow black alley and made his way to the gate. Here a movement and the gleam of something white set his heart bounding within him, and he stepped quickly to her side.

"At last!" he said, with passionate relief.

"Isn't it lovely and cool!" she murmured, making room for him beside her. "This is the best spot in the garden after a hot day."

"It is," replied Hugh, with conviction, " the very best. I have never known a day go so slowly in all my life."

"I suppose you have missed Wilfrid and your daily lecture," she said, with a laugh that closed in a sigh. "I wonder what is keeping him?"

"It was you I missed," he said in low, passionate tones. "You and only you. Nothing matters to me now except you."

"Don't say it," she said in a tired voice. "I have heard that townsmen think it the proper thing to talk like that, but I am country-bred and have never learnt the manner. Besides, I am weary and all the brightness has gone out of me, and I could not answer you in kind even if I knew how."

"Say nothing," he said, "until I have told you that I love you. I have never done anything else but love you from the moment I first saw you. I shall never do anything else as long as I live."

"Spare me," she said hopelessly. "How can you tell me that, knowing what you know?"

"Oh, Esther!" he replied, "I know that you are promised to another man, but do you love him? If you tell me that you love him, I must perforce be silent. Your happiness is more to me than my own, and if your happiness lay in a marriage with him I would go away, though it would seem like death. It is the belief that you do not love him that gives me courage to speak to you."

"Even if I did not, it would still be too late to talk of it now. We are to be married on the tenth of March."

"God forbid!" he exclaimed fervently. "Do you remember, dearest, at our first meeting, when I wanted you to do something for your own good, how resolute you were not to do it, and how, when nothing else would serve, I picked you up in my arms and so compelled your obedience? Do you never yield except under compulsion?"

She stood in the pale, diffused starlight and he in the dense shadow. So close together were they that any movement might have brought them in contact. The words, with the tender endearment, sank into her troubled mind, bringing the thought of the refuge that lay in his strength, the temptation to seize it and have done with the bitter struggle that was driving

177

her distracted.

"It would have been better," he said presently, "that you had died then, if you have no more compassion on yourself than this. Tell me, Esther, if this entanglement had not been, could you have cared for me?"

"What is the good of thinking of what might have been?" she answered sadly. "All the misery of the world is locked up in the thought of what might have been. How would it help you if I answered yes or no? It could not change the thing that is."

"Is that an admission that you could have cared for me?" he asked. "Is it an admission that you love me? Dearest, if you have no mercy for yourself, have some for me. I cannot give you up; I would sooner be dead than live without you. Even if nothing is to come of it, even if it is the last word that shall ever pass between us, yet tell me that you love me. Say it to me in so many words."

"If it will help you, knowing what you know and that it can make no difference in the result, then—then—" She stammered and shrank from him. "Ah, why did you come into my life? I was happy until I saw you, or I thought so."

"Then you do love me?" he said, stretching his arms out towards her.

With a quick motion she eluded him and was lost in the shadow of the path.

"Won't you understand?" she said breathlessly.

"That you love me," he replied; "nothing else."

"That I am pledged to another man; that I have given my irrevocable promise."

"You are mine," he said; "you cannot give away what belongs to me."

And he advanced towards the spot whence the sound of her voice had reached him.

"This is madness," she cried. "Don't you see that nothing—nothing can absolve me from a promise twice given? Have mercy on me."

"Have mercy on yourself," he replied. With a sudden

movement he gained the exit and commenced to close in towards the gate.

"Come to me, Esther," he said, "my will is stronger than yours."

There was no reply, and he moved cautiously forward. A sound of low sobbing arrested him, and putting out his hand, he touched her dress. She made no further attempt to escape, and he drew her into his arms.

"Pledge yourself to me, Esther," he said gravely. "There is no happiness in the world for us apart from one another."

"Oh, Hugh," she said brokenly, "how can I? How willingly I would, but what are my pledges worth if I dishonour myself to make them? Shall I make my happiness out of his misery?"

"And yet you would make his happiness out of mine. Is my misery of no account?"

"You will soon forget me," she said. "The days will come and go and bury up the past till the pain of it is lost and forgotten."

He stooped and kissed the wet cheeks. "Life would not be long enough to forget you in," he said. "Surrender yourself, my beloved, for I will never give you up, and sooner or later you will be mine. Why do you set this barrier between us? You love me, you do not love him; there alone is reason sufficient. Will you wreck both our lives in the vain hope to save this man suffering? For it *is* vain. What happiness can there be for him in a marriage with one who has no affection for him?"

"I have thought of it all," she said. "Every argument you use I have put to myself a hundred times, but they make no difference." With a gentle effort she freed herself from his embrace, and they stood together, her hands locked in his. "I am sorry for you, my dear," she said tenderly, "and I am sorry for myself; but I have told him, and he will not release me."

"What have you told him?" he asked, surprised. "Have you told him that you love another man?"

"Everything but that," she replied. "It was last night; he seemed upset at something and accused me of avoiding him. I told him then that I did not love him, that I would sooner be free, that I could not bring him happiness, and I asked him to release me."

"And what was his reply?"

"That his love would suffice for us both; that he would never give me up. Then I told him that I would marry him, and he appointed the day."

Hugh was silent a long while. "Esther," he said at last, "will you let this matter go into other hands? Will you allow Wilfrid to see him?"

"No, no," she said fearfully, "not for the world."

"He is acting a brutal part," Hugh said strongly after another reflective pause, "and no girl—you least of all—would have any chance with him. Do you suppose for a moment that a man of any honourable feeling would act in the way you describe him to have done? Don't you see that he is using your sense of honour to drag you into an alliance that is nothing short of a blasphemy? What if he does love you? So do I; so may many others. It does not give him the right to possess you. You are your own gift, and if there is any truth in the world it is this, that you cannot give yourself where you do not love."

Again he encircled her with his arms. "Say you love me," he said passionately, "me and only me."

"I do," she said. "I love you better than my life."

For one instant their lips met; in the next they had started guiltily apart.

"Esther!" exclaimed Roller's voice in sharp, excited tones.

"Yes," she replied.

Hugh stood alone in the darkness, his heart beating violently. He heard their retreating footsteps dying away in the direction of the house, until at length they became inaudible. What ought he to do? Or what ought he to have done? His brain whirled in the midst of the complex sensations that assailed him as he stood trying to resolve on his course of action. The storekeeper, no doubt, had heard the sound of their voices and come up stealthily, and in this case he had got no more than his deserts. Hugh laughed to himself with fierce exultation over his enemy as he recalled the completeness of the moment on which Roller's voice had fallen like a thunderclap. The indignity of his own position troubled him next, and he grew hot with a desire for action, preferably something physical and final. Then the intoxication of the knowledge that she loved him and only him allayed his anger and led him into sweet paths of self-communing, only to be rudely arrested by the thought of what might be happening in the house. At any rate, he decided there was no sense in staying where he was, and he made his way on to the lawn in time to discover Wilfrid leading his horse through the gateway.

"Well?" asked the latter, coming to a standstill. "How have you been getting on? I struck a rather interesting case and it has kept me later than I intended. The doctor made a curiously wrong diagnosis of it, between ourselves," he added, with professional pride, "but I twigged what was wrong in less than no time. Is Roller here? How have you been getting on?"

"Well and ill," said Hugh.

"Come round to the stables and let me hear."

Hugh related a portion of the events of the evening, and after the horse had been unsaddled and fed, they returned to the front of the house.

"I won't go in till he goes," said Wilfrid, looking towards the dining-room, where the windows and blinds were now drawn. "This may be the crisis, and professional etiquette directs me to stand by and give nature a chance. I hope he interrupted you at a sufficiently interesting moment."

"Pretty fair," said Hugh.

"H'm! Did he address you at all?"

"Not a word."

For twenty minutes they continued walking up and down discussing the subject, then Wilfrid got impatient.

"He might consider my feelings," he said. "I am dying for a smoke, and I want something to eat."

As if in answer to his words, the hall was suddenly illuminated by the opening of the dining-room door, and Roller came out. He passed down the path, looking neither to the right nor left, and going out on to the road, banged the wicket behind him.

"Dismissed," said Wilfrid slowly, looking reflectively towards the gate. "And now I can almost be sorry for the beggar."

CHAPTER XXIV

"SO that was the reason you desired to be free?" Roller said, as they entered the dining-room.

"That was the reason," she replied.

"Why did you not tell me so yesterday? You said some things hard for me to hear; why did you reserve that?"

"Would it have made any difference if I had told you?" she asked.

He seated himself heavily, without replying.

Esther remained standing, her fingers idly straying among the pages of a magazine on the table. After the first shock of his abrupt entry on the scene, Esther had accepted the situation with the calmness with which mankind usually accepts the inevitable.

She was keenly alive to, and absorbed in, the possibilities of the interview before her, but she was astonished at the coolness and apparent indifference with which she awaited the conflict. She had expected violence, bitter reproaches, furious anger, and it was perhaps the non-fulfilment of these expectations that was responsible for her present dangerous mood of acceptance.

"I cannot give you up, Esther," he said at last, rousing himself as though from a reverie; "not even now. Least of all can I give you up to this man. Have you spoken of love to him before? Was this one scene of many? Or was it the first and last?"

"It was the first," she said.

"Will it be the last?"

With the sound of Hugh's voice still lingering in her ears, with the passion of his kiss still stirring her blood, the girl stood silent.

"Answer me," he said, turning his gaze for the first time full upon her.

She met his look unflinchingly.

"I love him," she said. "I cannot cease to love him at your direction. You complained that I did not tell you the whole

183

truth; this time you shall have no ground for complaint."

"I trust you, Esther," he replied; "you cannot frighten me into releasing you. I know the whole truth now, and I am not afraid of it. Afraid!" he repeated scornfully—and for the first time the volcano beneath revealed itself in a flash of fire—"What can there be to fear in the rivalry of a gum-digger and a thief?"

She smiled slowly, and the smile drove him to frenzy.

"A thief," he went on, "who will descend to stealing trinkets from the girl he pretends to love."

Esther's face wore a look of bewilderment.

"What can you mean?" she asked.

"Mean?" he echoed, rejoicing savagely in the possibility of inflicting pain. "I mean that you were thrown into his society with money and jewellery, you left him with neither."

"You cannot really imagine that he was responsible for that?" she said, her lip curling.

"There is no imagination about it," he declared, with a brutal laugh. "I accused him to his face, and he did not deny it."

Esther stood rigid, watching him with blazing eyes.

"You told him to his face that he was a thief?" she exclaimed.

"I did," he replied. "I told him so more than once."

"I wonder you dared!"

"Esther!" he exclaimed, shrinking under the deadly significance of the words.

"No," she said wildly, "you shall not have the right to call me Esther. Wild horses shall not drag me to marry you now. You have committed a cowardly and unpardonable outrage, so gross and wicked that I wonder you are alive to tell it me. It is not true that you had any cause to suspect or dislike him. Until to-night there was not one word passed between us which might not as well have been said in your presence. He has never from the first treated you otherwise than as one gentleman should treat another, but you have continually made him a butt for vulgar insult, even in my presence, when, if you had had a spark of manly feeling, you would have known that he could not possibly answer you as you deserved."

Roller sat dazed in the midst of the whirlwind of his own creation. So accustomed had he become to the girl's unquestioning obedience that the possibility of her freeing herself without his consent had never seriously occurred to him. In the fierce blaze of her anger his own wrath for the moment died away, and only the desire to appease her held possession of his mind.

"Forgive me, Esther," he said. "It was the distraction of the thought of losing you that maddened me so that I hardly knew what I was saying."

"It is impossible I should forgive you," she replied; "there is no forgiveness for an insult so baseless and unprovoked. When I think of the kindness with which he treated me on that dreadful night, and remember that it was under my father's roof this indignity was done him, I stand loaded with shame. No, so long as I had for you one spark of respect, I was prepared to stand by my promise though I wrecked my life in doing so, but I will not tie myself to a man for whom I have neither respect nor love, and nothing shall persuade or compel me to do so."

"Is this, then, the end of it all, Esther?" he asked after a while. "Have you led me on and deluded me for six months to throw me aside in favour of the first man you meet more to your liking? What term do you think people will apply to conduct such as that?"

"It is not true," she replied, "that I have led you on or deluded you, or been anything else than completely frank with you all through our engagement. I have never professed any feeling for you stronger than liking and respect, and I have never given you reason to suppose that I entertained any. I was mistaken in you and in myself, and for that, in so far as it has led to disappointment for you, I am sorry, but there is no more to say."

"There is a little more for me to say, however," he replied, with a sneer, "and I fancy if it were said openly in the township it would bear a rather ugly interpretation. Until you met this man Clifford you had no fault to find with me. Even until he comes on a visit to the house there is nothing to lead me to suppose that I have lost favour with you. Then, however, on that very day, I ask you to name the time for our marriage, and you put me off for a fortnight. Why? Because you want to make sure of the new love before you are off with the old. Even so recently as last night you tell me again that you will marry me; but then you are not certain of him, and nothing but certainty will justify you in throwing over your chance of an establishment. To-night he has declared himself; I have served the purpose for which I was required; I am of no further use; I can go. And you avail yourself of the first possible pretext to dismiss me. There is the whole truth."

Her cheeks flamed at the coarse insult, but her voice remained steady as she replied, "Have it so; you can then feel nothing but satisfaction in escaping me."

"I know that you are quick-witted," he said, watching her, "and that in argument I am no match for you; but there is one thing I can do; and that is ensure the failure of your designs. You think that you can get rid of me and marry Clifford. Not while I live."

She looked at him, and for the first time there was a shadow of fear in her eyes.

He rose and crossed to the door, his face working. "Remember what I say," he said, pausing with his hand on the handle and regarding her steadfastly. "You shall not marry this man while I live to prevent it. You have tricked and deceived me; for months I have lived in a fool's paradise of your making, and your whole life has been one long lie from the moment when in this very room you promised yourself to me: therefore this man, of all the world, shall never be your husband. And that is my last word, to you." He stood a moment looking at her, then, opening the door, passed swiftly out of the room and the house.

She was still standing in the same position when Wilfrid and Hugh came in. Her face was pale from the stress of the scene through which she had just passed, and she looked at them at first with unseeing eyes.

"Dinner, Esther, if you love me," Wilfrid said after a keen glance, and he threw himself full length on the sofa,

There was something in the request, unfeeling and trivial as it seemed, which roused her and did her good, and Wilfrid knew as she turned to him that its effect had been calculated to a nicety.

"Poor thing!" she said, with quite the old mocking tenderness. "Where *have* you been?"

"Wrestling with death," he replied, "and worsting him."

They all three drew in their chairs to the table while Wilfrid discussed his meal, and though Esther and Hugh said little or nothing, yet in the rattle of Wilfrid's conversation, skimming lightly from subject to subject, with an undercurrent of serious feeling revealing itself here and there, the strain of self-consciousness vanished, and the cloud that had darkened their days seemed to melt and disappear.

"No news of the doctor?" asked Wilfrid. "Well, give me a cup of tea.

'Lo! I myself, when flushed with fight or hot,
Before I first have drunken scarce can eat.'

Have some tea, Hugh? Give the boy a cup, Esther—hang the expense."

After his wants were satisfied and Maria had cleared away, they still sat at the table while Wilfrid smoked his cigar.

"I shall have to return to town soon," he said; "my cigars are nearly all gone."

"I will provide you with cigars," said Esther, "if you will stop here until I am tired of paying for them,"

Wilfrid looked at her, and then turned to Hugh. "Isn't she the most perfect girl in the world," he said, "bar one?"

Hugh nodded, but his look spoke volumes.

The colour mantled in her cheek She sat leaning forward, her face pillowed in her hand, her whole attitude full of trustful repose. Her voice was low, and charged with the tired tenderness of emotional exhaustion. After the blistering words—yet repeating themselves in her mind—which, however baseless, had still wounded her self-respect, how sweet was the love and praise of these two men! Yet—and she shrank visibly at the thought—what if, after all, their praise were misplaced, and she were indeed as blameworthy as her rejected lover had told her?

How much Wilfrid guessed of the late interview is not easy to say, but he had never previously shown his cousin such deference as he did to-night. If he had deliberately set himself to annul every one of Roller's strictures he could not have shown a clearer perception of what was required.

But there was one trouble at the back of Esther's mind which remained untouched and undiminished, and that was the attitude her father would assume on hearing of the broken engagement. With which of his many moods would he receive the announcement, and how long would it be before he became reconciled to the fact that the marriage was not to be? Her father, it was true, had never displayed any pleasure in Roller's society, and had even shown symptoms of dislike for him, especially when, as occasionally happened, he had been contradicted under his own roof in matters concerning which the storekeeper was manifestly ignorant. But it was no certain corollary from this that the breach would be welcome to him, or that serious consequences might not result from the view he took of Roller's dismissal. Esther knew from past experience that a good deal in her father's reception of a new idea depended on the mood he was in at the time, and also upon the manner in which it was first presented.

But it so happened that the desire to break the news to the doctor carefully was rendered abortive by the fact that when he arrived he was already in possession of the facts, and his first words to Esther, even before any greeting had been interchanged, showed the source from which his information was derived.

"What nonsense is this Albert is telling me about your

breaking off your engagement with him? Write to him at once, and tell him it is all childishness, and that you are sorry for it."

Esther shook her head. "No, father," she said, recognising that her worst fears were realised, "I shall never marry Mr. Roller. I don't know what he has told you of what passed between us, but I shall never engage myself to him again."

"Pooh, pooh!" said the doctor. "We shall see—wait till I have got my boots off." And he retired into the house with that object.

But Esther was no longer fighting her battle alone, and the doctor's determination to give battle after his boots were off having been reported in all seriousness to Wilfrid, the latter was seized with such uncontrollable mirth that Esther, despite her misgivings, was compelled to join in, and her heart was greatly lightened in consequence.

"Stand to your guns, Esther," Wilfrid directed, "and if necessary, take your boots off also. Remember we are behind you and no retreat is possible. I have never gone back in my life, though perhaps I should be ashamed to confess it. As for Hugh, you know the sort of stubborn, immovable mass he is."

"But Hugh has got to go," she said. "Father must have heard something, because Maria tells me that he came into the dining-room while she was setting the table and asked her who the fourth place was for, and when she told him he said, 'Mr. Clifford will not be here to dinner!' in a voice that made her jump. So what ought we to do?"

Wilfrid whistled, and throwing aside his book, got quickly to his feet. "Where is Hugh?" he asked. "I must go and give him a gentle hint to make himself scarce till the storm blows over. We can't have him insulted again, for though the young man is roused into action only with difficulty, he is deucedly active when he gets going."

Hugh, in consequence, did not appear at dinner, and his visit, so far as the shelter of the doctor's roof was concerned, was thus brought to an abrupt conclusion.

The young man, however, was not to be immediately driven from the township, and when Wilfrid, smoking his cigar in solitude on the lawn, heard the cry of a morepork from the region of the orchard, he at once recognised it as one of Hugh's accomplishments, and bent his steps in that direction.

"Do you think she would see me?" Hugh asked eagerly. "If you told her I am here, would she come?"

"Like a swallow," replied Wilfrid. "Stay where you are." And he returned to the house.

Hugh opened the gate and came into the shadow of the path, and in a moment Esther joined him.

"Oh, Hugh!" she said. "I am sorry, but it cannot be helped. What will you do?"

"Go back to the camp," he replied, "for a few days until your father relents. He cannot hold out long if you stand firm."

"I will never give in," she said. "If it were a little thing I would obey him against my will, but this is my whole life."

He kissed her passionately. "You are mine, Esther," he said. "Remember you are fighting for me as well as yourself. It will only be for a few days, and then our happiness will begin."

It was not until the following day that the doctor opened the campaign by demanding of Esther whether she had written to Roller, as directed.

"No, father," she said quietly.

"Very well," he said. "I will send for him, and you can discuss the matter in my presence."

"I shall not see Mr. Roller," she said in the same tone. "I have nothing to discuss with him."

The doctor was staggered. The girl hitherto had shown herself so amenable to his caprices that this change of front came on him like a sudden reversal of the laws of nature.

"You *will* not?" he asked, with an emphasis on the will."

"No, father," she repeated; "I am sorry to disobey you, but I have made up my mind."

"It seems to me you have no mind," said her father. "Tut tut! my girl, you cannot play fast and loose with a man in this way. You must stand to your agreement. It appears from what Albert tells me there has been some sort of flirtation between

190

you and this young man Clifford. I am surprised at that young man, but since he has had the good sense to go away, we need say no more about it. Come, I will send the boy across to the store for Albert, and we will get the thing cleared up right away."

His tone was not unkind, and it seemed that he really did desire to have the business accomplished as pleasantly as possible. "What do you say?" he asked, his hand hovering over the bell on his table.

"Oh, father," said Esther, "have pity on me! I do not want to disobey you, or make you angry with me; but if I yield now I must wish that I had never been born."

It was impossible for him to disregard the anguish of her tone, and his hand fell irresolutely to the table. "Tell me what it all means," he said irritably.

"Father," she said, kneeling on the rug beside him and throwing an arm across his knee, "I do not love Mr. Roller, and I do love—somebody else. I did not know what I was doing when I promised to marry him. I have had to live my life alone, with no one to help me. God help me if I made a mistake, for there was no other to set me right Dear"—she went on, stealing an arm round his neck and gazing at him, the tears streaming unchecked down her cheeks— "do you remember how for years, when I was a little child, you would take me on your knee and shed tears over me as you told me of the mother I never knew? Have you forgotten her?"

"Forgotten " said the man uneasily, watching her with a strange awe.

"Father, would *she* have driven me into the darkness if I had come to her telling her that I had done a wrong that I could not retrieve except at the cost of my life's happiness? Would she have had no pity for me too? Oh! no, no; all my life her picture has hung by my bed, and I have seen her, beautiful face in my dreams, and I know that in her heart there would be nothing but love and compassion."

He laid a trembling hand on her head and continued to scan her face with the same intentness.

"Listen, dear," she continued—and it seemed to the man watching her that a spirit from the dead had arisen to plead for her—"when mother died, I know now, because I feel it in my heart, that for you the joy of life died with her. But how would it have been if by some cruel chance, her mistake or yours, you had been compelled, still loving one another, to live apart, beyond hope of reunion? —for that is the fate to which you would consign me. Could you have borne it? Can you think of her enduring it, and still have no pity for me?"

He drew a long breath, and his hand moved caressingly in her hair.

"Many and long the years have been, child," he said musingly; "and they have tired me, and I have been a failure every way. I see now how in the absorption of my grief I have missed something that might have been mine—a daughter's love."

"Oh, father," she said, with eager compunction, drawing his face down to hers, "I have loved you, but now more than ever, because I understand. Oh, my dear, my heart is sore for you—and see—I will not disobey you any more, and what you direct me I will do!"

"God forbid," he said tenderly, "that you should look at me with your mother's eyes and speak to me with your mother's voice, and I should send you, as you have said, into the darkness!"

So at the first encounter, to the touch of that loving spirit, the doctor capitulated, and his household was no longer divided against itself.

CHAPTER XXV

"YOUR attendance is requested at a farewell social to be tendered to his lordship the Earl of Baringbroke, on the occasion of his departure for the Old Country. Time and place: 7.30, on the 15th inst., at the 'Scarlet Man.' N.B. Bring your music."

Such was the notice that Hugh found pinned to his tent when he awoke a couple of mornings after leaving Parawai. The 15th inst. happened to be the following day, and, his curiosity aroused, Hugh decided to make one at the gathering. He was influenced also by the fact that he did not intend to continue long at his present occupation, and the occasion seemed to offer an opportunity of himself bidding farewell to a few men he had met and liked. It was dark when he reached his destination, and the ceremonies, to judge by the noise which issued from the new building, had already begun. Passing through the bar, he discovered a passage that led him into the midst of the scene of festivities.

Two rows of tables ran the whole length of the as yet incompleted building, and a cross-table was placed between them at one end. Here, in the position of chairman, sat Bart, with a Maori mere, lying ready to his hand. On his right was a short, thick-set individual of about middle age, with a beery but good-humoured countenance, whom Hugh identified as a digger of the name of John Dopping, while on the other hand of the chairman sat, greatly to Hugh's surprise, no less a person than Roller. Fully a hundred guests were present, and a more motley and diversely clad assemblage it would have been difficult to get together anywhere. The tables were loaded with a cold collation of baked and boiled meats, sweets, and other viands, and a gleaming row of spirit bottles, every one so far with its seal immaculate and intact, adorned their centres. For the present the meeting was contenting itself with beer, and Upmore and three or four assistants were kept busily employed in supplying orders from a tapped barrel in one corner.

Upmore's quick glance soon detected the new-comer, and he came over to him. "Bart has kept a place for you near the top of the table," he said. "We have got the quieter ones up there. Come and I'll show you."

He led the way up the room, turning now and again to make sure that the young man followed him, and finally pausing at a chair about the second or third from the top. This was already occupied, but on a word from the innkeeper its occupant rose and passed round the centre table to the opposite side of the room. "Who is that man?" asked Hugh, frowning, and following the retreating figure with his eye.

"What man?" asked the innkeeper, gazing blankly at the faces around him.

"The man who was sitting here and has just gone away."

"I hardly noticed him," said Upmore; "I just told him this was your seat, and he went."

Hugh nodded without relaxing his countenance and sat down. From the position he now held he was favoured with a three-quarter-face view of the three personages who occupied the places of honour, and he was probably not more than three yards removed from the furthest of them. His eye speedily met that of the storekeeper, and from that moment until the end came he never lost consciousness of Roller's presence..

After he had taken stock of those about him, Hugh looked round in vain for the guest of the evening, and it was not until the eatables were disposed of and the company had lit their pipes and settled down to steady drinking that enlightenment came. A few toasts were given and drunk with enthusiasm— "The Queen," "The Governor," etc., —and Bart again got to his feet to propose the toast of the evening.

"Gentlemen," he said (cheers). "Gentlemen, I say again (vociferous cheering)—I am not now alluding to those persons who continue to interrupt the chair (dead silence). It is now my pleasant duty to propose to you a toast which I am sure you will all drink with enthusiasm. You all of you know the Earl of Bolingbroke"—after a whisper from the person beside

him— "I should say Billingsgate"—after further whispering—
"Boosingbloke?" (laughter and "Keep it at that, Bart," from
the audience). Well, at all events, gentlemen, you know
John Dopping (loud cheers). You know 'Dop the digger'
(enthusiastic cheers and a chorus of "Good old Dop!"), and
when you know him, gentlemen, I will venture to say that you
know a—a man, gentlemen, who, be his name what it will, is the
equal of any two dozen of your ordinary earls ("Hear, hear!").
Gentlemen, for years past you have had in your midst, walking
about amongst you, sharing in your toils and pleasures, a
potential earl. For long it seemed that this virtue lying latent
in our friend Dopping ("Good old Dop!") was never destined
to reveal itself. But the wheels of circumstance, though they
grind slowly, grind exceeding small, and they have eventually
ground Dopping into a peer. By a fortunate concatenation of
unlooked-for but—knowing Dopping—we cannot doubt pre-
ordained events, the whole of Mr. Dopping's relations, or at
any rate, the most essential of them, have been annihilated in
a railway accident, and simple gentleman as he sits before you,
he is at this moment, by the rights of birth and inheritance, a
peer of the proudest and most glorious aristocracy of the earth
(cries of "Good on Dop!" and loud cheers). Gentlemen, I have
not to enumerate to this gathering the virtues for which his
lordship has made himself famous wherever the field of the
digger extends, they are all well known to you all (cheers). As
a friend in need, there are few of us here to whom he has not at
some time recommended himself, and as a boon companion
I challenge this company to produce his equal. I have further
to tell you that though this entertainment purports to be
tendered by the diggers, the whole of the expenses have been
borne by his lordship, and there will be—no collection (loud
and enthusiastic cheers). Gentlemen, I have no more to say. I
ask you now to charge your glasses and drink to the long life
and prosperity of the Earl of—Dopping" (loud and prolonged
applause, including "For he's a jolly good fellow " and "Three
cheers for Dop!").

"Shentlemen," said the Earl of Baringbroke thickly, rising

to his feet and beaming good-naturedly on the assemblage. "I have to shank you forsh magnifshent reception. I may shay that my feelings overcome me to such'n exten' that—hic (laughter and applause, during which the speaker's voice is drowned). When I shee 'roun' me men I have known many years, with'om—exshellent shairman jus' said—shared pleas-urean' toils, I feel—hic (loud applause and chorus, "Good old DOP!"). So, shentlemen—only to say how mush I reprociciate (cheers)—should say re-prixocate (renewed cheering)—in fact, re-cip-o-hic—" (tremendous applause, during which his lordship completes his remarks and sits down, still smiling with the utmost goodwill).

"The next item," said the chairman, "will be a song by Mr. Richard Harrowell: "The Exile's Return."

Hugh sat listening to the songs and recitations and the conversation of those around him, trying to read by external indications something of the life-story of those who came under his notice. A short distance down the table on the other side sat a tall, emaciated man in seedy black, whom he knew by the sobriquet of "the Parson." He was drinking with an appalling resolution, and his mirthless conversation was charged with the most dreadful oaths and blasphemies. Each drink he took appeared to nauseate him, and he grew steadily whiter as the evening advanced; yet the torrent of invective that flowed from his lips knew no abatement and, if possible, increased in virulence with every tumblerful of spirit he consumed. In spite of himself, Hugh's gaze returned again and again with a sort of horrified fascination to this creature. He seemed to be the butt of those around him, and apparently the withering retorts, betraying unmistakable evidences of education, with which he replied to the banter of his tormentors merely served to increase their amusement. The chief instigator of the attack was a little foxy man, known as "Six-and-eight"—and it may be said generally that whatever names these men may have inherited, or may have used with the object of obtaining credit at the stores, they were known by no others than those given on the field—who appeared to take immeasurable delight in drawing the lightning of "the Parson's" attention upon himself. Looking down the tables and noting the various groups into which the assemblage had by a sort of natural selection divided itself, Hugh wondered how often the tragedy being enacted before his eyes was repeated in various parts of the room. His reverie was interrupted by the voice of the chairman, now high and slightly unsteady. He was half singing, half reciting some verses that fitted in curiously with the young man's mood:—

"This is the lay of the digger, the song of the seeker of gum,
Sung in a kerosene twilight, to the tune of the kerosene drum;
The lay of the sick and the sorry, the men who have drawn
        God's wrath,
Warbled in tent and whare everywhere over the North."

Between Hugh and Roller three persons intervened; two were seated at the centre table and the other immediately above Hugh, on his left hand. One he indentified as Armitage, the second storekeeper of Parawai; the other two were strangers to him. One of them was a man verging on middle age, but plainly marked for the grave. His face was gaunt and of an unhealthy creamy whiteness, relieved only by a brilliant blot of colour in either cheek. His eyes were large and uncanny in their lustre, and he spoke in a beautifully modulated voice that had the trick of dropping every now and then into a minor key. While he spoke his eyes continually swept the hall, lighting every now and then on a face and lingering there only to lift abruptly again, in a manner which through some association of ideas reminded Hugh of a butterfly. His companion was a man perhaps a few years younger, whose chief characteristics were a prognathous jaw and a brutal laugh, that repeated itself almost with the regularity of clockwork. For a while Hugh heard only the tones of their voices, but at length a few words reached him which brought the blood to his cheeks, and after that the language of "the Parson" became tolerable.

How wonderful and mysterious were the bonds of sin and failure that united all these men together! Here were the scourings and scum of humanity, the top and bottom of the world's social system, driven by a multiplicity of causes to a common life. Again Hugh heard Bart's voice like an echo of his thoughts:—

"In the eyes of a woman we found it,
    In the kiss we construed as a sign,
In the leap of the steeplechaser,
    In the glow of the whisky and wine."

Presently from the bottom of the room and rapidly spreading upwards came a drumming of tumblers and a chorus which Hugh recollected to have frequently heard on Bart's lips:—

" The new-chum and the scum,
    And the scouring of the slum,
And the lawyer and the doctor and the deaf and halt and dumb,
And the parson and the sailor and the welsher and the whaler,
    When the world is looking glum
    Just to keep from Kingdom Come
    Take to digging kauri gum."

There was a cry of "Order!" and Bart, pulling himself together, took up the solo in a strong, not unmelodious voice.

"In the slighted, blighted North, where the giant kauris grow,
    And the earth is bare and barren where the bush-bee used to hum,
When the luck we've followed's failing, and our friends are out of hailing,
    And it's getting narrow sailing by the rocks of Kingdom Come,
There's a way of fighting woe, squaring store bills as you go,
    In the trade of digging gum.

CHORUS.

"And the new-chum and the scum, etc.

198

"In the scrubby, grubby North, when the giddy sun is set,
     And the idiot-owl cicada drops the whirring of his drum;
When the night is growing thicker and the bottled candles flicker,
     And the damned mosquitoes bicker in a diabolic hum,
There's a way of ending fret and of pulling down a debt
          In the task of scraping gum.

CHORUS.
"And the new-chum and the scum, etc.

"In the sloppy, floppy North, through the dismal winter rain,
     When the man is merely muscle and the mind is nearly
numb,
When the old, old pains rheumatic fill the bones from base to attic
     And a sound of words erratic sets the pannikins a-thrum,
There's a way of killing Cain and an antidote to pain
          In the task of hooking gum.

CHORUS.
"And the new-chum and the scum, etc.

"And the man of law has gambled through another man's estate,
     And the doctor's special weaknessat the present time is rum,
And the parson loves the clocking on a pretty maiden's stocking,
     And his sermons (mostly shocking) scare the neophyte
new-chum;
By the smouldering tea-tree fire,when the wind is howling higher,
They are cracking jokes that blister the Recording Angel's slate,
And the matters that they mention are too primitive to state
          At the scraping of the gum.

CHORUS.
"But the new-chum and the scum,
     And the scouring of the slum,
And the lawyer and the doctor and the deaf and halt and dumb,
And the parson and the sailor and the welsher and the whaler,
     When the Day of judgment's come,

Oh, won't they be looking glum,
As the mighty trumpets thunder and the harps go tinkle-turn,
And they've finished with the digging and they've scraped the final
    crumb,
And the bottom's gone for ever from the trade of kauri gum!"

For a long time the humming and drumming continued, and it seemed as though after this the assembly had little patience for further songs and recitations. As time wore on the drink began to have its effect in a loosening of tongues and as it were the letting down the barriers of a hundred dispositions, and only those performers with bull-like voices and perfect self-conceit managed to struggle through to the end of their items. From the bottom of the table on the other side of the room came an uproar of laughter and dispute with in the midst of it the sound of a high, querulous, maudlin voice; and here and there at other parts of both tables there were indications that the fighting drunks were getting under weigh. The sound of breaking tumblers came with increasing frequency. Men could be seen asleep with their arms stretched across the table, and one or two had retired into a corner, where they lay huddled up in serene unconsciousness of their surroundings.

Hugh himself had drunk next to nothing, and so far from being exhilarated by what he did take he had gradually lapsed into a mood of depression. So long as the gathering remained for the most part sober, it had possessed many points of interest which had served to amuse him and hold his attention; but the prospect of a prolonged and drunken orgy repelled him, and only the desire to save Bart from ending the evening in the dead-house prevented him leaving his seat.

As for Bart, he had by this time entirely lost control of the meeting, a fact of which, however, he remained in complete ignorance. Every now and then he would rise to his feet, thump the table vigorously with the club, pounding a glass or two in the process, and deliver a speech or other matter in a voice that never rose above the uproar.

No one paid the slightest attention to him, and each

occasion saw him retain his balance with greater difficuty.

Roller also had been drinking steadily, and was beginning to show the effects of the liquor he had taken in an increased insolence of manner. He had made a short speech in reply to the toast of the "Storekeepers," but had not otherwise taken an active part in the proceedings. Most of his conversation was addressed to Armitage, who appeared flattered at the other's attention and followed his remarks with a show of deep interest. Once or twice Hugh had found the eyes of the pair bent on himself, as though he were the subject of conversation, and as the evening wore on the insolence of their manner began to cause him annoyances The cold stare with which he regarded them had its effect on Armitage, who would turn away in a shamefaced manner, but Roller was not so easily daunted, meeting Hugh's looks with a sneering smile and continuing his remarks to his companion, no little apparently to the latter's amusement.

The innkeeper, looking somewhat haggard and anxious, was moving round the tables taking away the empty bottles and occasionally, when the opportunity occurred, purloining a full one. Except when addressed, he spoke to no one, but his hawk-like glance roamed hither and thither, taking in every incident. As for the guest of the evening, he had long since ceased to take any prominent part in the proceedings. He dozed peacefully with his chin on his chest, only rousing in response to a violent shaking from Bart, when he would drum solemnly on the table with the butt end of a bottle and request Bart to "give it a name."

It was shortly after midnight that Hugh observed a figure bearing a lantern come rapidly up the hall and approach Bart. He was clad in a long coat pulled up about the ears, and his hat was drawn down over his eyes, yet there was something in the manner in which he moved which enabled Hugh to identify his friend Jess Olive. The advent of this strange figure caused a lull in the noise at the upper end of the hall, even "the Parson" pausing in his diabolic eloquence to watch the scene.

Jess laid his hand on Bart's shoulder. "Come, lad," he said, "it's time to go home."

Bart, arrested in the act of rising to announce a fresh imaginary item, turned and looked glassily at the person who interrupted him.

"Why, it's Olive!" said Roller, with a laugh. "Where's Upmore? Here, Upmore, you're wanted."

Upmore approached and said something in a low voice to Olive.

"You can spare one," Hugh heard him reply; "it's only Bart I want."

"Put him in the dead-house," said Roller; "that'll settle him."

Upmore smiled cunningly and looked from one face to another.

"In with him, Upmore," repeated Roller, and a chorus of drunken approval greeted the suggestion.

Jess shrank back. "No, no!" he cried. "Let me take Bart away, and I will not trouble you any more. What difference will one make to you?"

The innkeeper looked doubtfully about him, but at length, in response to a whispered suggestion from Roller, he beckoned to his assistants.

Hugh rose leisurely and walked round to the back of the table. "It's all right, Jess," he said encouragingly, "you are not going in."

"Who's going to stop him?" asked Roller, turning in his seat.

"I am," replied Hugh, nodding; "he's not going in."

"Put him in, Upmore," said Roller slowly. "We'll stand by you and see it done. Don't let a gutter thief like that prevent you."

"The first man that lays a hand on him," said Hugh steadily, "goes down."

Roller gnawed his lip and looked savagely round the group.

"Are you all afraid of him?" he asked. Then, with a sudden insane fury, he seized his glass of spirits and threw the contents fair in Hugh's face. "Take that, you hound!" he cried.

Maddened by the repeated insults and their gross culmination, Hugh darted forward, and seizing the storekeeper by the collar of his coat, dragged him backwards on to the floor; then, turning him on his face, he pinioned his arms behind his back. "Get the key and open the door, Upmore," he said.

"What do you propose to do, Mr. Clifford?" asked the innkeeper, shrinking back.

"Open the door," thundered Hugh, "or I will put you in with him."

"Gentlemen," said Upmore, "I call you all to witness that I am not responsible for this. I am acting under compulsion, Mr. Roller, I am not a willing participator in this outrage."

"Blast you!" screamed the storekeeper. "Grab hold of him! he's breaking my arms."

"Lie still, you cur!" said Hugh, glaring round the dangerous-looking crowd that had now swarmed over the table and surrounded them. "If there is a man here with the heart of a dog," he said, "let him give me a hand to lock this drunken brute in the dead-house."

The Earl of Baringbroke, aroused from and partly sobered by his slumbers, had been watching the scene with beery good-humour, as though under the impression that it was an entertainment got up in his especial honour. He now rose, and removing his coat, laid it with elaborate care on the seat he had just vacated. He then rolled up his shirt-sleeves and spat on his hands. "Give it a name," he said.

"Grip hold of his legs," directed Hugh, and this after a brief struggle was accomplished.

"Now, up with him," and Roller was swung into the air.

Meanwhile Bart had watched the proceeding with a drunken solemnity, occasionally crying, "Order! order!" in shocked tones. At length, however, the full significance of what was occurring appeared to penetrate his dulled wits, and he got unsteadily to his feet.

"Gen'l'men," he said, "Cliffor' man o' genius. Put Upmore in too." And he went straight for the innkeeper.

A shout of laughter greeted the suggestion, and a still

louder shout followed when Bart, advancing, met the fist of some person standing behind Upmore and collapsed in a heap on the floor.

"I'll give a hundred pounds to the man who frees me," roared Roller, black in the face with impotent rage. "One hundred pounds! Do you hear, Upmore?"

"Make room there," said Hugh, beginning to advance. "Upmore, unlock the door."

The innkeeper shrugged his shoulders and began to lead the procession round the hall.

"Bear witness, gentlemen all," he repeated, "that I am acting under compulsion. This is none of my doing."

"One hundred pounds," repeated Roller, struggling violently.

"Make it guineas," suggested Bart. There was a big lump on his forehead, and he appeared to some extent sobered by the blow.

"I'll give two hundred," shrieked Roller, as they squeezed through the passage and across the bar.

"Think better of it, Mr. Clifford," said Upmore, as they reached the dead-house.

"Open the door," said Hugh inflexiby, "and stand aside. Look out to let go when I tell you, Dopping."

A dim light from the bar penetrated to where they stood, but was powerless to solve the gloom that lay beyond the open door of the dead-house. Only with difficulty were the leaders of the procession able to prevent themselves from being forced through the doorway by the pressure of the excited crowd behind. There was a brief struggle, a blow or two interchanged, then the door swung to, and the key was turned in the lock. An uproarious cheer greeted the completion of the performance, and the crowd began pushing and struggling back to the hall. Hugh pocketed the key and followed, a sound of furious kicking and muffled oaths pursuing him from the region of the prison.

When they reached the bar the Earl of Baringbroke took Hugh aside.

"Give me your hand," he said. "You are a man; but trouble will come of this."

Hugh gripped the hand extended to him.

"Thank you for your help," he said. "The fellow got less than he deserved, but then, it is always best to temper justice with mercy."

"If anything should come of it," said the Earl, "rely on me to stand by you. I should consider it an honour to help you in any way in my power."

Hugh again thanked him, and they re-entered the hall. A few regarded them curiously, but the majority apparently had already forgotten the incident, and were again devoting themselves to the bottles.

Hugh made his way to the top of the room, where Jess was still standing, anxiously awaiting their approach. Hugh threw the key down on the centre table.

"Gentlemen," he said, "you were all witnesses to what occurred previous to my laying a hand on the man, and I leave you to decide the duration of his punishment. When you think that he has had enough, there is the key and you can let him out."

He took Olive's arm and looked round for Bart, but the latter was nowhere to be seen. Having scanned the tables without discovering anything of him, he re-entered the bar. The place was dark and deserted, but a sound of voices came from the dining-room beyond, and here Hugh discovered the innkeeper screwing down the lamp. Hugh looked about him, surprised to find that the man was alone.

"No," said Upmore, in answer to his inquiry; "isn't he inside? But surely you are not going yet?" he added.

"Yes, I am," said Hugh curtly. "I have had enough of it. You'll find the key inside, and can please yourself what you do with it after I am gone. Come on, Jess."

"Aren't we going to find Bart?" Jess asked when they were alone.

"We can take another look, if you like," said Hugh, "but it seems to me he is gone already."

They again went round the hall, scrutinising every face, but without success, and finally gave up the search and passed out into the starlit night.

Hugh drew a breath of relief as he looked up into the clear sky, and after a while the anger that had possessed him melted away. Jess, still carrying his lantern, drew close to him and linked his arm in his with a little laugh of apology. Hugh whistled cheerfully, and so they went forward along the silent road.

CHAPTER XXVI

WHEN Upmore turned away from the door of the dead-house after seeing the exit closed on the storekeeper, instead of following the others he stepped aside into the dining-room, which was almost in darkness. A glance revealed the person of whom he was in search, and he closed the door and turned up the lamp.

Brice, for it was he, grinned and showed his discoloured teeth, but Upmore, gnawing his moustache, apparently did not share in the other's amusement.

"You're a deep un," said Brice, with an admiring chuckle. "What's to do next?"

"That's the point," said Uptnore thoughtfully. He crossed the room, then walked softly back on tiptoe, and, opening the door, looked out into the deserted bar. Satisfied that there were no listeners, he allowed the door to remain partly open and placed himself in a position that would command a view of anything occurring outside.

"Look 'ere," said Brice in a whisper, "let's finish Roller and Make t'other chap swing for him. We've got fifty witnesses to swear that he slung 'im in there, and who's to say 'e didn't crack 'im on the 'ead before he shut the door?"

"Listen," said Upmore, holding up his finger.

For a man with a cracked skull the storekeeper indeed was making an extraordinary amount of noise, and Brice at once recognised the futility of his scheme.

"What then?" he asked again.

Upmore was on the point of replying when his eye caught a motion outside and he pointed hurriedly to a recess behind the door. Brice slipped across, and when Hugh and Jess entered there was apparently no one present but the innkeeper. The latter, after following them to the hall, remained in the doorway of the inn until the lantern was a considerable way from the house, then he returned to the dining-room.

"Goin' 'ome, eh?" said Brice, rubbing the side of his nose with a fiat forefinger. "He's as slippery as a darned eel. Hanged if 'e 'asn't the luck of a Chinaman."

"The point I was debating," said Upmore, "was whether we couldn't get Roller to take the job off our hands. It might be a job that would suit him very well now."

Brice regarded him with an admiration verging on awe.

"The difficulty," continued Upmore musingly, "is to get the strength of his hand without disclosing ours."

The other became suddenly thoughtful. "What difference would that make to my little commish?" he asked anxiously.

"Eh? None. The thing is—it has got to come off somehow."

"He's that darned slippery," repeated Brice, leaning forward and looking apologetically at the innkeeper— "first there was the little go we 'ad on the gumfield —'e 'ad all the best of that. Then there was the time I dropped in promiscuous like and found 'amilton's kid there—that was a point to 'im too. Then there was a couple o' other times when I reckoned I 'ad the drop on 'im, but 'e dodged me both times."

"Yes," said Upmore, "the thing has been bungled, and the worst of it is he has his suspicions aroused, and that makes it all the harder."

"I'll tell you what," said Brice; "I'll tackle it right off to-night. This time I'll make certain of it."

"How," asked Upmore hopefully.

"I'll kerosene 'im," said Brice, with a malignant grin. "Get me 'alf a tin o' kerosene and a bit o' a pannikin. The tea tree's grown up that thick round the tent that I can get right in be'ind and slop it on without 'im surspectin' nothin'; then—" He struck an imaginary match on his trousers, and a puff of the breath conveyed the rest.

Upmore received the scheme with a show of respect, but he did not discuss it. "Stay here," he said, "or go into the hall if you like, till I have a talk with Roller. The hall will be better, so that if anyone proposes to let him out you can take steps to prevent it. I've got another key upstairs."

He turned down the lamp, and groping his way up the dark, steep stairs, returned presently with the key.

The dead-house was wrapped in complete silence as the

innkeeper, bearing a lantern in his hand, rapped on the door with his knuckles.

"Who's there?" asked a hoarse voice.

"Me—Upmore. Is that you, Mr. Roller?"

"Who the devil d'you expect it is?" asked Roller not unnaturally.

"I'm coming in, Mr. Roller; but don't try to get out until I tell you, or it may lead to worse trouble. Do you hear what I say?"

"I hear. Come in, and be hanged to you!"

Thus cordially invited, the innkeeper lost no time in turning the key, and slipping in edgeways he closed and locked the door behind him.

"I am in absolute terror of my life with that young man," he said breathlessly, holding up the light to get a good view of his companion. Then his voice changed suddenly to another key. "What's this?" he asked sharply.

The dead-house, as revealed by the light of the lantern, was a place sufficiently gloomy to justify the worst fears of its most imaginative occupant. In shape it was a strongly built lean-to, high at the back, but barely providing standing-room at the front. It was lighted only by a few panes of glass near the ceiling of the bar, and thus the only light that reached it even in daytime was, as it were, second-hand. A rude bench nailed to the wall in one corner provided the only resting-place above the level of the floor, and with this single exception the place was absolutely bare of anything in the nature of furniture or fittings. The walls and floor were in a filthy condition, and the rat-holes in the lining boards sufficiently accounted for the fetid odour with which the room was charged. The bottom panels of the door, as well as the lower lining boards, were everywhere dented and split, as though from the furious kicking of half-maddened drunks, with possibly a percentage from those who, having slept off their debauch, found themselves temporarily forgotten and resented it. It was, however, nothing of all this which arrested the innkeeper's attention and caused him to break off in his conversation with Roller. His eye was attracted by a figure lying huddled together in one corner, its face turned to the wall.

"Who is it?" he asked, casting his memory back with the possibility of discovering some flotsam from the wrecks of the past few days.

"That brute chucked him in with me," Roller explained, with a shrug of the shoulders. "I expect he's drunk; he tumbled down there as soon as he got in."

The innkeeper tiptoed across and lowered the lantern to the level of the man's face. "It's Bart," he said, touching him with his foot. "I expect I'd have had to bring him in here, anyway." He stooped down and shook him violently by the shoulder, eliciting nothing more intelligible than a drunken snore.

"Well," said Roller impatiently, "what are we stopping here for?"

"It's this way, Mr. Roller," said Upmore, rising and looking furtively at the storekeeper; "you haven't given me much reason lately to feel friendly towards you."

"Oh, well," said Roller, "we'll forget all that. I've something else to think of now."

"That's spoken like a gentleman," said Upmore, setting down the lantern and seating himself on the bench. "And I suppose, then, the matter of the guarantee may be considered finally settled?"

"Yes," snarled Roller, "I tell you I am not going to bother any more with it."

"That's satisfactory, anyway," said Upmore easily; "very gentlemanly indeed."

"Confound you! said Roller, after a pause. "Why don't you open the door?"

"It's this way, Mr. Roller," said the innkeeper, looking around him as though in admiration at the scenery, "that young man's got a down on the pair of us, and I'm thinking what he'd do if I let you out."

Roller contemplated the speaker with savage disgust. "Let me have a fair chance at him face to face," he said, "and we'd see what he'd do."

"He was rather severe on you," Upmore admitted. Then he gave vent to a low cackle. "Very funny you looked, Mr. Roller, if you'll excuse my making the remark."

"Shut your mouth!" said Roller fiercely, moving feverishly up and down the room. "Where is he now?" he stopped suddenly to ask.

"He *may* be on the road home."

"I'd give something to get my grip on him, drag him in here, and—"

The innkeeper waited for the conclusion of the sentence, but as nothing came he leaned forward and asked suggestively, "Why not? Mind you," he continued cautiously as Roller came to a standstill, "I've got nothing against him myself; he's never given me offence; it is the gentlemanly manner in which you have cried off with me that makes me feel that I would like to help you to—get square with him."

"How can it be done?" asked Roller eagerly, opening and shutting his hands. "I'll get even with him if—if—"

"There's a chap outside," the innkeeper said musingly, "who'd stick a knife into him if he had the chance, he's got that much of a down on him. Not, of course," he broke off, changing his insinuating tone in response to some fancied shrinking on the part of his victim, "that you'd go as far as that, except, maybe, by accident, but still, if you got him to help you, you could mark him a bit or even bring him back and give him a day or two of this."

"Who is he?" asked Roller.

"Brice is his name. —Yes, but all that is forgotten. I was talking to him not ten minutes ago, and one of the things he said to me was, 'Mr. Upmore,' he said, 'Iused ter 'ave a down on Roller, but now hang me if after this I ain't on his side '—those were his very words."

The storekeeper continued to pace doubtfully up and down the floor.

"I don't care to put myself in the power of a man of that stamp," he said, gnawing his finger.

"Very well," said Upmore indifferently, "it was merely a

suggestion. Perhaps it will be better to leave him alone. A man who can cut you out in a love affair and throw you into a place like this *is* rather a dangerous customer to tackle."

Roller started and glared savagely at the innkeeper. "Where is this man?" he asked.

"I'll arrange it all for you," said Upmore, rising. "Just sit down a minute while I find him and get your horse ready."

Leaving Roller seated on the bench, Upmore let himself out and made swiftly for the hall.

The festivities here still continued, but not more than twenty or thirty men remained at the tables. The remainder had either wandered out and forgotten to return, or were lying asleep round the walls of the room. Brice had placed a chair on the centre table, and was sitting there with a whisky bottle grasped between his knees. His speech was slightly thick.

"Come down from there," said Upmore sharply, "and give me the key."

"I'm a-comin' down," said Brice, suiting the action to the word.

The innkeeper led the way into the bar and looked him up and down with an expression that cowed the half-intoxicated ruffian. "Do you know what you are about?" he asked.

"In course," said Brice half sulkily.

"Well, get along the road and wait till Roller comes up. Finish the job this time, or—" A look of cruel significance completed the sentence.

"Give us a bottle o' soda," said Brice, his spirits thoroughly dashed.

Upmore stepped into the bar, uncorked a bottle, and poured the contents into a tumbler. "Now," he said, when the stuff was consumed, "keep out of everyone's sight and wait for him on the brow of the hill."

Brice nodded, and pulling his hat down over his ears, lurched heavily out into the night.

After a moment the innkeeper made his way to the stables, brought out and saddled Roller's horse, and led it round to the verandah; then he stood awhile in deep thought. At last he roused himself, and again entering the hall approached the centre table, scanning the faces of those around it as he advanced.

"I am going to let Roller out, boys," he said, "and I should like one or two of you to come and see it done, so as to be on the safe side. Mr. Armitage, would you mind stepping out on to the verandah? And perhaps his lordship would also oblige? There is no need to let him see you, but in case of accidents I should like one or two witnesses to the fact that he left here safe and well."

Curious as was the request, it was made in such matter-of-fact tones that the men in their muddled condition accepted it as perfectly natural, and two or three accompanied the innkeeper to the verandah, and allowed themselves to be placed in a dark spot, out of reach of the light from the doorway.

These arrangements completed, Upmore returned to the dead-house.

"It's all right," he said in response to an impatient ejaculation from Roller; "your horse is ready. I have put a rope on the saddle in case you should need it. You will find Brice waiting for you on the top of the hill."

"Is there anyone about?" Roller asked.

"Not a soul; they're all busy inside. Come along." He flashed the light in Bart's face, who lay with his mouth wide open snoring loudly, and, turning, led the way out.

Roller passed quickly through the house and scrambled on to his horse.

"Good night, Mr. Roller," said the innkeeper clearly.

Roller muttered some response, and wheeling his horse, galloped away up the road.

"Where's he going?" asked Armitage, coming forward with the others.

Upmore, in the dim light of the bar, appeared dumb-foundered and looked questioningly from one to the other. "I thought he was going home," he said. "What can he be going to do along there?"

Armitage had a muddled idea that something was wrong, but could form no connected idea of what it was. The Earl of Baringbroke had attended merely out of good-nature and was anxious only to get back to his seat, standing erect being a position attended with some difficulty.

Roller pulled up on the brow of the hill and, looking round, was startled to discover Brice almost immediately at his elbow.

"That you, guv'nor?" asked Brice, laying hold of the stirrup-iron.

Roller dismounted, and they stumbled along the dusty road side by side, the storekeeper leading the horse.

"What do you suggest?" the latter asked presently, coming to a standstill.

"Shove a knife into 'im," said Brice; "it's quick and easy.

> 'There was a lady fairly fair,
> Who—"

"Pst!" hissed the storekeeper. "Are you drunk, or what?"

"Take it at 'what," said Brice, lurching up against him. "Do you expect a man to be dead sober for ever?

> 'She went to take the early air,
> And she had jewels rarely rare.' "

"If you want all the country to know where we are, you couldn't do better than you are doing," Roller remarked savagely.

"Mum's the word," said Brice, "I took 'alf a bottle to wunst, and it caught me on the sudden. What's your idea of it?" he asked in a hoarse whisper. "Somethin' lingerin', eh?"

"No knives," said Roller. "I want him in my power, bound hand and foot, then we'll see."

"Pretty large order that," said Brice. "He's as slithery as a flounder and strong as a lion. Did you ever feel the weight of his fist?"

"Never," replied the storekeeper, writhing.

"Well, you're likely to," said Brice. "I shouldn't be surprised if 'e broke your neck before the night's out.

'She met young Fairleigh Palifax,
And he was fairly fou—'

Beg pardon, guv'nor, mum's the word."

The red distorted remnant of a moon was coming up over the shoulder of a neighbouring ridge as the pair came in sight of the tent and halted among the tea trees on the margin of the road.

"Tie up the horse," said Brice, who in the imminence of action appeared to be sober. "Are you right? Then keep low and take care where you are going."

Stooping into the cover of the bushes, the pair crept stealthily forward to within touch of the back wall of the tent. Brice put back a hand to stay the other's advance, and crouched, still listening intently; then he began backing cautiously out till they reached a track some distance away.

"Slithery as a darned eel," he remarked in a whisper. "I don't believe 'e's there at all."

"We'd better make sure," Roller suggested.

"Come on, then," said his companion, and they crept round to the front of the tent, Brice finally crawling in under the fly. After a moment he stood erect. "Sold again," he observed in a low voice from within the tent.

Roller followed, and by the aid of a match looked contemptuously round on the possessions of the man who had dispossessed him. Their very slenderness increased his desire for vengeance. "What next?" he asked impatiently.

"Name the game," said Brice, snuffing out the match with his fingers and stepping out into the open air.

"Where does this man Olive live?" Roller asked.

"Up the hill," said Brice. "Come along." He thrust his hands deep in his pockets, and set off through the scrub. Roller untied the horse, and led it across the road, and for some

215

distance through the tea tree, until the track they had started on became too overgrown to follow further, when he came to a standstill.

"Hurry up, guv'nor," said Brice; "we'll have the daylight on us directly."

The storekeeper secured the horse to the bushes, and they continued their advance until the fern-log cabin of the King of the Diggers loomed out against the sky above them.

"This is another pair of shoes, you know," said Brice, stopping and scratching his ear. "If 'e's 'ere, there's two of them, and they've got a door. The best plan 'ud be to fire the shop, and shoot 'em as they come out."

Roller drew back at the cold-blooded suggestion. "I want one man," he said, "and I want him alive. Help me to that, and I'll pay you well for it."

"Blest if I see 'ow it's to be done," said Brice, after a moment's reflection. "You can't cop a man like that same's a skylark; you've got to wing 'im first."

They crept up to the flat land on which the cabin stood, and after reconnoitring around it, drew off to discuss the situation.

"Man to man's no game at all," said Brice; "we want 'alf a dozen for a job like this. They're no spring chickens either of them."

"I have brought the rope," Roller said. "I was wondering whether we could put it across the doorway, so that the first man who came out would trip over it."

Brice grinned audibly. "Clifford would be the first all right," he said, "and if 'e goes down I could manage 'im—always supposin' 'e's inside. As for t'other bloke, you'd 'ave to stand by to plug 'im in the eye as soon as he turned up."

Roller nodded. They discussed the details, and then returned to the door.

In a few minutes the trap was laid.

CHAPTER XXVII

"JESS," said Hugh suddenly, as the dip of the road extinguished the lights of the inn, "have you forgotten what they did to you the last time you visited that place?"

"No," replied Jess.

"And yet you put yourself in their power again. Why are you so foolish?"

"Do you not sometimes help your friends?" Jess asked.

"Yes, but Bart is used to it. The darkness is nothing to him, while to you—"

"Darkness is something to every man," Jess replied irritably. "Even though they don't know it, it acts just the same. All diseases and misfortunes have their beginning in the night-time. Did you think the black gum leaked out of the trees while the sun was shining?"

"Darkness has its horrors, no doubt," Hugh said; "but it has its delights as well. What about sleep?"

Jess drew closer to his companion. "I will tell you about sleep," he said in a whisper; "when God saw the darkness, He was afraid, and He made sleep that we should not know it was there." He leaned forward and peered up into Hugh's face. "I call that kind of Him," he concluded triumphantly.

"You should not have gone," Hugh repeated, "and you must never attempt such a thing again."

Jess turned away and for a space was silent. "I have tramped this bush many many years," he said sadly at last, "and no man knows it as I do. I have seen men come and seen them go, and none are left here now that I knew in the old days barring only him. Where have they gone? God have pity on me, where are they?"

"Now, Jess," Hugh said, with gentle remonstrance.

"Drunken and mad and diseased," muttered Jess, stopping short. "I see them. Spade and spear—devils and men; but the bush was silent all the while."

He paused abruptly and, holding the lantern above his head, peered anxiously about him. "Where are we?" he asked.

"Close to my tent," Hugh replied. "I will come up with you and see you safe home."

Jess moved forward irresolutely, every now and then shrinking close to his companion.

"What is it, Jess?" Hugh asked at length.

"The darkness," exclaimed Jess pitiably, dropping the lantern, which was instantly extinguished. "Oh, the horror of the black night!"

Hugh recovered the lantern, and again lighting it, held it up. "Come along," he said cheerfully. "Don't give way."

Holding the light low to guide their steps, he led his companion off the road on to a track which led round the low, scrub-covered hillocks in the direction of Olive's `cabin. By degrees Jess, who had at first trembled violently, grew calmer.

Olive's cabin stood on a little flat half-way up the side of a hill. It was constructed of the stems of tree ferns sunk into the ground side by side, the roof being thickly thatched with palm leaves. A wooden door, secured by a lock and staple outside and a bar within, formed the only break in the solid walls.

Jess unlocked the door, and taking the padlock inside, slipped the bar to behind them. The interior of the hut was thatched between the fern stems with rushes to exclude draughts. At the further end was a fireplace and chimney of corrugated iron, a few embers smouldering on the hearth. To the right and left of the fireplace were a couple of narrow bedplaces, filled with the dry, elastic stems of the climbing fern, and covered with mats of native flax. The blankets lay neatly folded at the head of the beds. In the centre of the cabin was the sawn section of a tree, forming a low, solid table. The whole place presented an appearance of cleanliness and comfort; the tin-ware and crockery were bright and clean; the hard earth floor was smooth and dustless; the large oil lantern, which Olive proceeded to light and suspend from the roof, had its glass polished to the utmost degree of luminosity.

Once inside Jess became his old self on the instant.

"Sit down," he said, disencumbering himself of his coat and hat. "There is no sense in going back to your tent to-night; and there is a reason why you should not go."

"Very well," said Hugh willingly. "What is the reason?"

"I have a message for you from Bart," Jess said, feeling in the pocket of his coat. "What happened down there made me forget it but here it is." He handed Hugh a soiled and twisted piece of paper..

Hugh opened the paper and found a bill in the name of Higgins for sundry supplies; on the back a short message was scrawled in pencil, and holding the sheet up to the lantern, Hugh deciphered it as follows: —

"CLIFFORD,—You have more enemies than one, and they are men without scruples. Do not sleep in your tent again. Do not sleep on the field again. If you know why any man should desire your life, you will guess whom you have to fear. Take this warning from your well-wisher—BART."

Hugh crumpled the note up, and looked inquiringly at his companion.

"Yes," said Jess, "I know what it is. He asked me to read it. You must obey him."

"Do you know what his reasons are?" Hugh asked.

Jess shook his head.

"Depend upon it, they are good," he said.

He seated himself, and his blue eyes regarded Hugh steadfastly.

"Tell me, boy," he said gently, "is it true that you have won her heart away from that man?"

"Yes," replied Hugh simply, "it is true."

"Be good to her, boy," said Jess almost inaudibly. "Let that one life be without a cloud."

"God help me to make it so, Jess," the boy answered.

"Who is your enemy?" Olive asked.

"Unless it is Roller, I can think of no one. He has good reasons for disliking me, but it is absurd to suppose he would go the length Bart seems to anticipate."

"Jealousy is a fierce passion," said Jess. "Often in the night, when I cannot sleep, I listen to the voices of the bush, and it is among them."

He began divesting himself of his clothing, but stayed his hand when the task was half completed, and spreading out the rugs, lay down and covered himself up. Hugh followed his example, removing only his boots and coat.

"Do you keep the light burning?" he asked.

"Screw it out," said Jess. "Home is like the sunshine to me at all times."

Hugh obeyed, and the cabin was plunged in darkness.

"When the wind is howling," resumed Jess, "I hear the voices of the evil spirits—hatred and jealousy and lust and madness, and there is murder in the throats of them all. Only when the nights are still do the beautiful things come out and encourage one another."

A morepork, hunting for rats, alighted on the projecting roof-pole of the cabin, and gave vent to a prolonged harsh shriek, followed by a mysterious "koko." The sound of a person shouting or singing floated up from the direction of the inn.

"What else do you hear?" Hugh asked, as Jess remained silent.

"Sometimes I hear the sound of a tree falling far off in the bush, and then I know that I shall sleep no more that night. I hear it lying awake, or I start from my sleep with the sound in my ears, and that is the worst of all the noises of the bush. For it is like some hope destroyed. Sometimes"—he lowered his voice to an awed tone—"I have even for hours lost faith in the goodness of God."

"Sleep, Jess," said Hugh; "there are none but the beautiful things abroad to-night."

Jess was silent.

A lonely breeze, presaging the advent of the morning, touched the roof of the cabin with a stuttering message and was gone. The shouting or singing came again, still indistinguishably faint, and was lost abruptly in the silence.

Hugh, dreaming a tree had fallen in a dream forest, awoke

to find the crash in his ears. So realistic was it that he lay still listening, unable to believe that the sound was merely a figment of the brain. Hearing Jess stirring, he called him softly by his name.

"Yes," said Jess, "I heard it fall. Strange that it should happen to-night."

And he sighed.

Suddenly something struck the roof of the cabin and slid down the dry, rustling thatch to the ground.

Hugh started up, and feeling about for his boots, felt his hands grasped in a trembling hold.

"Boy," whispered Jess fearfully, "thee evil spirits have come at last."

Hugh gripped the other's hands in swift, stormy reflection.

"Jess," he said persuasively, "listen to me. These are no spirits, but men like ourselves. Perhaps they are those of whom Bart has warned us, and there may be truth in the worst he has suggested. Nothing can harm us if we stand together and help one another."

The speech had its effect, Jess returning him grip for grip.

"Have you any weapons?" Hugh asked in a whisper.

"None," said Jess.

Suddenly the silence was again broken by a loud hammering on the door. Hugh was on the point of stepping forward when Jess held him by the arm. "Boy," he whispered cunningly, "they want us to open the door; we will keep it shut."

Hugh by a motion of the hand signified assent.

The next indication of the presence of the enemy was a slight rattling of the door-bar, followed by heavy, muffled blows, as though from the shoulder of a person testing the resistance of the lock and hinges. Hugh stood braced for all emergencies, but the door held. After a moment or two the blows ceased and all was again still.

"What is the next move, Jess?" Hugh asked, his spirits rising. "A sortie ought to be effective now, I should say."

"Wait," said Jess; "they may be tempted to show who they are, and it's a good thing to know one's enemies."

There was an interval of quiescence, then the walls of the but began to tremble and there was a sound of clawing and rustling in the thatch. Hugh felt Jess slip quickly away, and half a minute later there was a howl of pain and a heavy body slid with a thud to the ground.

Jess bad prodded the party on the roof with a gum spear.

The next event was the sound of running footsteps and a violent blow on the door. Hugh darted forward, and setting his foot against the bottom of the door and his hands on the upper part, braced himself for the shock. Again and again it came till the cabin reeled to the furious onslaught, but the stout slabs of the door received the blows uninjured. Presently a thought struck Hugh, filling him with fierce amusement.

"Stand aside, Jess," he whispered loudly, at the same time slipping the bolt and drawing back. "If he doesn't go through the other side we'll collar this beggar, at any rate."

There was a rush, a loud clatter of the door, and something pitched heavily over the table into the fireplace. Then followed a spluttering as of someone spitting out hot ashes and loose teeth and segments of oaths.

Hugh grinned to himself as he stood with his eye on the doorway awaiting further developments.

They came with tragic suddenness. From the impenetrable darkness of the region of the fireplace came a spurt of flame, followed by several others in rapid succession, as the contents of a six-shooter were emptied in all directions through the cabin.

"Stand clear, Jess," Hugh cried, creeping forward along the bed. A bullet whizzed past his ear, burying itself in the thick wall of the cabin. There was a scrambling in the fireplace, followed by an oath as the retreating enemy barked his shins against the table, then the moonlight in the doorway was obscured. A sound of cartridges being knocked out and replaced warned Hugh that the situation was becoming desperate. He was preparing himself for a spring, when the door swung to with a crash and the bar fell into the slot.

"Are you hurt, lad?" asked the anxious voice of Jess, and at the same moment the flame of a match illumined the cabin.

"Not a scratch," said Hugh, looking thankfully at his uninjured companion. "Shall we lock ourselves away from one man?" he asked in the next instant

"There is another lurking about outside," said Jess. "I saw him against the sky—a short, thick-set man. What chance would we have unarmed against ruffians like those?"

Hugh looked round for something in the nature of a weapon, but in vain. A few knives, such as are used for pig-sticking, lay on a shelf in one corner, but the English hatred of a knife caused him to avert his eyes. "If there were only a stick of any kind," he said restlessly, "pistol or no pistol, I would tackle them."

Meanwhile Jess had lit the lantern and set it on the floor in front of the table in such a position that while the door end of the cabin was illuminated the rest remained in shadow. He now drew Hugh into the darkness by the fireplace.

"Listen," he said, "let us see what they will do next."

A sound of voices was audible some distance away, as of two persons in angry dispute, but the words were indistinguishable. Presently this ceased, and for three or four minutes silence prevailed. Hugh, tired of inactivity, approached the door, and silently slipping the bolt, looked out into the night. The open space in front of the cabin was flooded with moonlight, and had any person been present he must have stood revealed. No one was in sight. He stepped out and made a circuit of the cabin, scanning the surrounding bushes for the slightest motion which might betray the presence of his enemies, but nothing stirred. Returning to the front of the cabin, he found Jess gazing intently down the hillside,

"They have gone," Jess said; "I heard their voices. Listen!" he broke off suddenly, holding up his hand.

A sound of talking floated up through the still air from the bottom of the hill.

Hugh brought a couple of seats out of the cabin, and the pair sat down with their backs against the door.

"What can be the meaning of it?" Jess wondered. "All the

years I have been on the field I have never known a thing so shocking as this. That man has the disposition of a wild beast."

"They seem to be searching for something," said Hugh, who had been listening intently to the noises below.

"Perhaps their horses are there," Jess surmised.

It may have been a quarter of an hour later that Hugh discerned a glow in the sky straight in front of him. "Can that be the dawn, Jess?" he asked.

"No," replied Jess, "it's a fire." Suddenly he laid his hand on Hugh's shoulder. "They are revenging themselves on you, my boy," he said; "that is your tent."

Hugh laughed unpleasantly. "I suppose I shall have an innings some day," he observed, as a brilliant flame shot suddenly up into the night.

"You shall," said Jess; "only be patient."

The flame from the tent died down as suddenly as it had arisen, but the fire, spreading to the tea tree, became visible as a bright band of gold creeping across the field, and gradually increasing in length as it advanced. Clouds of red and orange-coloured smoke hung above it and drifted away backwards, until everything beyond the gilt line was dimmed or concealed. Now and then, as some bush of loftier growth was enveloped in the fire, a gorgeous flame-blossom sprang and quivered for a few moments above the pervading level. In time the fire was checked by the road, and dying out in the centre, it spread away east and west in a great semicircle over the hillocks.

Hugh and Jess again barricaded themselves in the cabin, and did not awake until the day was several hours old.

CHAPTER XXVIII

THEIR first act the following morning was to endeavour to discover Bart. With this object
they ascended the hill behind the cabin, and skirting the ridge for a distance of half a mile, dived into a deep gully, at the upper end of which Bart's whare was erected. The hut was constructed of rushes with a low sliding door of wood. Around it a small piece of land was inclosed in a stake fence, and in the centre of this was a red rose bush in full flower. Surmounting the fence by the aid of a log roughly hewn into steps, Bart's visitors slid back the door and entered the cabin. The place was empty, and had evidently not been slept in the previous night. The blankets were folded, as is usual, to prevent them being blown by the bluebottle fly, but everything else was in a state of more or less disorder.

Jess looked round and shook his head. "His spade is here," he said, "so he cannot be on the field. The dead-house has got him, after all."

Over the bed was a single shelf, containing ten or a dozen volumes, several of which were elaborately bound in leather. Hugh removed one from its resting-place and discovered opposite the fly-leaf the bookplate of a famous English college, and an inscription to the effect that the volume was presented to Charles Horace Medway for "English Literature." Most of the others were somewhat similarly inscribed, and Hugh finally turned away from the shelf with a feeling of commiseration for their absent owner.

"Poor Bart!" said Jess, who had observed Hugh's occupation. "He has parted with everything else. Even in the maddest of his debauches, when to obtain liquor he would sell a month's labour ahead of him, he kept those."

"Let us find him," said Hugh suddenly, with a frown. "The inn will be the best place to look for him."

They went out into the inclosure, where Hugh's gaze was again arrested by the rose bush. He noticed that the soil around it was kept loosened and free from weeds and the plant wore a lusty and well cared for appearance.

"Don't, boy," said Jess, as Hugh put out his hand to secure a bud. "Bart would resent it."

"Why so?"

"Who knows?" Jess replied vaguely.

They made their way out of the gully, and striking a track through the scrub, soon reached the road. The country here was black and unsightly from the recent fire. At various points arose thin columns of smoke, and away on the horizon dense clouds marked where the bush was still burning. Of the tent nothing remained but the charred poles, and of its original contents only the metal portions of the tools and implements were left unconsumed. Hugh kicked over the articles on the ground, disclosing a few books with their backs and edges burnt away.

"There was nothing here of any value," he remarked, "and but that these men thought to do me an injury, I might feel relieved that I am saved the trouble of dealing with my belongings."

They returned to the road and made their way along it to the inn.

In the bar they found Upmore, busy transferring the dregs of the bottles to a quart measure. He looked leaner and greyer than usual, possibly from the effects of a night of wakefulness, and Hugh noticed that the bottle he was emptying rattled against the lip of the measure.

"We have come for Bart," he said at once. "Where is he?"

"I'm sure I couldn't tell you," said Upmore indifferently, setting down the empty bottle. "I haven't seen him since you left."

"I'll take a look through the dead-house," Hugh said without ceremony.

"Will you?" the innkeeper replied nastily. "Not without my permission, I suppose?"

"Have you the key on you?" Hugh inquired.

"I might," said the innkeeper, "or I might not."

"Better look," Hugh suggested. "I should be sorry to put

you to the expense of a new lock."

Upmore showed his teeth slightly. "That would be a bit of hard luck," he thought.

Hugh turned resolutely towards the passage.

"Stay a moment," said Upmore quickly. "You can satisfy yourself that he is not inside. If you had made the request civilly in the first place, there would have been no trouble."

"Very well," said Hugh, diminishing nothing of his curtness of manner.

The innkeeper led the way along the dark passage and pointed to the open doorway. There was a strong smell of soapsuds and damp wood mingling with the usual odour of rats. The place had evidently been only recently scrubbed.

"We had to swab it out," Upmore explained; "it was in a filthy condition."

"Is there no one in the new building?" Hugh asked as they returned to the bar.

Upmore shrugged his shoulders. "Search the whole house, if you like," he said. "I have already told you he is not here."

Nothing mollified, Hugh began a search of the building, and he did not desist until every room down to the kitchen had been explored.

"Well," asked Upmore, bending his dark eyes upon them as they re-entered the bar on the conclusion of the search, "are you satisfied now?"

"He is not here," Hugh replied.

"Just so," said Upmore. "Take another look round, if you like," he added obligingly.

Outside on the road the two men came to a standstill.

"You know more of his habits than I do, Jess," Hugh said "Can you form an idea of what has become of him?"

Jess Olive shook his head. "He may have lain down and gone to sleep somewhere along the road," he said. "We can do nothing but await his return."

Looking across the blackened landscape, a thought struck both men simultaneously, and they turned to one another with an equal gravity in their eyes.

"Let us look," Hugh suggested. "In any case he would not have wandered far from the road."

They spent an hour tramping over the crackling ground, blackening themselves against the charred stems, but what they dreaded to find remained undiscovered. Now and again they stumbled against a digger, his face, hands, and clothing sooted like those of a sweep, but none of them had seen anything of Bart or had come across any sign of him in their wanderings.

Their search at length brought them again into the neighbourhood of Clifford's camping-ground, and happening to cast his eyes towards the road, Hugh observed a horseman, holding a spare horse, pulled up by the roadside and gazing blankly around him.

The rider was Wilfrid.

"So this is the end of it," he said, indicating the spot where the tent had been as Hugh hurried up.

"Yes," replied Hugh, "it's a case of clean sweep."

"Not so very clean," remarked Wilfrid, looking at a black smudge on Hugh's nose.

"How is she?" the latter asked.

"Well," replied Wilfrid, producing a letter from the breast of his coat, which Hugh received and regarded with a beating heart.

It was the first missive he had received from his sweetheart; the first time, indeed, that he had seen her writing, but he had no difficulty in identifying the writer on that account. No wonder he stood looking at the note as though it were too precious to be opened and read!

"There is something inside as well as out," Wilfrid remarked drily, and the young man blushed and broke the seal.

The contents were brief but charming: "My dear Hugh" (*Her* dear! Was it conceivable?), "father wants you to come back and—so do I.—Your Esther." His Esther! His! His And then that exquisite "so do I," so sweetly simple, so full of divine promise! He read the note through several times, and but for shame he could have spent the day in its perusal. When he raised his eyes the tawdry landscape was bathed in the golden haze of paradise. God was good. The world was beautiful.

"I have brought a horse for you," he heard Wilfrid saying, and he cast a grateful eye on the animal that was to transport him into the heaven where his lady dwelt.

"Will you come right away, or is there anything you have to do?"

The necessity for answering the question brought Hugh back to the world, and he turned doubtfully to Jess, who had just come up. Something vaguely unhappy in the latter's eyes touched and sobered him, and he looked at Wilfrid.

"Wilf," he said, "Bart is missing, and Jess is anxious about him. Let us see if we can find him before we go."

Wilfrid looked with speculative interest at Jess, and dismounted from his horse. "Is there any reason to suppose something serious has happened to him?" he asked, when he had been put in possession of the facts.

"No," Hugh replied hesitatingly. "Only that he apparently left the inn, and has neither gone home nor been heard of since."

"What time did the fire start?"

Hugh gave the required information, and after further discussion Jess set out to search the scrub on the unburned side of the road, while the mounted men rode over the blackened waste, scanning the field in all directions. It was past midday before the three met again at Olive's cabin to report progress. Meanwhile over twenty diggers had been encountered and questioned without eliciting any information. Most of them had been present at the social and had a more or less hazy notion of the last time they had seen the missing man; but none of them were able to speak of him later than when he accompanied the crowd to the door of the dead-house, and stood with the others outside in the passage. The rumour, however, that Bart was missing and was supposed to have been caught in the fire spread rapidly across the field, and before night fell there were numerous searchers, especially on the track of the conflagration, where something gruesome might possibly be discoverable.

During the afternoon Hugh, on the understanding that Wilfrid would not communicate them to Esther, related the events of the previous night, including the attack on the cabin, and so interested did Wilfrid become, especially in connection with the mysterious warning received from Bart, that he decided, and persuaded Hugh, to pass the night on the field, in order that the search might, if necessary, be resumed the following morning.

"You owe it to him in return for the warning he gave you," Wilfrid had said. "Who knows but for that you might have taken no precautions?"

"I was thinking of Esther," Hugh replied.

"We will send her a note. Esther is an intelligent girl, and she knows better than you can tell her that you would sooner be with her than out here. She will love and respect you all the more that you sacrifice your inclinations in the cause of one who may have made a much more momentous sacrifice for you."

"What makes you think so?"

"I don't think so. I say it is possible. There are two things clear to me, and there is an unpleasant significance about both of them."

"What are they?" Hugh asked.

"He was close to you when Roller was thrown into the dead-house and he was never seen by the crowd again. I argue from that that he was either forced in or he went in of his own accord."

"That would account for the sudden way in which he dropped out of sight last night," Hugh admitted. "What is the second thing?"

"Just a little remark you let drop as to the condition of the dead-house this morning."

Hugh turned suddenly and looked full at his companion, then he rose from the chopping-block outside Olive's cabin, where he had been sitting, and paced restlessly up and down.

"I wonder," he said, "if they would send us a good man

from Auckland, if I were to ride into the Bay and wire to the inspector?"

"Wait a day or two," Wilfrid suggested. "He could not leave Auckland anyway before Monday, and that gives three clear days. After all there may be a quite simple interpretation of the business."

The sun was setting. Jess, who had returned for the sixth time from the gully over the ridge, moved busily in and out the cabin, preparing the evening meal. Occasionally he came to a standstill and peered anxiously out through the waning daylight. All day long he had complained at intervals of the darkness, and it was evident that recent events had had an unhappy effect upon his disordered mind. The two men had ceased to discuss possibilities with him, and none but cheerful topics were alluded to in his presence.

After the meal was over Hugh and Wilfrid took their seats outside. A native, on his way to the settlement, had been intercepted, and by him Hugh had sent a message to Esther. Before the twilight failed Jess came out of the cabin and looked wildly around.

"Did you hear?" he asked in a whisper, his blue eyes shining with an unearthly light. "They are killing a child. I heard it scream once, and then it moaned—moaned."

"Lie down and get some sleep, Jess," Hugh entreated.

"Sleep!" said Jess, in tones of awe. "With that sound in my ears and the trees falling all night long! God gave us sleep that we might never know the darkness, but the voices of the night steal through and tell us what God sought to conceal." But he turned back into the cabin.

"Is he often like this?" Wilfrid asked thoughtfully.

"I have never known him so disordered. Bart used to say that Jess lived in the front room, and that behind it lay the chamber of horrors."

"Figuratively that is a correct and striking image. Sometimes the curtain of separation trembles and thins, and darkness floods the whole house. But who knows what the figure really represents?"

Throughout the day the atmosphere of the field had been dimmed with smoke, and away to the south-east a bank of brown cloud lay all day long on the hillocks. Now, as darkness gathered, that portion of the sky grew slowly roseate, and tongues of bright flame flickered momentarily in the heart of it. The fire, steadily advancing across the inflammable scrub-lands, had reached the standing bush, and the fate of twenty miles of magnificent forest was sealed.

The Stars came out dimly and close at hand through the hazy air as the two men sat smoking and talking. Occasionally a cricket shrilled out to his mates, who answered at various points down the slope, but there was no other sound.

"Tell me the truth, Hugh," said Wilfrid. "Do you think that man last night was Roller?"

"No, I do not."

"Then who was he? Let us make an attempt to get to the bottom of this."

"Do you remember my telling you of a man with a spade? The same man who subsequently invaded my tent when Esther was there? Well, I have a fancy that he and my visitor of last night are the same."

"What is it that has made him attack you time and time again? It can be no common cause that inspires a man to make continual and murderous assaults on another."

"I have not the least idea in the world."

"Maybe he is merely the instrument of someone else. The whole thing is an inexplicable mystery. For what are the usual causes of attempted murder? Let us thrash the thing out. First, there is hatred, but that, unless we are dealing with a maniac, necessitates a motive, and apparently you have given no man any. Then there is jealousy, but at the time the first attack was made upon you love had not entered into your experience of life, therefore we must dismiss that also. Thirdly—and lastly, as far as I can see—there is greed, the desire to possess something which your continued existence debars someone from obtaining. Can that be made to explain the facts? Hardly.

You stand in no man's light unless it be your brother's."

Wilfrid paused suddenly, and there was a long interval of silence.

"Is this an educated man?" he asked at length broodingly.

"Very much the other way" Hugh replied. "He is even exceptionally illiterate!"

"There must be a motive and a strong one. His motive is probably money, but since he can obtain nothing directly, there must be someone behind, whose instrument he is. Who is that someone?"

He rose, and dropping the butt of his cigar, stamped it out with his heel.

"That someone," he said, "is your uncle. Mind you, it is a long and wild shot, but just possibly it may have hit the mark."

CHAPTER XXIX

THE theory Wilfrid had formed led him early the following morning to the hotel, intent on testing its worth by the first means that occurred. Hugh, Jess, and half a dozen others, including the Earl of Baringbroke, who, with characteristic good nature, had returned from the Bay on hearing of Bart's disappearance, had meanwhile resumed the search with an energy and thoroughness that seemed to promise success.

Wilfrid pulled up in front of the verandah, his eye scanning the building with an interest it had never hitherto possessed for him. The innkeeper's name in white letters over the door drew more than a passing glance, and he was still thinking of it when he entered the bar.

He found two persons present in addition to Upmore. One was a freckled man with red skin and hair so light in colour as to appear almost white; the other was a big, ungainly fellow with a long neck surmounted by a small head. They were both more or less grimed from working in the track of the fire, and the face of the bigger man was swollen and discoloured as though from some severe pugilistic encounter. They gazed doubtfully and even suspiciously at Wilfrid as he entered, and the conversation he had heard in full swing while outside' came to an abrupt cessation.

"Good day, gentlemen," said Wilfrid, looking smilingly round the group. "A charming day."

The freckled man spat viciously on the floor, and was understood to make some reference to the weather of a depreciatory character.

Wilfrid, with unabated good humour, turned to Upmore, still keeping the corner of an eye on the men on the seat.

"I have looked in," he said easily, "in connection with the disappearance of this man they call 'Bart.' "

"What about him?" Upmore asked.

"It is feared he may have been caught in the fire some time during the night before last, and it is proposed to make an exhaustive search of the field."

"Well, you'll find the field outside," said the innkeeper, indicating the doorway.

"Blow me," said the big man, chuckling, "if that ain't a good un."

"In order that the search may be pursued with additional energy," Wilfrid continued, fixing a smiling gaze on the last speaker, "I am commissioned by his lordship the Earl of Baringbroke to offer a reward of a hundred pounds for such information as may lead to the discovery of the missing man or of his body."

There was a silence that appeared to be filled in with reflection. Wilfrid noticed a momentary gleam of cunning in the eyes of the freckled man, and he made a mental note of it for future use. Then he turned to Upmore.

"I have a notice here to the effect I have stated, which it is proposed, with your permission, to fasten up in a conspicuous position on the verandah."

"Don't trouble to ask my permission," Upmore replied. "Placard the house all round if you feel the least inclination to do so. I am merely here, it seems, for the convenience of the public."

"Thank you," said Wilfrid feelingly. "I felt sure of your co-operation. This is the notice. We are having a few copies struck off in type, and they will no doubt be here some time during the day or to-morrow."

"Read 'er. out, boss," said the big man. "Let's 'ear what she says."

Wilfrid spread the copy out on the counter, and read as follows: —

" '£100 REWARD.

" 'The above reward will be paid to the person or persons giving such information as will lead to the discovery, alive or dead, of Charles Horace Medway, *alias* Higgins, *alias* Bart, a gumdigger. Height 5 feet 9 inches. Age 36 years. Of fair complexion. Tawny moustache, otherwise clean-shaven. Grey eyes. Was dressed in a brown store suit, nearly new. White palm hat. Was last seen on the 16th instant, between 12 and 1 a.m., in the vicinity of the dead-house at the "Scarlet Man." Information to be given to Dr. Wilfrid Hamilton, of Parawai, or the undersigned, from whom, on fulfilment of the conditions, the reward may be obtained.

" 'BARINGBROKE,

" '(At the whare of Jessamine Olive).' "

"By gum, it ought to fetch 'im," said the big man admiringly, slapping his leg. " 'Tawny complexion, otherwise clean-shaven, *alias* Higgins' Durned if you 'aven't touched 'im off like a lookin'-glass."

Wilfrid looked pleased to the verge of fatuity. "Charge these gentlemen's, glasses, Mr. Upmore," he said. "We'll drink to the speedy claiming of the reward."

The toast was duly honoured, Wilfrid contenting himself with-a glass of ginger ale.

By the aid of some postage-stamp margins he secured the notice to the wall outside, and bidding the company a cheerful good-day, mounted his horse and rode off.

His visit had resulted in the acquisition of two fresh pieces of information: one was the innkeeper's christian name, and it formed the first link in the chain of circumstantial evidence which was soon to enmesh Upmore in its folds; the other was the certainty that Bart's whereabouts was known to one, if not the whole, of his recent companions, and that that one had it in his power to secure the reward if he chose. This, however, threw a dread complexion on the man's disappearance. If his fate were known and not instantly revealed, it must be because his continued absence was due to no accident, but to some cause it was necessary to conceal. It became, then, unlikely that the search now being prosecuted would be fruitful of results. Far more stringent measures would need to be taken to unearth the mystery.

On his way back to the cabin he encountered Hugh, and the sight of the young man determined him on a course he had been debating *en route*.

"We can do no more here," he said. "Baringbroke has the thing in hand, and we may safely leave it to him. Let us ride into Parawai and ring up the police."

"Very well," said Hugh, nothing loath; and they turned their horses on to the road.

A short distance past the inn they came suddenly on two men seated among the bushes on the roadside, apparently in deep conversation.

The men started on hearing the approach of the horses, and one of them threw himself back as though to escape notice. Wilfrid recognised his recent companions and nodded genially to the sandy man as he cantered by. A curve of the road took them almost immediately out of sight.

Hugh, looking somewhat excited, pulled in his horse. "That is the man," he said, "the one who leaned back. I could swear to him anywhere."

"You will have the opportunity of doing so before long," Wilfrid replied. "Where are you going?"

"Back," said Hugh.

Wilfrid wheeled his horse across the road.

"Stand aside, Wilf," said Hugh, his eyes smouldering.

"Don't be a young fool," was the response.

Wilfrid, however, was no match for a man who had spent the greater portion of his life on a stock farm, and in a few moments he found himself galloping in Hugh's wake round the bend. He was greatly relieved a moment later to discover that the men, probably anticipating what had actually occurred, had removed from where they were sitting and were now no longer in sight.

"Come, Hugh," he said impatiently, as the young man, after galloping in and out among the bushes, still showed signs of continuing the search; and Hugh, with a last fierce glare across the field, turned to follow him.

"You are a headstrong young beggar," Wilfrid remarked amiably, "and it is not the first time I have told you so."

"H'm!"" said Hugh.

"Is that all you have to say for yourself? If your father had thrashed you when you were a boy you might have grown into a decent, respectable citizen instead of a—a—"

"Try again," Hugh said, with a slow smile, his anger beginning to evaporate.

"Mule," Wilfrid concluded as he set his horse in motion.

An hour's canter brought them in sight of the township, and they dismounted at Doctor Hamilton's gate.

The doctor was in the garden, and came forward to greet them with considerable friendliness. He had formed a strong liking for Hugh, which had been only momentarily interrupted by the affair of the broken engagement, and he now allowed his liking to display itself.

"I am glad to see you, my boy," he said. "We were expecting you yesterday, but Esther tells me you were detained looking for someone who is supposed to have met with an accident. I hope you succeeded in finding him."

"No, sir; I am sorry to say he is not found," Hugh replied.

"Dear, dear! The man they call Bart, I am told. Well, let us hope it is nothing serious. The boy will take your horse round to the stables. Esther is in the house somewhere. You know your way about."

"Thank you, sir," said Hugh, colouring and looking longingly at the open doorway of the house.

The doctor smiled and then sighed. "You will excuse me if I get back to my paper," he said. "I was in the middle of a very interesting case when you arrived." And he returned to his seat on the lawn.

The "very interesting case" must have been one attended by unusual difficulties, for for half an hour the doctor did not turn a page, and the downcast eyes which regarded the sheet fixedly at one point were full of sad reverie.

Was he, perhaps, thinking of his young wife, dead for nearly twenty years, or of the daughter who had sprung up into womanhood unperceived? Of the old, old story unfolding itself afresh and imagining itself to be original; or of the story that opened so brightly and finished so abruptly so many weary years ago?

He was startled to feel an arm round his neck and a kiss lightly implanted on his brow. Esther, clothed in a new and dazzling beauty, knelt beside him.

"Look, father," she said, stretching a hand out to Hugh, "this is your son, your eldest, and youngest, and only son. How do you like him?"

"Very well," said the doctor, regarding the pair with kindly eyes.

"I have asked your daughter to marry me, Doctor Hamilton," Hugh said, "and she has promised. I love her sir, and will do my utmost to make her happy. I have as much money as we shall need—but that is nothing. They say I am a bit headstrong in my temper, but I will try to cure that. I will try to make her a good husband."

"Wasn't that nicely said?" Esther asked, giving her father's neck a little squeeze and looking with a heightened colour on the manful form of her lover as he blurted out his aspirations.

"Very, indeed," the doctor replied, stretching a hand out to the' young man. "So it is a love match, my children?"

"Yes, sir," said Hugh. "I loved her from the first moment I saw her, and she loved me."

"Well I never!" exclaimed Esther, opening her eyes.

"You know you did," Hugh said, turning a serious gaze upon her. "You told me so not five minutes ago."

Esther gasped and then broke into a merry laugh.

"Oh, you simpleton!" she said; "I will never tell you anything like that again." But her looks belied her.

"I know of no better foundation for marriage," said her father gently, "than love. Though men of learning and intellect have again and again set their seal to the doctrine that there are other matters of greater and more enduring importance, yet love has this advantage over them all, that it is the only foundation justified and sanctioned by nature. If I look into my own life," he continued, softly stroking Esther's hand and gazing with unseeing eyes across the lawn, "I could not without blasphemy breathe one word against a marriage founded on love alone. May your happiness be as great as mine was.

May it be—as mine was not—enduring."

Dinner was over half an hour ago. The darkness of a moonless night had settled on the little township, relieved only by the scattered lights of the settlement and the flashing of the constellations overhead. Away back in the native village a huge fire made a brilliant opening in the darkness, and sounds of chanting and shouting betokened the progress of some native celebration. From the open casements of the dining-room a band of light fell across the lawn, but all the remainder of the garden was bathed in a restoring blackness.

The three young people were perambulating the lawn, crossing the band of light at intervals and again plunging into the darkness. Hugh and Esther preserved a happy silence, but Wilfrid had struck a vein of talkativeness and was exploiting it generously in their behalf.

"Tell me when I bore you," he said, with a thoughtfulness that did him credit. "If you would sooner do a little spooning, say the word."

"Turi, turi!" said Esther.

"Which means 'shut up,' I believe. Well, to resume. I went into the hotel, and there, seated on the bench, were two of the ugliest customers my eyes had ever lighted upon. They did not seem pleased to see me, strange to say, and the little sandy one appeared to take the utmost offence at my boots, which he continued silently to compare with his own during the whole time I remained there. The man with the swanlike neck—"

"And a small head?" Esther asked.

"Yes, I see you identify him."

"Oh!" exclaimed Esther, "and the other one will be Sandy George. I remember he told me something horrible about Sandy George."

"Good," said Wilfrid. "Sandy George exactly fits him, and I am glad to have that little extra bit of information. Well, I could see by their faces that they knew what I was after before I opened my lips."

There was a slight motion in the eleagnus hedge of the

garden and Esther drew back with a shiver.

"Are you cold?" Hugh asked, with instant anxiety.

"No," she said, "but talking of that man always makes my blood run cold."

"Then we won't talk of him," said Wilfrid. "There are a thousand subjects for a night like this. Look at the Milky Way, trembling like an arch of white fire."

They crossed the band of light and were again immersed in the shadow.

"What is going on back there?" Wilfrid asked, indicating the Maori settlement, as a long, weird wailing filled the air.

"A bone-scraping," Esther replied. "They have been bringing some of their ancestors up from the Kaipara and are preparing the bones for burial."

"Pah!" said Wilfrid. "How the savage imagination delights in the horrible! After all, the education we give them only amounts to a starch-glaze. They lose it in contact with their kind, and constant intercourse with the white man is needed to preserve it."

"I am not sure you are right," Esther remarked. "The bone-scraping is or was in a sense a religious ceremony. It bore some relation to the after life. But nowadays the young natives look upon this and similar ceremonies merely as occasions for gorging themselves with meat and kumeras, and that, I suppose, is an effect of education."

"Why are you so silent, Hugh?" Wilfrid asked suddenly. "Are you at peace with all men."

"Yes," Hugh replied slowly; "I am content now to cry quits."

"What about the folks at home?"

"I have written to them; they will have my letter by this."

Wilfrid drew a breath of relief, and they passed again out of the shadow into the light.

The wailing in the native settlement had ceased, and in that direction all was quiet. Only the intermittent shrilling of the crickets disturbed the silence.

The lamp in the little office across the road had been turned out several minutes since, and the road outside the garden was buried in darkness.

Suddenly, without warning, breaking ruthlessly on the serene stillness and beauty of the night, came the report of a pistol close at hand. Hugh started violently, and Esther shrank back, leaving the two men for an instant close together.

"Get her inside," said Hugh, in a strange, uncertain voice.

Wilfrid, his heart frozen with the terror of what he suspected, turned sharply to his cousin. "Run in, Esther," he commanded.

For an instant it seemed as though she would obey him, but a moment later her arms were round the swaying form of her lover. "Oh, my dear one!" was all she said.

His eyes smiled on her as he sank to his knees, and then to the ground, dragging her down with him.

"Quick, Esther," said Wilfrid, in ringing tones. "Rouse the house and bring lights. Keep calm; everything may depend upon you."

She rose instantly, and without a word fled into the house.

CHAPTER XXX

THE clock in the dining-room was striking three in the morning as Wilfrid pulled the gate to behind him and crossed the road to the store.

In the office the light, which had been extinguished earlier in the night, was again burning brightly as it had burned for many hours, while its owner, a prey to terror and remorse, paced restlessly up and down.

Wilfrid, his face pale and a look of battle in his eyes and nostrils, closed the door behind him, and stood looking in silence at the storekeeper.

"Tell me how he is," Roller said, throwing himself into a seat.

"There is a chance," Wilfrid replied slowly.

"Thank God for that!" Roller exclaimed, burying his face in his hands.

Wilfrid sat down, staring moodily at the floor. "Have you sent the messages?" he asked.

"Yes. Reynolds is on his way here now."

"Understand that though I have yielded to your entreaties and come to see you, I do not abate one jot of the vengeance I intend to take for this. If there is a particle of guilt attaching to you, better for you that you should hold your tongue, for there is no mercy in my heart."

"I must tell you," Roller replied, starting to his feet, "let the consequences be what they may. I was drunk or mad or both. When he threw me into the dead-house I was like one insane, and that fiend Upmore came to me, taunting me and offering suggestions. I took them. I met Brice on the hill and we went together to Clifford's tent, but he was not there. Then we went to Olive's whare and tried to make him come outside, but he kept the door bolted. I swear I meant him no greater injury than he had done to me. I wanted to get level with him. But one of them prodded Brice with a spear while he was on the roof, and after that he was beyond my control. He broke down the door and fired at them. I swear I did not know he

243

was armed till that moment. After, when he came away, I quarrelled with him, and when I had found my horse I left. I did not go into the 'Scarlet Man' again. I came straight home, and I have never left the house since. God is my witness that I have had no hand in this."

Wilfrid fixed him with a gaze that sought to read his soul, but Roller stood it unflinchingly. "If you have concealed anything from me," Wilfrid said slowly, "you have wasted your breath. If that is the truth and the whole truth, then you have nothing to fear. When Reynolds arrives, as he should do by daylight, you will sign warrants for the arrest of Brice and Upmore, and you will then accompany us and help to execute them." He rose and took a pace or two up and down the office. "What of this man Bart?" he asked, coming to a standstill.

"I know nothing of him either, beyond the fact that he was in the dead-house with me. He came in with me, and when the door closed he went into a corner and lay down. He was still there when I left, lying in a drunken sleep."

"Did Upmore turn the key on him?"

Roller reflected awhile.

"I would not be sure," he said, "but I believe he merely pulled the door to, as though he intended to go back."

Wilfrid stood a moment in thought, then turned to go.

"I advise you to get some sleep," he said. "We shall probably be on the road in less than two hours."

When Reynolds came a difficulty arose, and it required all Wilfrid's masterful nature to overcome it. The sergeant was accompanied by two constables, one a full-blooded native. They turned through the slip-rail into the yard behind the store, and Reynolds dismounted and followed Wilfrid into the office. The latter gave an account of the event of the night, and also of what had preceded it on the field; then he stated what he proposed to do.

"Arrest Upmore and Brice, eh?" Reynolds said. "What's the ground?"

"You know the legal terminology better than I do. Attempting murder and inciting to commit murder. It may be the capital crime itself before the day is out."

"Where is your evidence?"

"I have already told you the evidence. Brice has made repeated attacks upon him, dating from three or four months ago right up till last night."

"Who have you got to swear that? Brice attacked him with a spade, but unless and until this man recovers you are unable to produce evidence to prove it. You say that he broke into Olive's cabin and fired at him. Will Olive swear to that?"

"Well, at all events, Miss Hamilton will swear that he is the man who entered Clifford's tent armed with an axe."

"That might be something," Reynolds admitted doubtfully, "but not much. Not sufficient, in the absence of anything else, to send him for trial."

"Good heavens, man!" said Wilfrid impatiently, "and can't we get something else? It is as certain as the sun has risen that Brice is the man. It is in order that we may have leisure to look round for evidence undisturbed that I am urging the arrest of these men immediately."

"Don't get impatient," said Reynolds good-ternperedly. "When it comes to actual business you will find nothing to complain of about me, but I want to see where I am going before I start. Well, now—supposing I stretch a point and arrest this man —what about Upmore? It would be ridiculous to think about arresting him. The evidence against Brice is as poor as it can be, but it amounts to conviction compared with what you've got against Upmore."

"If we could get them under lock and key," Wilfrid said, "heaven knows what might not turn up."

"Just so, but when you arrest a man you have got to produce evidence that you had good reason for doing so."

"Could we not get an adjournment? Surely in a serious case like this the police are not bound to show their hand right away?"

"I doubt it," said Reynolds. "And then, what kind of fix are we in if we get the adjournment and it does us no good?"

"Look here, sergeant," said Wilfrid, "you are not taking the right view of this. This is likely to be a *cause celébre*, and it may mean the making of you."

"Or the unmaking, for that matter," interpolated Reynolds; but there was a reflective twinkle in his eye which showed that the shot had gone home.

"A man has got to speculate at times," Wilfrid went on, watching the effect of his words, "if he wishes to distinguish himself, and here it seems to me is the chance of your lifetime. If the theory I have suggested to you prove false, what difference will it make? Probably a wigging from headquarters, and all is well again. If, on the other hand, it prove correct—and I would stake ten years of my life on it—then it means fame, promotion, all kinds of good things. I give you the theory as a free gift, and my mouth is sealed for ever as to where you got it. Surely no man ever had such a chance before and hesitated so long before he took it."

"By gad! I'll do it!" said Reynolds, with sudden resolution. "I look to you to stand by me, Doctor Hamilton, because the risk I am taking is greater than you seem to suppose."

"Done," said Wilfrid. "I will provide you with a case against both of them that will send them to gaol for life, and perhaps to the gallows."

Accordingly the warrants were drawn out and signed, and the five men set off. On the outskirts of the township they came on a group of natives, mounted on small, weedy horses, who were evidently on the lookout for them. The news of the attempted murder had already travelled a considerable distance round the settlement and across the field, for the Maoris, like all aboriginals, are indefatigable purveyors of news. The sight of the police riding into the township at dawn suggested that something sensational was likely to occur, and after that to find and saddle their horses was merely the work of a few minutes.

On the road the natives surrounded the cavalcade like a cloud of mosquitoes, riding now in front, now behind, now to either side, where they guided their horses through the scrub with an extraordinary quickness and dexterity. All the while they kept up a sharp fire of jocular conversation, calling and signalling to one another as though their business were that of scouts for the main party of Europeans in the centre. In this manner the party reached and surrounded the inn, and Reynolds and the two constables dismounted at the door.

Upmore, hearing the approach of the horsemen, came out into the passage, and the sergeant signalled him on to the verandah.

"Cuthbert Upmore," he said formally, "I arrest you on the charge of inciting and abetting one Robert Brice to commit murder, and I warn you that anything you say may be used in evidence against you." At the same moment he produced a slip of blue paper from his pocket and handed it to the innkeeper.

Upmore took the warrant, looking round the watchful group like one in an evil dream. "The charge is absurd," he said at length; "I haven't the faintest idea what it means."

Reynolds signalled to the Maori constable, who crossed over to Upmore's side.

"The next thing is to search the house," said the sergeant, making his way into the bar and beginning the search by breaking open a bottle of beer; "and I suppose afterwards we had better close the place up. All this is devilish irregular, you know," he added in a whisper to Wilfrid. "You needn't smile; I'm not alluding to the beer. But we're in it now, and shall have to keep on."

The key of the dead-house was found on Upmore's person, and to this place the first visit was paid.

"Nothing here apparently," said the sergeant, looking round,

Wilfrid was holding a candle near the floor and gazing curiously at a dark circular stain on the boards in one corner. "Have you a knife, sergeant?" he asked.

Reynolds produced the required article and Wilfrid proceeded to sink a small square in the boards and split out the included portion: this he divided into two halves. "Slip them into an envelope," he said, "and return one piece to me when I ask you for it."

The sergeant turned the bits of wood over with a puzzled expression, but finally he stored them away in his pocket-book.

The rest of the house produced nothing which appeared to connect Upmore with the present charge, but there was a small bundle of yellow papers, which Wilfrid, after a hurried glance through, handed to Reynolds, with injunctions to preserve carefully. "There is your promotion, sergeant," he said, his eyes glittering.

"Good," said the sergeant. "Now to capture the other man."

Upmore was left in charge of the native constable, while the rest of the party set off in search of Brice.

The whare occupied by this man in partnership with Sandy George lay about a mile and a half to the southward of the inn, and was gained after crossing a tract of rough and difficult country. Reynolds drew up his forces on a hill overlooking the hollow in which the shanty was situated.

"We had better take it from all sides," he said. "He may have gone, but, on the other hand, if he expected us at all, he would probably not expect us quite so soon."

"Don't forget that he may be armed," Wilfrid cautioned him.

"I hope he is," replied Reynolds; "but if he has any sense at all he will have got rid of his weapon long ago."

Reynolds made his arrangements, and when the others had started he and Wilfrid allowed their horses to scramble down the hillside. Reaching the bottom, they dismounted and proceeded on foot to the front of the shanty. Sandy George was discernible, moving in and out, as they approached, but he did not notice them until they were upon him. "Morning, Sandy," said Reynolds, looking over the little man's shoulder into the whare.

"Mornin'," said Sandy sulkily.

"I see your mate's inside," Reynolds continued. "Sleeping a bit late, isn't he?"

"Oh, it's him you're after," said Sandy, looking relieved. "Yus; he's got a sorter cold on him—bin coughin' all night."

Reynolds grinned and pushed past into the shanty, followed by Wilfrid. Brice was on his back, snoring loudly, but he started up and made a grab towards the head of the bed as the sergeant touched him with his foot. Both his visitors had their eyes fixed on the hand groping under the pillow, but it came forth in a moment, empty.

"What's up, mates?" Brice asked, looking from one to the other.

"I want you," replied Reynolds, producing the warrant and reading the charge, concluding with the usual warning.

"You've come to the wrong shop this time, Reynolds," said Brice, getting slowly to his feet. "Somebody's been kiddin' you."

The sergeant watched his opportunity, and with a deft, quick movement betokening long practice clapped the handcuffs on his wrists.

"I'm a bit short-handed, Bob," he explained apologetically, "or I wouldn't do it."

For a moment the ruffian looked nasty, then he appeared to submit.

"Blow me," he said, ""if you ain't that smart, you are in danger o' cuttin' yourself. Get along outside before I knock the brains outer some o' yer."

Reynolds laughed as though at some monstrously good joke, at the same time pushing his prisoner boisterously out into the open air. On the way he found time to whisper a caution to Wilfrid to be on his guard.

The others, however, had now come up, and Brice, recognising the futility of trying to escape, sat down on the ground.

"There's the man that ought to 'ave the darbies on," he said, suddenly catching sight of Roller, "not me. Wait till I get up before the beak and we'll see who's who."

"I'm afraid we'll have to take a look round, Sandy," said Reynolds. "just step inside and tell us what belongs to you, and—we'll look at those first."

The search of the whare, however, proved fruitless, neither

pistol, nor cartridges, nor anything of an incriminating nature being forthcoming. Wilfrid soon desisted from the search, and when Reynolds went to look for him a few minutes later, he found him a little distance away, busy chopping at a standing tree with a tomahawk he had borrowed from the wood pile.

"What's up now?" Reynolds asked, with expectation, for in their acquaintanceship of a few hours he had already come to regard the young doctor's actions with considerable respect,

Wilfrid handed him a couple of partially flattened bullets. "I noticed this tree," he explained, "because it seems to be the only one about, and it struck me it might be worth while looking at it. When a man gets a pistol and a few cartridges the next thing he wants is something to aim at, and here it is quite conveniently handy."

"You ought to be a detective," said the sergeant, with enthusiasm.

"Thanks," said Wilfrid. "I suppose you mean to be polite. Well, that seems to be all there are. Add them to the other little lots. They'll help in the promotion."

A quarter of an hour later Brice was mounted on a horse borrowed from one of the natives and escorted back to the inn. He whistled softly when Upmore was brought out and placed beside him between the two constables.

Reynolds, after a short interview with Mrs. Brandon, decided to leave the house open, but he locked and sealed up the door of the dead-house. Then he rejoined Wilfrid.

The litter took him aside and shook him warmly by the hand. "You are a credit to the force, sergeant," he said. "I imagine for a case of this gravity you have put up a record for the colony."

Reynolds laughed as he returned the other's grip. "I've enough now for an adjournment," he admitted; "but for heaven's sake keep going, or we shall end in the mud. What about the samples from the dead-house?"

"Yes, you can give me one of the pieces now. Of course, as soon as you have got your men under lock and key you will come back here. Nothing must be left undone to discover this man Bart, and that reminds me, I will give you the note he sent to Clifford."

"What is your theory about him?" the sergeant asked, stowing the paper away in his pocket-book.

"Murder," said Wilfrid, lowering his voice. "Evidently he had in some way become aware of a plot against Clifford, and probably while endeavouring to frustrate it or learn more he met his death."

"Then the stain in there—"

Wilfrid nodded. "That is what I suspect," he said. "Well, good-bye, sergeant. You can easily communicate with me on the wire if it is necessary, and in any case I shall expect to see you back here to-morrow."

A few minutes later the party had separated; Roller and Wilfrid galloping back to the settlement, while Reynolds with his two prisoners, and still surrounded by his crowd of natives, headed for the Bay.

CHAPTER XXXI

THE weary hours of waiting dragged slowly by while in the darkened room Youth wrestled strenuously with Death. All that the science of man could accomplish had been performed by the young doctor the night before. It had been one of those conflicts of daily, nay, hourly, occurrence of which, save when we are perforce witnesses of them, we hear nothing.

Wilfrid had had imperatively presented to him a task from which Doctor Hamilton had drawn back, declaring it to be impossible; a task, indeed, which would have tried the skill and endurance of the most gifted surgeon, and by force of will and keenness of intellect he had borne it through. If the young man's constitution were, as it appeared, flawless, then he would survive and be none the worse for the injury. That was the sole dependence. In the meantime there was nothing to do but wait.

Wilfrid was lying on the sofa in his room, trying to recover from the nervous strain of the last twelve hours, when Esther opened the door. He started up at once and looked expectantly towards her.

"I came to see if you would like something to eat, dear?" she asked. Her face was pale and her eyes large and brilliant, but her manner was tender and collected as of old.

"Come and sit down," he said cheerfully, making room for her beside him. "I have done great deeds to-day and praise is sweet to me."

"There are no words good enough for you," she said softly. "Father has told me, and though I don't understand, I believe." She took his hand and raised it impulsively to her lips.

"I wasn't thinking of that," he said, flushing. "I was thinking of vengeance. Reynolds has got them both, and if there is any justice in the country they will never be free men again."

She drew a quick breath and her eyes sparkled.

"Does that do you good?" he asked.

She sat silent a moment, looking straight before her; then turned to him, her face full of entreaty.

"Tell me the truth, Wilfrid," she begged. "Let me know the worst."

"Soon," he replied, "I will tell you, but now I cannot, because I do not know. I think he will recover, but it may be it is willed otherwise. You are a brave girl, and your conduct throughout the night has been beyond praise. You have asked me for the worst and I will tell it you. If his case had been merely described to me, I should have said as your father said, that it was hopeless."

She drew a quivering breath, and his eyes regarded her with an affectionate scrutiny.

"But," he continued, "Hugh has a clean record and his constitution is magnificent; with such men the word 'hopeless' hardly exists." He rose to his feet and paced the room, moved beyond himself by the desire to say something that would do her good. "Belief," he said at last, "is treacherous ground, but I do believe, nay, at this moment I am certain that all is well."

In the morning Hugh's fate still hung in the balance, but his condition was such that even Doctor Hamilton began to wonder whether the "impossible" might not after all prove amenable to the latest surgical science, as exemplified by a man fresh from a great London hospital.

Shortly after eight o'clock Wilson ran across from the store with a wire for Wilfrid. The sender was Reynolds, who had great news to communicate.

"Constable Howell reports" (ran the message) "Olive found missing man 11.30 last night. Apparently dying from injuries to head. Leaving here instanter. Probably bring him through this afternoon. Prisoners safe.—REYNOLDS."

Wilfrid stood a moment, then went across to the store to interview Roller.

"Can you find room for him?" he asked, after the storekeeper had read the message.

"Certainly," Roller replied. "I'll see to it at once."

It was in the dusk of evening, when the first faint stars were becoming visible, that four horsemen, riding in a square, carried the unconscious form of Bart over the boundary line between the gumfield and the fertile lands and brought him at last into the settlement. It needed no experienced eye to recognise that his case was hopeless. Whatever might have been the result had his injuries been attended to at first, the long hours through which he had lain concealed in a dry water-hole covered with brushwood had carried him beyond the reach of human help. The most that was possible was to restore him to a brief consciousness, and this Wilfrid, after a discussion with Doctor Hamilton, decided to attempt.

The delicate operation of trepanning was successfully performed, and for a while the patient rallied, so that Jess, who had constituted himself his nurse, became inspired with the hope that Bart would pull through.

"He has a very strong vitality," he said pleadingly to Wilfrid.

The latter shook his head. "Don't deceive yourself, Jess," he said; "it is all up. Our duty is to get from him a deposition of what occurred in order that the guilty may be punished. I shall go and lie down for an hour in the next room, and you must call me as soon as he attains complete consciousness. After that the end will be near."

Reynolds, on hearing from the constable the condition in which Bart had been found, had considered it his duty to communicate the facts to the Stipendiary Magistrate, and that gentleman had accordingly accompanied the sergeant on his journey to Parawai, and was now quartered in. Doctor Hamilton's house.

About three o'clock in the morning Bart opened his eyes and looked at Jess. He did not speak, but there was consciousness and reflection in his gaze. Jess slipped out and communicated the news to Wilfrid, who at once crossed the road for the magistrate.

Meanwhile Jess had again taken his seat at the bedside of the man whom for many years he had loved and befriended as a son.

"So the road parts here, Jess," Bart said quietly.

"For a little while, perhaps," Jess replied.

A sound of approaching footsteps became audible.

"They want you to tell them what happened to you," Jess said, as the magistrate and Wilfrid entered the room.

A small table with writing material was brought to the bedside, and at this the magistrate took his seat. Then he turned to Wilfrid.

"Does he know?" he asked.

"Tell him, Jess," said Wilfrid.

Jess turned his face to the bed. "Boy," he said tenderly, "you are going to die."

"Yes," said Bart.

"Tell the magistrate the truth, and all the truth."

"What does it matter?" said Bart wearily. "Let it rest."

"We cannot save you," said Jess entreatingly. "Let us avenge you."

"Vengeance!" replied Bart. "Give me vengeance for life, not death."

"Tell him about Hugh," Wilfrid said softly.

"Listen, Bart," said Jess; "you were fond of the young un. You tried to save him. Take vengeance for him if not for yourself."

"Is he dead?"

"Not dead, but near it. They shot him down at his sweetheart's side, and he is at death's door now."

"Well," said Bart, and was silent.

The magistrate dipped his pen in the ink and looked expectantly towards the bed.

"It was some days ago," came the low, weak voice at length. "I was sleeping at the inn. I came downstairs in my stockinged feet for a drink. I heard talking in the dining-room and stood at the bottom of the stairs, waiting. I heard the voices of Upmore and Brice. They were quarrelling. I judged that Brice had been asking for money, and that Upmore was reproaching him for not earning it. I understood that Brice was to make away with Clifford. I did not hear Clifford's name, but I guessed he was the man from what was said. Afterwards I attempted to warn him. On the night of the social, when Roller was thrown into the dead-house, I got pushed in. I was dizzy from a fall I had sustained and went and lay down. While I was there I heard Upmore come to the door, and something induced me to feign sleep. I heard Upmore persuade Roller to attack Clifford. He was to join Brice outside and they were to go to Clifford's tent. When they went they left the door open, and after a while I got up and went out into the passage. . . . I was still dizzy—I had been drinking a good deal—and I had to put my hand on the wall to steady myself. I was still in the passage when Upmore came back and found me. He held the light up to my face, and I suppose he guessed that I had heard him. I tried to get away, but he dragged me with him into the dead-house and locked the door. I lost command of my temper at that and began to call him names. I told him what I had overheard between him and Brice. He grew very white and sat on the bench gnawing his nails and watching me. Presently he got up and went out. . . . He came back in half an hour. He had something in his hand and I did not like the look of . . . I was still dizzy and had been sitting on the ground. I tried to get up, but he was too quick for me. . . . He struck me."

There was a long pause. The magistrate took down the last word and carefully blotted the sheet.

"Is that all you remember?" he asked.

"I remember hearing Brice's voice — it seemed a long while after, but all is confused. . . I remember lying in the open air and watching the Southern Cross swing backwards and forwards. . . . But maybe it was all a dream. . . . No, that is all."

"Now," said the magistrate, "I am about to read the statement you have made, knowing yourself to be on the point of death. If there are any errors, or if there is anything you desire to alter or add, tell me, and after, if you are able, you will sign the document."

The deposition was read and approved, and the hand of the dying man was guided to the sheet.

"What shall I sign?" he asked.

"Your name," said the magistrate.

There was a long pause, then the hand seemed suddenly inspired with an unnatural vigour and moved rapidly across the paper.

The magistrate took up the sheet and read—"Charles Horace Medway." "And that is your true name?" he said.

"Yes," said Bart, "I have never forfeited the right to sign my name, and no man in the world has a right to it but I."

The magistrate looked at him with a speculative interest "Is there any relation you would like to communicate with?" he asked.

"Relation!" exclaimed Bart harshly. "In the Land of the Lost a man has no relatives, and that is the only advantage it possesses."

"Ah, Bart," said Jess pitiably, "the darkness is closing in upon you now. Send them a word of forgiveness before you go."

"No," said Bart. "No death-bed relentings for me. I die game. God bless you, Jess—if there is any meaning in the words—but this you don't understand. Give me a drink, and let me die as I have lived."

He lay back white and exhausted from the passion of memory that stirred him. Wilfrid administered a stimulant that brought a momentary colour to his cheeks, but the dews of death were already beginning to gather on his brow.

"Bart," said Jess brokenly, "say good-bye to me before you go."

"Good-bye, Jess," he murmured, with closed eyes. "There may be vengeance for me, but who will take vengeance for you, old friend? But the world is only a little while, and the universe itself—isn't a great matter, and sleep's—best of all."

There was a long silence.

"Jess," clearly, "take care of my rose tree. You know."

The rest was the rambling of unconsciousness. In the last minutes his mind wandered back to his youth and away to his ancestral home. Again he was a boy at college, bird-nesting in the glorious English lanes, rejoicing, boy-like, in his youth and strength. Then a note of sadness seemed to creep in. His voice became alternately rebellious and wistful. Just at the last he raised himself and said in tones of indescribable weariness, "Yes, mother, I will try."

And there was the story of his life.

CHAPTER XXXII

IT is the morning of a day two months later.

The first heavy rains of the approaching wet season have fallen, and the atmosphere, long charged with the dust of the roads and the smoke of burning bush, is restored to its original freshness and purity. In the garden of the doctor's house the chrysanthemums and cactus dahlias are in full flower, and there is a last magnificent burst from the mignonette.

On the verandah, wrapped in a huge coat, sits Hugh. The shadow of the Valley of Death has not quite left his countenance, but his eyes are bright, for he is looking on the face of his sweetheart.

"All your arguments," he is saying, "are nothing. I remember that he lost you, and conceiving what that might mean there is not an ounce of bitterness against him in my heart. They tell me he has acted well since. It is certain he must have suffered out of proportion to his offence; so, if it is any satisfaction to him to know it, you may tell him when you write that my hand is ready for him."

"I knew you would say that, dear," she says. "I cannot forget that whatever justification I had afterwards I did wrong him at the first."

"Stuff and nonsense," says Hugh.

His illness has made him a privileged being, and his rudeness goes unreproved.

A figure comes along past the hedge, and opening the gate, enters the garden.

"It is Jess," says Esther, and she calls him by his name.

"Poor old Jess!" says Hugh; "Bart used to say he was the only perfect Christian on the field and to add that he was mad."

Jess greets them and takes his seat on the step of the open doorway.

"The stone is up," he says musingly, "and I have planted the rose bush on his grave. I thought I would wait till the rains came, and it ought to grow now."

"I am sure it will," says Esther, and Hugh also murmurs a

belief in the recuperative powers of the transplanted tree.

"What is on the stone?" he asks.

"Just 'Bart'," says Jess, "and the date. He told me years ago to write no more, and I obeyed him. He thought he was dying then, but he pulled through. He was not a man to die easily. Perhaps the desire was too strong."

"Why should he wish to die?" Esther asks, her face full of tender feeling.

Jess shakes his head.

"That is part of the story of his life," he replies. "I should have liked to put a text on the stone, but he was not great on scripture and I have let it be."

Jess sits musing awhile, then turns to Hugh.

"What news from Auckland?" he asks.

"Brice has a life sentence, and we are expecting a wire from Wilfrid any moment as to Upmore—or Hilton I suppose we ought to call him. His case was to conclude last night."

"He was an inhuman man," says Jess. "There are tales all over the field of what the police discovered under the floor of the dead-house. Bank-notes and jewellery, and some say— bones."

"Yes," says Esther, with a shiver, "and to think that all these years he has been free in our midst! Oh, Hugh," she breaks off suddenly, "what shall I say about the brooch and ring? The police will give them up presently and Mr. Roller has begged me not to return them to him. He thinks if I send them back it will mean that there is no real forgiveness."

Hugh, remembering the scene between himself and Roller, frowns thoughtfully; then, drawing a hand across his brow, he seems to wipe away the last trace of bitterness.

"Then keep them," he says.

Presently through the gateway comes Doctor Hamilton, bearing the expected telegram. His face has lost much of the irritable look that once characterised it, but the habitual sadness is accentuated. He is looking forward to the day, now near at hand, when the daughter he has learned to prize too late shall be no longer with him.

"Sentenced to death," he says, handing the paper to Hugh.

There is a long silence.

"Well," says Hugh at length, "it's an awful end, and it is not nice to think that he is a blood relation, but if ever a man deserved his fate it is he."

Jess rises from the shadow in the doorway and with a little shiver seats himself afresh in the full sunlight of the verandah step.

"I do not like the new man," he says, "but he cannot be worse than Upmore. Of all the men I have met, of all who have crossed the field during twenty years, there has never been another like him. He was the evil spirit of the field."

"And he dispensed spirits worse than himself," says Hugh.

"And so it will go on," says the doctor, "till the last pound of gum is taken from the land and the singular communion is dissolved for ever."

"And what then?" Esther asks.

"Then," says Hugh, "it will be a desert. The traveller in those days will see the country choked with impenetrable scrub, with here and there in the midst of it the abandoned houses rotting into the ground."

"No," says Jess, rising to his feet, "there is a better day coming. Every year the settler is extending his landmarks and rooting himself like the trees he displaces. As the gum goes he advances."

He turns his face beyond the settlement—a look of inspiration in his eyes. "I see the apple orchards and the vineyards of the future," he says. "The men we know—the reckless, the hopeless, the unhappy—are gone to their appointed places. I hear the voices of the children at play among the thick-leafed trees. I hear the mothers singing at their work. Over all the land rests the peace of God."

Night has settled on the field.

In more than five thousand shanties the diggers are at work scraping their gum. Over three-quarters of a million acres the scratch of the gum-knife is heard mingling with the shrill cry

261

of the crickets.

In the "Scarlet Man" a little crowd is assembled, for the news of Upmore's conviction has reached his quondam home, and there are many eager to discuss the particulars. "The Parson" has drunk himself white in the face in commemoration of the event, and "Six-and-eight," who seems to attend him everywhere like a shadow, is taunting him with the fact that he is still sober.

"It has cost your reverence eight shillings already," he is saying, "and you ought never to have attempted it. You know very well that you have never got drunk yet under nineteen-and-six, and all you have is thirteen shillings."

"Six-and-eightpence is your charge for a professional opinion, I believe," says "the Parson." "May you burn in hell till I pay you!"

"Nineteen-and-six is the lowest price for oblivion," says "Six-and-eight," wrinkling his cruel little face, "and you haven't the money. Fancy not having the money! How tragic! Let us pray."

The new publican is apparently only new in the sense that he is fresh to the "Scarlet Man," for he is evidently a complete master of his business. During a couple of days past he has been pouring the dregs of the drinks, consisting of stale beer, watered spirit, and so forth, into sundry large tumblers under the counter, awaiting his opportunity to dispose of them. A native, approaching the confident stage, calls for a "long shandy," and is served with one of these tumblers, into which sufficient lemonade has been poured to promote effervescence. He gulps part of it, then, pulling a horrified grimace, expectorates freely. "Ehoa!" he says reproachfully.

"What is it?" asks the innkeeper, with innocent anxiety, coming forward with a spoon. "Fly? Piece o' cork?"

No one takes much note of the occurrence, and the half-poisoned native becomes in time reconciled to the villainous mixture. By-and-by he would drink kerosene, for that matter.

Night takes another turn of his wheel. The lights in the

scattered shanties are going out one by one. The sound of the scraping dies away. The moreporks fly soundlessly across the dreary scrub lands.

THE END

www.ingramcontent.com/pod-product-compliance
Lightning Source LLC
Chambersburg PA
CBHW071135260626
47162CB00003B/799